The Lineage
War Torn Trilogy Part Two

KIMBERLY HUMPHREYS

Copyright © 2021 Kimberly Humphreys
All rights reserved.
ISBN: 9798508829469

Scripture quotations are taken from the Holy Bible, New Living Translation, copyright ©1996, 2004, 2015 by Tyndale House Foundation. Used by permission of Tyndale House Publishers, Carol Stream, Illinois 60188. All rights reserved.

CONTENTS

	Acknowledgments	*i*				
1	The King's Lineage	*1*	15	Greatest of These	*100*	
2	Bloodlines and Battle Plans	*5*	16	Ammo	*110*	
3	The King's Word	*12*	17	Schemes and Tea	*116*	
4	A New Home?	*19*	18	Zyandite Pledge	*120*	
5	Running Water	*25*	19	Heartfelt Worship	*126*	
6	Accusations	*32*	20	Holy	*136*	
7	Pumpkin Cream Cake and Coffee	*37*	21	The Arena	*143*	
8	Culture Shock	*45*	22	Reactions	*156*	
9	A Thousand Gardens	*54*	23	Worthy Enough?	*163*	
10	Quandii	*58*	24	Homecoming	*170*	
11	Prophecy and Politics	*63*	25	Military Traditions and Change	*175*	
12	Fallen	*78*	26	Breakdown	*180*	
13	The Call	*85*	27	A Light in Darkness	*184*	
14	Death of a Nation	*95*	28	Confirmed	*186*	
				Epilogue: The Man Across the Sea	*195*	

ACKNOWLEDGMENTS

I want to thank you, dear reader, for caring about Kira, Ruger, and precious Nadia's journey.

I would also like to thank my family, especially my husband and oldest daughter, Vivian. This book would not be what it is without you.

Though this may be a fictional account of God's leadership and love, but in real life, He is sovereign, and in control. Whatever you're going through, not only is God there, but He is bigger. I dedicate this work to Him.

The earth is the LORD's, and everything in it. The world and all its people belong to him. Psalm 24:1

CHAPTER 1
THE KING'S LINEAGE

Across the dark landscape of Auctairea, only the city of Quandii has light.

The glow from the city's artificial lights reflects off the sky, as those who inhabit around the city's borders live in tents. As usual, they retire to bed just before dawn.

Auctaireans fortunate enough to live within the city stagger home from their night of debauchery.

Most of the residents are half-naked, with various tattoos over their pale skin. The hair color ranges from yellow, to blue, to black, and many mixtures in-between. In a word, these people are a mess. A hungover, drugged out mess.

Nothing is natural.

Nothing is sacred.

As the sun rises, the black cloud cover slowly morphs into gray. It's an average morning in the land of the indecent, where in the chaos there's no such thing as brotherly love.

Across the wooded landscape, where land meets the sea, a different scene takes place. Zyandite occupation is orderly, cohesive, and strong.

On one of many runways on Saffarion Airbase, hundreds of soldiers march from physical training singing an old cadence. The voices are uniformed and to the enemy, frightful.

A man steps out of the hanger, making the cadence stop.

From across the runway, Ruger sees the relief on his soldiers faces. As he follows Lieutenant Coltner out of the hanger, the soldiers part the way. Pain from the bullet wound in his thigh lingers, but Ruger manages to walk without a limp. A few nods are exchanged as he scans the harden eyes in passing. The sour taste of kepweed haunts the back of his throat, but to his relief, nothing needs to be said.

The eyes of his soldiers say it all.

Whatever happened in Ruger's absence has made them afraid. Now they stand straight-backed and encouraged.

Their King is alive.

His eyes promise resolve, while the fever that once overcame Ruger threatens to return. Hoping he won't need the second antidote Kira gave him, Ruger's chest warms at just the thought of her. He glances back at the opening of the hanger. The cargo plane is so high it's merely a dot against Auctairea's gray clouds. Just the assurance that Kira and Nadia are on their way to Zyandite curves his lips into a smile.

"Would you like to change, my King?" Lieutenant Coltner asks. "I can show you to your quarters."

Ruger checks the time on his tablet. The daily briefing should be underway. "No." He grins. "I need to drop in on my generals."

Lieutenant Coltner's face tightens. He points his hand towards a single-story building on the other side of the runway. "They'll be meeting in there."

Ruger's green eyes focus on the surrounding airfield. It's comforting to see so many Zyandite vehicles and soldiers moving about, but the chill of the Auctairean air still feels foreign in his lungs. He misses the warmth of Zyandite. The cold mixed with anticipation for the political battle ahead stiffens his already strained muscles. He hasn't felt this disgusted with his generals since the day he was crowned...

THE LINEAGE

Standing on a balcony at the castle, Ruger was too nauseated to stay inside. The party behind him was far too loud for his liking, especially as General Kentwood bellowed out a song written about his great-grandfather, King Kentwood. Ruger desired to get back to the war, but the generals insisted on a party.

The warm Zyandite night was enough to calm his nerves. Staring at the stars, Ruger knew the Lineage would find a way to make his coronation about them. Presented by the Church, Ruger became the people's choice for king, but that didn't damper the Lineage's bias against him. Not only was he the youngest king crowned, but the first to have never been married. It's a double black eye for the Lineage, so they chose to elaborate on themselves. All while Zyandite soldiers fought on a foreign soil...

The King's coronation was supposed to be a celebration for all of Zyandite, but General Kentwood saw it as an opportunity.

Ruger's moment of solitude was broken by General Kentwood introducing him to Lorie Faulkner.

Her features were slim and youthful. Her dark hair was in an elegant ponytail above high cheek bones, plump lips and hazel eyes. Wearing a navy-blue gown that shimmered in the moonlight, Ruger should have been taken by her.

Yet all he saw in the many shades of hazel in her eyes was an undeserved arrogance, the very arrogance most of the Lineage share. For Ruger, it was repulsive.

Cheeks still red from singing, General Kentwood stepped onto the balcony, his arm linked with Lorie's. "King Anstone, this is Lorie Faulkner. Not only is she King Faulkner's great-great-great-granddaughter, but she also has four generals in her bloodline. Her impeccable Lineage would suit everything yours lacks." He smiled as though this was a jovial subject.

Keeping his anger in check, Ruger nodded at Lorie once, just to be polite. "Excuse me." He returned to the distractions of the party, just to calm his racing heart. Deciding to give his first order as King, Ruger asked to be taken back to Kaddain.

It only took a few moments to load the helicopter. Once in the air, Ruger couldn't help but smirk at the generals' disappointment. His leaving clearly made them look bad. Disgusted by their prejudice, Ruger always believed Zyandites weren't supposed to worship bloodlines or let its people take credit for the actions of the past. On the contrary, Zyandite is supposed to be strong, Christ-centered, and free.

Individualism is God's gift, but how can individualism be achieved if everyone is judged by the accomplishments of the dead?

No one can help what their ancestors did. All anyone can help is what they themselves do.

That night, Ruger made a promise to himself that he would never marry. He didn't want to have children who would be scrutinized over a past they couldn't help.

No, Ruger decided his line would be cut off.

That would have been his fate except, God had another plan.

The memory of seeing Kira for the first time melts the Auctairean cold off of Ruger. The wisdom and strength in her brown eyes tamed by intentional kindness was unlike anything he's seen.

This Auctairean proved with one look that Kira not only knew the horrors of life, but has suppressed the evil of resentment from enclosing her heart. Her eyes, and their many shades of copper, are eyes Ruger knew could understand his heart.

What he does isn't about bragging rights or handsome uniforms. To be a soldier means so much more than protecting the homeland from being conquered. For Ruger, it's to protect what he loves; faith, the sacred family unit, and innocence, ensuring your homeland won't have to face the evils of this world. Kira knows these things because she's seen the contrast. She knows what he protects Zyandite from. Not only were her eyes keen to the wisdom many of his countrywomen lack, but the sensation of her touch was electric. It was unlike anything Ruger had experienced. He tried to convince himself that it was just the fever messing with his mind, but the more his health improved, the more he was captivated by her.

Now he stands underneath the overcast sky of Auctairean, and frowns at what the generals' reactions will be once he informs them of his plan. They can't know he intends to marry Kira until this war is won, or else it'll be a distraction. Ruger knows the generals won't take this sitting down. He lifts his chin high, ready for the battle today, and every one that's to come.

THE LINEAGE

"Sir," Lieutenant Coltner stops before the metal door and tilts his chin. A soft breeze rustles his blond hair over his stern blue eyes. "When your vitals went blank, the generals ordered us not to search for you. It's like they expected it. When they enacted the Slayden Rule..." He looks at the ground, fear breaking away at his courage until he overcomes it and looks up. "They've lost my trust."

Ruger raises a brow. "While your doubt is justified, a kingdom divided by civil war will collapse." Ruger quotes Mark 3:24 before letting out a sigh. In his heart, Ruger knows the sabotage his men are so certain of, may very well be true. "Pray for my discernment."

"Yes, my King." Lieutenant Coltner opens the door.

The artificial lights are welcoming, causing Ruger to frown. Here, the military has electricity while Kira suffered without it for years. He knows the city of Quandii still has utilities and the unfairness makes his blood boil.

Lieutenant Coltner glances back at Ruger with an unspoken anticipation before leading the way into a conference room.

In a society where military lineage is essential for leadership, this son of a preacher never thought he'd be King. Ruger Anstone walks into the room, which might as well be a lion's den. All of the generals' wool and brass are straight and polished.

Ruger's civilian clothes under armor are tattered, and his face is unshaven. In the center of the room is a long table with two rows of Charge Commanders. All but one stands in reverence of the crown. Their eyes widen in shock at the sight of their king, while most carry a tinge of regret. Only two seem happy to see him alive, making the suspicions of his men come to life before him. Of course, they are the only men inside the room not born under the purity of the Lineage.

Slowly eyeing each of the generals, Ruger's lips curve into a smirk. No matter how perfect their uniforms or bloodlines are, these men have never intimidated him, not even now, when at least one of them wants him dead.

CHAPTER 2
BLOODLINES AND BATTLE PLANS

At the head of the table, General Marshal sits in the king's place. He's the only soldier who remains seated in the presence of their king. His pale blue eyes are a contrast to his black hair, light complexion, and narrow face. Frowning, General Marshal looks at Ruger like he's just seen a ghost.

"Hello, men," Ruger greets before taking the chair across the table from General Marshal. As Ruger sits down, the soldiers retake their seats.

General Marshal presses his thin lips together, and crosses his well-defined arms.

Ruger looks at the assigned displays for the vitals of the thirteen highest ranking Zyandites. Each screen is four inches wide and is never supposed to be turned off. He notices that General Marshal's heart rate is quite sporadic, revealing the fear hiding behind his façade of indifference. Meanwhile, Ruger's screen is blank.

Ruger's brow furrows upon noticing a screen at the bottom row is off. Eying his men, General Baxton isn't anywhere in sight, raising Ruger's suspicions.

"It's good to have you back." General Jordan Brice isn't much taller than Ruger. His blond hair, playful blue eyes, and beige complexion accentuate his oval face. Jordan is just two months younger than Ruger, and has felt the agony of defeat and the relief of victory with him, both in training and in war. When Ruger was crowned, he assigned Jordan Brice to become head of the King's Charge, which promoted Jordan from major to general in a day.

"King Anstone!" General Kentwood finally greets, with a face that's too round for his rank. His mauve lips curve below faded brown eyes.

"General Kentwood," Ruger greets before looking at General Brice. "Jordan," Ruger says, since they have been on a first name bases for years.

Jordan gives Ruger a knowing look, confirming the rumors of betrayal.

"Now that I'm back, alive…" Ruger pauses to study the reaction of his generals. Some chuckle, others become uneasy. "Can someone brief me on the status of our invasion?"

General Brice doesn't waste time. "Yesterday, we obtained air superiority. Our men have secured Auctairea's rural military bases. The border is ours. Only the city of Quandii remains protected by Auctairean machines."

"That's impressive," Ruger acclaims.

"I couldn't agree more, King Anstone," General Marshal says. "In fact, we just discussed using the Flatiron." His face becomes smug.

The room is silent. All eyes wait for Ruger's response.

Ruger looks around in shock at their lack of wisdom. "How long has it been since we Flatironed Kaddain?"

"Five months," General Marshal answers proudly.

"It will be six months, next week. I know, because I'm the one who ordered it." Ruger's brow furrows. "I've been on the ground of this wretched place and there's nothing I'd like more than to wipe Auctairea off the face of the earth, but…" Ruger's tone softens. "There's hope among the people here. Even if there wasn't, I won't put our soldiers smack dab in a global conflict. If we Flatiron both of our neighboring countries within a half of a year, we'll provoke the rest of the world to retaliate."

"Is our king more concerned about the actions of men than that of God?"

Everyone looks at General Mayes, shocked by his question.

General Mayes glares at Ruger from a pre-aged face and receding hairline. All his years in service have taken a toll on his gray eyes, since their color is hard to make out from under the cataracts.

"I won't concern myself with the actions of any man, including yours," Ruger retorts before looking at General Marshal. "I'm not afraid of the GPU, but after two major wars in such a short period of time, I'd rather spare our men from another conflict. Once we take down Prime Minister Joplin's mechanical army, Auctairea will be rendered defenseless. We can easily destroy all of its filth without using the Flatiron."

"Perhaps God wants us to gain world dominance?" General Marshal oversteps his bounds with such a statement, and everyone in the room knows it.

Instead of correcting him, the generals wait to see if Ruger will obey him.

Ruger understands the predicament he is in. There's an invisible coup happening right before his eyes. Though his heart is enraged, he keeps his cool. "How shortsighted," Ruger is harsh, but takes no pleasure in watching Marshal cower at his tone. "First off, Zyandite never has been, and never will be a dictatorship." Ruger's aghast at just the suggestion of such an idea, and makes certain to show it by twisting his face into a glare. "Do you even realize how many people we'd have to kill, in order to gain that level of power?" Ruger shakes his head at General Marshal, dismissing him as though he were a child.

Intimidated by Ruger and unable to hide it, General Marshal coils inward, causing a stir of uneasy glances from the other generals in the room.

Ruger watches them, hoping this moment will wake them up from their folly.

"General Marshal isn't seriously considering world dominance," General Kentwood says with a nervous chuckle.

"As a Zyandite General, he shouldn't have suggested it," Ruger sneers. With confidence, he takes a long look at his blank vitals before peeling off the rubber film that holds the sensor behind his ear. Ruger drops it on the table with disdain, before crossing his arms. "There's suspicion breeding in the hearts of our men. They fear that one of you is illegally seeking the Zyandite crown. After the negligence you've displayed, I don't blame them." Ruger raises his voice at the complacency before him. "I must see how I was disconnected from ZyanBell, and why an extraction team wasn't ordered after I crashed!"

"King Anstone, in our defense, your vitals were the worst ever recorded in Zyandite history. We figured no one could survive a fever that high. Do tell us, what plagued you?" General Fisher, the Commander of Zyandite's Medical Support Charge, asks.

Ruger has always respected General Fisher, perhaps because he is one of the few Generals who isn't arrogant. He takes a different tone in answering him. "A local poison, from a synthesized plant called kepweed; some of the natives lace their bullets with it." He briefly points to where he was shot. "It was a struggle, but by God's grace, I'm still here." Ruger looks back at the monitor. "I see that General Baxton's vitals are down as well."

General Fisher stares at the floor. His eyes are heavy with regret. "General Baxton died in his sleep."

"When?" Ruger's surprised since General Baxton was of good health the last time he saw him.

General Fisher avoids eye contact with Ruger.

"Last night," Jordan answers. He leans towards Ruger before whispering, "General Baxton was the people's choice for the crown."

"There was already a vote?" Ruger shouts.

"Yes," Jordan answers coolly. "The Generals chose Marshal, the people chose Baxton, but the Church chose you." He smiles. "A major hiccup happened when your survival was prophesied. Voter turnout was at a record low."

"A prophecy?" Ruger is taken aback, since there has not been a prophecy on this grand of a scale in Zyandite for decades. Yet even so, he knows that under the Slayden Rule, with one king-hopeful dead, not even the Church would be able to stop the generals from crowning their choice. "When would've General Marshal been crowned?"

"Tomorrow morning," General Kentwood says. His disappointment isn't lost on Ruger.

Ruger frowns. "How many days were they competing for the crown?"

Everyone stirs except Jordan, who answers boldly, "Twenty-four hours."

In shock, Ruger leans back into his chair. "That's the fastest competition in Zyandite history!"

"Divided kingdoms always fall, and with no disrespect intended, King Anstone…" General Danning interrupts, with his mop of brown curls out of regulation bouncing above his brow. "I think we should consider how we address each other, since our conduct affects every soldier. Instead of accusations, we should bring solutions to the table."

Jordan momentarily stares at Ruger with an unspoken irritation for this long winded General, before directing his glare at General Danning. "Yet how quickly you forgot why our King was shot down."

General Danning's upper lip curves at being interrupted, but Jordan ignores him and turns to General Stockton, who holds his head down in reverence.

"That unmanned jet would have shot me down, if you hadn't led it to the forest." General Stockton looks at Ruger with his hazel eyes full of gratitude. "You crashed, so I could deliver the key to our men." He shakes his head. "Turns out it was for nothing."

Ruger can see the sorrowing brimming from this young General's eyes. He knows that pain, and tries to soften its sting. "I'm glad you survived."

General Stockton stares at the floor, his eyes broken by grief for the soldiers who didn't.

"The point is King Anstone, you were shot down. What did you expect us to do, surrender?" General Marshal's tone is irate.

"The nerve," Ruger snarls.

General Marshal doesn't back down, and folds his arms over the table to lean forward. "It is my right as a Charge Commander to be bold in my decisions. Put yourself in our shoes. Imagine if I was king, was shot down and had a record breaking fever before my connection to ZyanBell was lost. What would you have done for Zyandite?" General Marshal's tone is not quite as arrogant, but Ruger is still unnerved by a general already behaving as though he were king.

"I won't travel down a road of the hypothetical because that would be a waste of my time. Since you all like history enough to enact the Slayden Rule, what I will do is remind you that as your King, I can demote a Charge Commander to a Private, like that." Ruger snaps his fingers at General Marshal, who immediately sulks into his seat.

A firestorm in defense for General Marshal fills the air, giving Ruger a headache. He pinches the skin above his nose to sooth it.

Of all the voices shouting, the hypocrisy of General Danning is revealed, since his voice is the loudest. "You weren't even first in battle!"

"Enough!" Ruger commands, silencing the room. "I was first in battle, in the air. I was shot down, poisoned, and cut off from ZyanBell. The trap was set. The enemy was supposed to think I was with the Calvary on the border, but knew exactly where I was. Now, come to find out that General Baxton died, only adds to my suspicions. I know in time the truth will be revealed, because that's how God works. When the truth is found, I will deal with it. Until then, we must focus on winning this war." Ruger stands. "Every last one of you should be concerned with victory in battle instead of victory in title, and frankly, I'm ashamed of you."

"You may think that's what I want, but with all due respect to the crown, you're wrong!" General Marshal yells.

"Okay, that's enough." Jordan stands, "How long has it been since you've slept, or even showered?"

"There's no sleeping in Auctairea, at least not for innocent women and children," Ruger begins without taking his eyes off of General Marshal, who sweats under his stare. "Even with how much I hate Auctairea, I will not use the Flatiron to destroy it. Auctaircans may be the very essence of evil written about in Psalm seventy-nine, but even they have hope." Ruger braces his palms on the table to lean forward. "Yet no matter who our foreign enemy is, it's wrong for any Zyandite to hope his king falls."

After a long moment of silence, General Danning is the first to speak,

"Of course, King Anstone."

Ruger sits back in his seat. "General Kentwood, order Colonel Lock and Major Cantor to investigate General Baxton's untimely death. General Marshal, you will oversee the groundwork of the machines and since communication is a bit fuzzy, you will take inventory by hand." Ruger points to where his vitals should show with a smirk.

General Marshal's eyes widen in horror at being put on the front line.

"Yes, sir," General Kentwood says before standing up. He stops at the doorway and waits for General Marshal, who follows his King's orders with reluctance.

"Guess I should be more careful where I sit," General Marshal tries to joke, but no one laughs as they watch him slowly leave the room.

"If he informs his wife of your new position for Sampson Tidal's heir, she'll blast it all over Zyandite airwaves," General Danning says with a laughter that's almost threatening.

"If he informs his wife of our tactical position, they'll both be guilty of treason," Ruger says.

General Danning's smile fades.

Ruger presses his fingers together while refocusing his thoughts on the mission. "I need to see plans, every niche, every road and every entry way to Quandii."

General Brice opens his tablet to display the blueprints of Quandii, through a projected image against the wall across from Ruger. General Brice points to the old radio station. "We were told the Hive was hidden here, but once we flew in, drones were waiting for us."

Ruger pulls out his tablet, and shows General Brice the coordinates Kira gave him. "The Auctairean, who saved me, said that Prime Minister Joplin would only trust his brother to operate the machines. His name is Hugh Joplin, and this is where he lives. The signal is controlled by an antenna, hidden up here." He points further south, "The Quandii Tower."

Jordan zooms in on the first location. It's in an upscale neighborhood, on the north side of the city. He scrolls to the tower. "That tower was said to be abandoned, but the road to get there is a conduit for Auctairea's military."

Ruger crosses his arms. "We'll have to create a diversion." The pain in his leg demands attention, but he repositions in his seat and ignores it. "We'll send a full battalion, right on the main highway." He points at the largest roadway that enters the city. "Meanwhile, you and I will lead a squad right up to the fence line of the neighborhood. To avoid being spotted by radar, we'll move in on horseback. With most of the machines protecting the main entry, we'll catch them off guard at the Hive, while General Brice takes down The Quandii Tower."

General Mayes clears his throat, "My King, I think this is a good plan, but how do you expect to take down the Hive without the key?"

Ruger's surprised at such an inquiry. He thought it was obvious. "The old fashion way."

That draws err from everyone but Jordan, who raises an eyebrow at the other Generals' lack of imagination.

"By blowing it up! That'll be more effective in shutting down the machines than any virus," Ruger confidently states.

The generals know at least one of them should have guessed that, causing several sheepish nods and smirks to fill the room.

"I need to speak to my men, so they know I'm alive," Ruger's tone is somber.

General Danning frowns and eyes Ruger's civilian clothes with disapproval, since appearance is everything to most generals. "After you've changed first, I'm sure?"

Ruger's indifferent regarding his appearance, and only wants to assure his men. "No."

"Should we attack at dawn?" General Danning asks, looking away in attempt to hide his displeasure at King Anstone's lack of saving face.

"They'll be expecting that. We'll strike tomorrow afternoon," Ruger says.

"Yes, King Anstone." General Danning begins to coordinate the king's orders on his tablet.

"Jordan, call in a formation at the hanger." Ruger hands his tablet to General Danning. "You must reconnect me to ZyanBell within the hour."

General Danning's mouth gapes before taking the tablet. "Of course, King Anstone."

Ruger doesn't like the expression of his Satellite Charge Commander. Trusting his discernment, Ruger decides to no longer trust General Danning, unless he earns it.

Jordan types in the order for an immediate formation. "It should take about thirty minutes for everyone to arrive."

"Good. I will release you all, but first, we must pray." Ruger waits for every soldier in the room to bow their heads before bowing his own. "The great and powerful I Am, we thank you for this chance to defeat an enemy who mocks your name, and murders your people. When we attack Auctairea tomorrow, please, give us wisdom, strength and victory. In the mighty name of Jesus Christ, amen."

"Amen," the rest of the room says in unison.

"God willing, we will have victory," Ruger says before leaving the room with Jordan.

Now that they're alone in the hallway, Jordan whispers, "We'll need victory in more places than just Auctairea."

Ruger's shoulders stiffen. "You don't believe my disconnection from ZyanBell was an accident?"

Jordan raises a brow. "No."

"Please, tell me you have proof?"

Jordan shrugs. "The outcome makes their plans obvious, but they've mastered hiding anything that could stick." He frowns. "You should've seen the generals on the night you crashed. They were giddy."

Letting out a slow breath, Ruger never thought he'd be in the position of fighting his own. The rage against anyone who'd betray his flag burns in his eyes. Muscles tense, Ruger's hands ball into fists. The whirl of anger intensifies with the pain in his leg. For General Baxton, and himself, Ruger turns around, ready to deal with his generals on foreign soil.

CHAPTER 3
THE KING'S WORD

Like a boulder in his stomach, God warns Ruger to stand down. His anger calms and morphs into wisdom. If Ruger were to deal with his generals with only half-truths, it would obliterate the morale of his men. The generals would deny it. Without proof, he could be imprisoned. Ruger knows this victory can only come from God. After a silent prayer, his fists unclench.

Still, Ruger can throw a wrench in the generals' plans. "Cut off General Marshal from ZyanBell. I can't risk him sharing our tactical positions."

"General Danning will reinstate his account the moment it drops."

"Not his account, just his tablet."

"I see." With a chuckle, Jordan types a code into his device. "Done."

"Good." Ruger turns to Jordan and frowns. "For Zyandite's sake, why didn't you compete for the crown?"

Jordan's eyes flicker with pain. "Deep down, I knew you were alive. How could I betray you?"

Ruger understands the torment his friend's been under, all while trying to hold Zyandite together. "I'll let you off the hook this time, but if anything happens to me, you're the best man for the job."

THE LINEAGE

Jordan shakes his head and mouths 'no,' before opening the door. The sunlight is so dim, there's no need for their eyes to adjust as they step outside. "Are you sure you don't want to change before addressing the troops? A fresh uniform might make the generals back off a bit."

"I didn't become a soldier to look pretty," Ruger's quick to retort.

Jordan grins.

The hanger comes into view, where hundreds of soldiers file into formation. These men deserve a leader who serves them. The self-seeking have no right to lay the burden of orders upon them; they're Zyandite's defenders, who are strengthened by God. General Marshal's ploy for world dominance sets Ruger's heart on fire. "Find me proof, and I'll execute whoever betrayed Zyandite."

"You won't hear any complaints from me," Jordan says.

Soldiers wait in formation before a makeshift platform, where Captain Hiledal sets up a tablet to record Ruger's message for the troops unable to make it into the hanger.

Ruger walks up a black tarp that covers a crate under his feet, and is greeted by thunderous applause. At this distance, he can't decipher every face, but those he can see, display relief at the sight of him.

"Thank you," Ruger's voice isn't magnified by a microphone, but as soon as he speaks, the cheering stops.

"I want you all to be aware that the chaos within your leadership is over. I'm still your King," Ruger shouts so those in the back can hear him.

The applause begins once more and Ruger looks at Jordan, who nods once with knowing eyes. Ruger finds himself hating politics more than Kaddain and Auctairea combined.

"I also," Ruger's voice cuts the applause to a halt. "Owe you an apology. I should've been in battle when our brothers fell." Ruger takes in a deep breath. "After my jet was shot down, I was hit with a bullet laced with poison from a synthetic plant called kepweed. By God's grace, a Christian widow took me in, and gave me the antidote. Out of all the battles I've fought, I never thought I'd almost be taken out by a plant."

The hanger fills with the melody of laughter.

"I see my crash as the will of the great I Am. It gave me the chance to see how truly evil Auctaireans are, and how they treat women and children. The truth of our enemy must be known. I've always said that purity is the only thing that can destroy evil. Purity comes in many forms. Unfiltered, honest truth is one of them. As Christians we are commanded to guard our hearts, to guard our eye gates and our ear gates. Much like Kaddain, there are things in Auctairea that will haunt you for the rest of your lives. Be prepared for it, and don't let it harden your hearts. As warriors, we are called by God to seek justice. The persecution against Christians in Auctairea was not voluntary, as we assumed. I learned of something called the Great Cleansing. In a single night, the Auctairean government used their mechanical army to hunt down and kill nearly every Christian who wouldn't renounce God." He holds a hand up to calm the angry chatter from the crowd. "However, I was able to convert an Auctairean soldier to Christianity. His family was slaughtered during the Great Cleansing. Out of fear, he denied God. Now, he's like Peter, giving me hope. As for the rest of them, they're vile, godless, selfish creatures who are in love with their sin. They wouldn't be merciful towards anyone weaker than them, not even children. We can try to convert as many as we can, but for those who choose to fight, we must overcome them. We invaded Auctairea to defend Zyandite's borders, but as surely as we live, we will overthrow Auctairea to take vengeance for God's people."

His soldiers cheer.

"Even with the vile actions of this people," Ruger begins, silencing the applause. "We know God desires that none shall perish. I have no plans to Flatiron this nation. God willing, we will have victory, not just in battle for our borders, but for the hearts of these broken people!"

Jordan watches as every soldier slams their right fist into their chest, giving a loud, harmonious salute to their King.

"May the great I Am bless you all!" Ruger returns their salute before stepping off the makeshift stage.

"It's good to have you back," Jordan says, but Ruger hardly hears him over the thunderous applause.

Ruger's focus is on his men. A line to greet him and shake his hand is already forming. Jordan stays by his side as various service members wait their turn to speak with their king. These men don't care what their king is wearing; they're just happy he's alive.

A lot of information is made known to Ruger, by his men. He learns just how close Zyandite came to complete division. Not only were his men suspicious of sabotage for Ruger's crash, but General Baxton's suspicious death almost caused a rebellion.

Jordan knows he must convince Ruger to leave the hanger, or he'll stay here all night to talk with the troops. "The King has gone far too long without sleep, and who knows how long since he has had a shower?" He says before plugging his nose.

The men laugh.

Ruger waves goodbye, before following Jordan down the hall.

"I suppose I don't need to brief you anymore," Jordan half-jokes as they make their way outside, where rows of temporary barracks lie ahead.

"Not unless they missed something." Ruger's face is stern, now that he knows just how bad things were in his absence.

"They never do."

"Thank the great I Am for that."

Jordan glances at Ruger's limp. He may hide it well, but Ruger's obviously in pain. Instead of leading his best friend to his quarters, Jordan turns to the right. Avoiding the fight, he doesn't say a word while walking to a small, gray trailer, leading Ruger to his surgeon.

Kind brown eyes greet Ruger. Doctor Tanner's dirty blond hair rests at her shoulders. This woman is twice his age, and allows her motherly care to hold authority over her king. "My worst patient." She smiles. "It's good to see you alive."

Ruger glares at Jordan, who can't contain his smile.

"I knew you wouldn't come here willingly," Jordan admits.

His lips curve, but the smile doesn't touch Ruger's eyes. "Fine. While I'm wasting my time here…" He gives Dr. Tanner a sheepish grin before looking back at Jordan, "Message Rhonda for me. Let her know what I've gotten her into. Be sure to tell her that Kira Westin and her daughter aren't just refugees I'm sending home, but family."

Jordan's eyes widen. He and Dr. Tanner exchange an uncomfortable glance.

Watching the door close, Jordan takes a seat in the hall and pulls out his tablet. Waiting for a few rings, he smiles once Rhonda's face appears on screen. Like her brother, Rhonda's skin is naturally bronzed, and her eyes are a vibrant green beneath thick, dark hair.

Rhonda's eyes scan Jordan's face with heavy anticipation. "Do you have word of my brother?"

"Yes, he's alive."

Rhonda gasps and fumbles with her violin. The screen momentarily shows the ceiling while she puts it away. "I was in session," she informs before the camera refocuses on her face. "I've been praying and praying."

"We all have." Jordan stares at her with admiration. "I'm afraid you're going to have to cancel your classes for a while."

"How badly is he hurt?"

"Not bad. He was shot again, this time in the leg." Jordan smiles to assure her. "He's walking with barely a limp."

Rhonda places a hand on her heart. "Praise the great I Am!" Her eyes brighten. "Thank you for letting me know, General Brice."

Jordan's cheeks flush. "I hate it when you call me that."

Pressing her lips together to hide a smile, Rhonda shrugs.

Soaking her in, it takes Jordan a moment to get back on track. "That's not the only reason I called."

"Oh?"

Jordan looks around before leaning forward. "It was a woman who saved him—"

"An Auctairean woman saved my brother?" Rhonda interrupts. "I'd definitely like to meet her."

"You will. He's sent her home."

Rhonda's eyes widen. "What?"

"Yeah…" Jordan takes in a nervous breath through his teeth. "He needs you to be her translator. So far, all I know is she's a Christian, and has a small child. They should be arriving there in about three hours."

"Have they been tested?"

"Yes."

Rhonda's shoulders loosen. "Well, I'll happily be their translator, and take them to a hotel—"

"No, he wants them to stay with you." Jordan's smile fades. "I think he's in love with her."

Nearly dropping the tablet, Rhonda gasps and covers her mouth with one hand. "What gives you a crazy idea like that?"

"He called her his family."

Rhonda's eyes fill with horror. "An Auctairean…" She shakes her head. "Who is she?"

"Kira Westin."

"Oh, Jordan…" Rhonda giggles. "She's married. There's no way Ruger could be taken by a married woman. He'd never!"

"He said she's widowed," Jordan whispers.

Rhonda gasps.

"I'm not happy about this either. I need you to keep an eye on her. Makes sure she's not a spy."

Rhonda's face becomes pale. "I need to speak with my brother, where is he?"

Jordan glances at the closed door. "He's in Dr. Tanner's hands."

***

"So, you've been shot, again?" Dr. Tanner motions for Ruger to sit at the exam table.

Ruger reluctantly takes a seat. "I'm feeling much better now."

"Last time you said that to me, you had a layer of skin hanging from your side." She scowls.

Ruger only shrugs.

"Okay, where have you been shot this time?"

"My thigh." Ruger nods at the wound.

She pulls out a white tube attached to the ceiling and points its lens directly above Ruger's thigh. "It's a burn!"

"That's from the kepweed," Ruger says. "It's the most painful thing I've ever experienced."

Dr. Tanner gives him a playful look, "King Anstone finally admits he can feel pain…" She shakes her head. "I don't believe it."

"If I didn't have the tolerance God gave me, I probably would've died," Ruger is matter of fact with his tone before he looks up to see the concern in her eyes. They remind him of his mother.

Dr. Tanner wastes no time in cutting the fabric of his pants and examines the wound. "Word on the street is an Auctairean took care of you."

Ruger chuckles. "Word on the street moves fast."

She pulls the bandage off. It's clean, making her nod in approval. "She did a good job. Still, it needs Zyandite care." Dr. Tanner pulls a wand out of the drawer. The orange glow stimulates his cells to rapidly heal. The process is warm, but not enough to hurt. Ruger watches both holes in his thigh fill-in where the bullet went through.

"General Fisher sent me a message regarding kepweed," Dr. Tanner mumbles while focusing on his injury. "I half-expected you to tough it out."

"I would've." Jordan may not be in the room, but Ruger glares in his direction anyway.

Dr. Tanner smiles, "General Brice is a true friend."

"He is, but most aren't," Ruger says before furrowing his brow. "What happened to General Baxton?"

Sadness fills Dr. Tanner's eyes. "They say he died of a stroke but..." She glances at the door, before whispering, "The generals didn't allow me to conduct an autopsy."

"They didn't *allow* the King's Surgeon access to a Charge Commander's body?!" Ruger can't help but shout.

"No." She sighs. "I believe it's by God's grace you're alive." Dr. Tanner tilts her chin. Ruger would have to be blind to not see the warning in her eyes.

Frowning, Ruger glances at his healed wounds. "Thank you," he says before standing.

"Don't you go running off," Dr. Tanner uses her tablet to take a blood sample from his arm. Waiting for the results, her shoulders relax once they come back clean. "The poison isn't in your blood stream."

"Kira gave me an antidote."

"Kira?" Dr. Tanner smiles, "What a charming name."

"She's a charming person."

His tone causes Dr. Tanner to tilt her chin and study his face. "You care for her?"

"She left me no choice." Ruger reaches into his pocket and hands her the syringe Kira gave him. "Here's the antidote. Kira grabbed it out of a medicine cabinet in the hanger. There's probably more. Send a few medics to investigate. I don't want our guys to suffer like I did. Without Kira, I would've died." He looks at the door, ready to bolt, but Dr. Tanner places a hand on his arm. She's never done anything like this before, making him focus on the concern in her eyes.

"Since you care about this woman, send her to Tunaunda. If…" She bites her lip and looks at the floor. A storm brews in Dr. Tanner's eyes, before she has the courage to look back at him. "It's possible the generals killed one of their own. What would they do to an Auctairean?" Her warning is soft, but stabs straight into Ruger's heart.

"That accusation is too serious to speak of without proof."

She holds her head down. "You're right, but I've never seen the generals behave like this, and I'm worried for our country."

"You're not the only one." Ruger looks at the doctor and regains control of his racing heart. "Have faith. God will protect Zyandite."

"I had faith that you were alive, and here you are." Dr. Tanner crosses her arms. "Now, I recommend three days of rest before you join the fight."

Ruger presses his lips together. "We invade Quandii tomorrow."

Dr. Tanner watches him walk away and shakes her head.

"Poor Doctor Tanner," Jordan pouts before revealing Rhonda's impatient face on his tablet.

Ruger's eyes brighten at the sight of his sister. "I'm sorry I didn't call you, but my account's still disconnected from ZyanBell."

Rhonda does her best to hold back tears, but is unsuccessful. "Jordan said you were poisoned?"

"Yes," Ruger takes the tablet in his hand and is disappointed to find Rhonda crying.

"Were you also drugged?"

Raising a brow, Ruger shoots a glare at Jordan. "What did my Charge Commander tell you?"

Jordan merely shrugs.

"That you fell in love with an Auctairean!" Rhonda's tone is hysterical.

"I did," Ruger can't help his smile. "Once you get to know Kira, you'll love her too. Be kind to her, and her brave little girl. They risked everything to save me."

"I understand that, but…" Rhonda's entire face creases with worry. It's a look Ruger hates seeing. "What about the Lineage?"

Ruger doesn't reply. His mind is too focused on the battles he's about to face. The war with Auctairea is bad enough without having to fight his own generals. Ruger thinks of John 8:32:

And you will know the truth, and the truth will set you free.

To protect Kira and Nadia from the Lineage, Ruger knows what he must do…

***

CHAPTER 4
A NEW HOME?

After exiting the aircraft, Kira and Nadia step onto Zyandite soil. Their hearts are full of peace while the highlights in their brown hair reflect the sun.

Nadia clings to her mother's side, her copper eyes scanning the airport. Ambulances full of the wounded soldiers who flew in with them are almost out of sight. A warm, moist breeze muffles her hair. Under a clear sky, the rolling hills beyond the cityscape are covered with cacti and oak trees. This world is a perfect mix of country and municipality. It's unlike anything Nadia's seen, but now that she's noticed the woman waiting by a white car down the runway, she can't bring her eyes to look at anything else.

Kira's head is held high, revealing the platinum cross necklace she was forced to hide in Auctairea. A thousand emotions whirl within her, varying between gratitude, serenity, shock, and fear. Letting out a slow breath, Kira approaches who she hopes is Ruger's sister. She was so hopeful upon first arriving here, but now, her refugee status makes her feel naked.

"Hello, my name is Rhonda Anstone, welcome to Zyandite." Rhonda's Auctrah is as flawless as her smile. With innocence intermixed with green, Rhonda's eyes only match her brother's by color.

"Thank you," Kira says. Her light brown eyes are soft as she looks at Nadia, who hides behind her. "This is my daughter, Nadia. We're grateful to be here."

Rhonda bends to Nadia's level. "My brother told me that you're a very brave little girl. I'm so blessed to know you, Nadia, my friend."

Nadia's pink lips curve into a smile. Rhonda's words give her the courage to step out of hiding. "You're as nice as Ruger."

Rhonda places a hand on her heart and straightens her posture. "Thank you." Her dress is crafted with swirls of black floral jacquard over emerald silk. It's simply elegant. Kira glances at her fraying black shirt and pants and Nadia's black leggings and purple tunic that are far too big for her tiny build. Embarrassment tries to creep into her heart, but Kira stops it before it can take root. She gave up the worship of a wardrobe a long time ago, and isn't going to let herself be brought down by something as frivolous as clothes.

Rhonda gestures towards the vehicle. "Shall we go? I'm sure neither of you are used to Zyandite sun."

Kira laughs. Looking up, the heat from the sunrays feels comforting on her skin. "It's a welcomed change."

"Wonderful!" Rhonda's face is animated with joy, before she frowns at something beyond Kira.

Kira turns to see several vehicles approaching. They're painted with different logos, and she doesn't have to be able to read Zyandish to know they're media.

"What is it?" Nadia clings to Kira's waist.

"Reporters," Kira explains before forcing a smile. "They're harmless."

"Um…" Rhonda's tone is stressed, proving Kira may be wrong. "Let's go."

They rush to Rhonda's vehicle, but the caravan of reporters is too fast. They're surrounded within seconds.

These women ask questions all at once. Kira can't understand a word of Zyandish, but in an automatic response, she smiles her best for the cameras.

Rhonda's smiling too, but addresses these women through her teeth. She finally says something that makes them notice Nadia. They immediately back off.

Looking at their young faces, Kira doesn't like how disappointed these reporters are at the sight of Nadia, and wraps a protective arm around her shoulder.

After opening the door to her car, Rhonda motions for Kira and Nadia to go in first. She gives a tight smile to the reporters, who know better than to get too close.

Nadia hesitates. "I've never been in a car."

"We have to go, now," Kira says, while glancing back at the reporters, who spectate on their every move.

"Okay." Nadia follows her mom into the vehicle and sits across from Rhonda. The tan leather is soft and Kira digs for their seatbelts, to find there are none. A tinge of fear causes her brow to crease. With the way Nadia is looking at her, Kira keeps her reservations to herself, and forces a smile.

"Sky-mode," Rhonda shouts in Zyandish, and her own yelling seems to surprise her.

The driver on the other side of the glass doesn't say a word. His gray hair is cut short and styled in a perfect wave over his brow. Kira thinks he's far too sagely to be a mere driver. Within seconds, the car lifts from the runway.

Nadia gasps.

Kira helps Nadia sit back properly. "It's alright. You used to be driven around all the time when you were a baby."

Rhonda eyes Nadia compassionately. "I can have him park somewhere to give you a break?"

Nadia shakes her head. "If I was able to handle this when I was a baby, I can handle it now."

"You're as tough as your mother," Rhonda says, forcing a smile before glancing out the window.

The group of reporters shrinks the higher they're lifted from the ground. Rhonda's shoulders relax. "I apologize for the press. They shouldn't have known you were here." She nervously shrugs.

Kira's heart races so fast she can hardly concentrate. Here, she thought they were safe. It's what Ruger promised, yet he didn't want anyone to know they were coming. "Why did Ruger want to keep our arrival a secret?"

Rhonda's eyes widen. "Oh..." She waves like it's no big deal, but Kira can tell otherwise. "The Lineage, they um, won't like his decision. My brother decided to hold off until after the war is won."

Needing clarification, Kira tilts her chin. "You mean of his decision to send an Auctairean to Zyandite?"

A miniature storm brews in Rhonda's eyes, before she forces a smile. "Yes. Something like that."

The sensation to run crawls over Kira's skin. She rubs her arms as though she were cold. Looking around, they're in the air, so there's no way to get this vehicle to stop. It's not like there's anywhere safe to run to. "How much danger are we in?"

Nadia looks away from the window and her eyes bulge. Kira hates scaring her, but she has to know the truth.

Rhonda shakes her head. "None." Her eyes dart to the side. It's subtle, but Kira catches it. "Zyandite welcomes Christian refugees. What the Lineage are upset about is a threat to their purity."

Kira grimaces. "What?"

Rhonda pinches the middle of her forehead and closes her eyes. "I'm the worst person to explain this." She opens her eyes and doesn't bother smiling. "I'm not Lineage myself, but Farrah, the Lead Pastor's wife, is an immigrant. It's better if she explains. I'll invite her over once you're both settled."

"Lead Pastor is an official government role here, correct?" Kira asks.

"Yes."

Kira's shoulders relax. If the Lead Pastor's wife is an immigrant, perhaps they're not in danger, and this is merely Zyandite's version of celebrity gossip?

Rhonda reaches over to place a hand on Kira's arm. "I don't know much about what you've been through, but you saved my brother's life. I'll forever be grateful, and don't want you to worry. This isn't Auctairea, okay?"

Wondering if she'll ever feel safe again, Kira forces a smile for Nadia's sake.

Straitening her posture, Rhonda motions towards her window. "Why don't we go on ground-mode, so you two can see the city?"

"This is your vehicle, not ours." Kira can't deny the distraction would be a blessing for Nadia.

"Ground-mode, please," Rhonda says to her driver. Her tone is softer than when the press was hounding them.

The driver glances back with a flicker of anger in his eyes. Kira's spine tightens, but then he smiles. Kira reminds herself that this is Zyandite, and she shouldn't be paranoid.

Their vehicle gracefully lowers to a highway onramp.

"I think I like sky-mode better," Nadia says while holding her tummy.

"Yes, but look." Rhonda points at the window.

High-rise buildings reflect the brightness of the sun like tall, gold curtains. Smaller buildings along the road carry unique architecture, with various arches and carvings. A few women happily walk along the sidewalk, wearing colorful dresses and bright smiles.

Nadia no longer holds her tummy, and scoots closer to the window. "Wow."

"Brustonite is Zyandite's capitol. If you look over there, you can see the tip of the castle's tower."

"I can see it!" Nadia points.

Kira smiles before noticing Rhonda's brow is furrowed.

"How long has it been since you've been up to date on current events?" Rhonda asks.

"Five years."

"That's practically a crime!" Rhonda frowns. "Well, a lot has changed in Zyandite over the past five years."

"Sounds like a lot has changed around the world…" Kira whispers, before staring out of her window. As they venture out of the city, there are at least eight lanes on this freeway in both directions. Every car keeps a perfectly safe gap. There's no sign of aggression, no tailgating, and no one is cutting anyone else off. It's perfect highway harmony and foreign to her eyes. "You have a driver, but do they?" Kira asks.

"Pardon me?"

"Self-driving cars?"

Rhonda laughs. "No."

"How is everyone so polite then?" The last time Kira drove in Auctairea, a semi-truck was dangerously tailgating them. Nadia was strapped in her car seat in the back. Kira kept a safe distance from the vehicle in front of her, and was driving over the speed limit. A motorcycle cut her off, and the semi-truck had to drive off the side of the road to avoid hitting them. Seeing it almost rear-end her made Kira scream. Shivering, Kira pushes the memory out of her mind to enjoy the serenity that surrounds her now.

"Well, perhaps there's less aggression in Zyandite because everyone's armed," Rhonda suggests. Her body language displays her innocence and security. Kira hopes that one day, Nadia will feel that free.

"Such a contrast," Kira whispers. "In Auctairea, only the rich were allowed to possess a weapon."

Rhonda's brow rises. "*A* weapon, as in only one gun?"

"Yes."

"Oh goodness, I couldn't imagine that." Rhonda places a hand over her heart. "We don't have limitations like that here."

The reporter in Kira can't help but to question this. "So, if it's mandatory to be armed, does Zyandite ration bullets?"

"Absolutely not," Rhonda holds in a laugh. "We can afford our own ammo. I certainly don't need anyone telling me how much or little to have."

Kira appreciates Rhonda's candor, and the tightness of her smile loosens. "I just assumed that since the government issues weapons, they'd control the ammo."

"Firearms aren't issued. Parents are required to buy them when their children turn fourteen. It's only mandatory because of our founding. Citizens shouldn't be dependent on the government to defend them." Rhonda frowns. "My brother said that you survived in Auctairea by reloading your ammo. We take that art very seriously in Zyandite, and I'm impressed an Auctairean pulled it off."

"Thank you," Kira whispers, before looking out the window again. The sight of how polite every driver is still catches her off guard. It seems as though everyone drives with other people in mind, rather than just looking out for themselves. The display of kindness inspires Kira to pray they'll be that empathetic towards her and Nadia.

Rhonda straightens her posture as their vehicle exits the freeway. These roads have a few restaurants and gas stations in-between patches of wilderness, where yellow grass, oak trees, and a few cacti thrive. Turning into a neighborhood, most of the houses are three stories tall, with chain link fences around the yards. The gaps in-between is quite substantial, but not exactly acreage. Each home is painted differently, most with bright colors.

Kira can see the rows of colorful houses that are a good distance behind, and while they're all different, the architect consists of similar qualities. Various points that look like upside down cones and lacy trim along the gutters gives proof they were all designed by the same builder. The most glorious detail each home shares, are the large sprawling oak trees in their yards.

"This way, come on!" Rhonda rushes out to open the little gate, before a cobblestone pathway to her emerald green front door.

Nadia bounces out of the car. "It's so pretty, mommy, look at all the colors."

"You should see it at Christmas! Every year there's a prize for the most festive homes in Zyandite. Someday, I intend to win it." Rhonda swings open her front door, which was left unlocked.

"Wait!" Kira shouts.

Rhonda looks at Kira like she's crazy.

"Your door was unlocked! We should check the entire house to make sure it's safe."

Her green eyes widen before Rhonda asks, "Safe from what?"

"From The Commons—I mean criminals. Anyone could be hiding in there." Perspiration builds on Kira's forehead while memories of Auctairean horror fill her mind. Even before the collapse, Auctairea was known for its crime. Kira glances back at the car and doesn't like the perturb expression on the driver's face. She doesn't want to scare Nadia, but Kira's survival mechanism has kicked in, and flight seems to be their only option.

CHAPTER 5
RUNNING WATER

After a long awkward silence, Rhonda gives Kira a sympathetic smile. "There hasn't been a home invasion in Zyandite for over seventy years."

Saliva builds in the back of Kira's throat. Crime statistics aren't enough, she needs her rifle. With it being in Auctairea, Kira's palms sweat at the helplessness of being unarmed.

"You've been through so much," Rhonda says softly. "Let me assure you that you're completely safe here." With a grin, Rhonda raises her skirt just enough to show the handgun strapped on her ankle. "I'm well trained." She winks before stepping inside.

Kira's shoulders drop with her heartrate. "Okay," she whispers, wishing she could leave the slime of Auctairea behind.

"Is it really ok, mommy?"

Taking Nadia by the hand, Kira nods. "I think so." She lets out a sigh. "We've got to trust God."

Stepping inside, Rhonda's home is decorated with dark wrought iron crosses and frames. The décor could be considered gothic, but is somehow still bright. Every light is on and the walls are a delicate gray, with a shimmering white trim.

Rhonda glances over her shoulder. "See, perfectly safe."

"Wow," Nadia mumbles as she soaks in the artificial lighting.

"Aren't the light fixtures beautiful?" Kira murmurs. She glances around, still feeling nervous. The one time she forgot to lock the door in Auctairea, a man got into her house. Nadia was young enough to be swaddled on Kira's chest when it happened, but if she hadn't been carrying her rifle, who knows what he would have done to them. Even though he ran out screaming, after that encounter, Kira was never careless with her locks again.

"Yes, they are," Nadia says, bringing Kira out of the fog from Auctairea.

Rhonda watches Nadia's awe at electricity, and her eyes water. She shakes it off before walking up the spiral staircase. "I hope you ladies are hungry. I've got a roast in the oven."

"Your oven works?" Nadia asks.

"Oh, yes." Rhonda glances back at Kira with a frown. "I can't fathom what it would be like to have modern technology stolen. Your government truly crossed a line."

Kira's never taken sympathy well, and doesn't respond as she follows Rhonda upstairs. There are several photographs of a young girl and boy together, mostly outside with bright rays of sunlight gleaming down on them. Some include a happy couple, who seem very proud of their children. "Ruger was adorable." Kira points at one for Nadia to see.

"Do you have anything like that of me?" Nadia asks.

Kira frowns. "No."

"You can take pictures together, now." Rhonda opens the second door in her loft, revealing a large suite. The inside of the room is a deep emerald green, with black baseboards and a large bed that's covered with a green comforter and tan sheets that look like silk. The carpet is a glowing green that reflects the many lights from the wrought iron chandelier hanging perfectly centered from the ceiling.

"This is beautiful," Kira whispers.

"Thank you." Rhonda's head bobs with pride for a moment. Walking up to the first doorway before the black dresser, she opens it. "This is your closet." Inside, there's a large golden gift bag tied with a fancy green bow. Rhonda steps over to the second door on the other side of the dresser. "This is your bathroom."

The floors and counters are all gold, before black cabinets. There are two blown glass sinks that shimmer with gold speckles over brown swirls. A separate room for the commode sits before a golden tub and tall shower, separated by blocks of white tile that's laced with gold and brown swirls. The tile sparkles from the sunlight shining down from a rectangular window which is high enough to provide privacy. The light fixtures above the mirror and all the water fixtures are a dark bronze. Even in her prime and all the luxuries Kira once knew, she never saw a bathroom this elaborate.

Nadia is not nearly as impressed with the bathroom as she is of the round window in the bedroom. Just before the glass, there's a seating area with various pillows of different shades of green. "This would be a perfect reading area."

Kira smiles, before noticing the fireplace on the other side of the bed. It's smaller than the mantle was in her living room, but the crown molding is painted the same black as the baseboards, making it a sophisticated centerpiece. "This isn't your room?"

"No, my room is down the hall. Don't worry, you're not putting me out." Rhonda pulls out a tape measurer from her purse. "Before I leave you two alone, I need to get your measurements. That way, I can order clothes."

"That's extremely kind of you." Kira almost does not want to accept such generosity.

"My brother insisted." Rhonda kneels to take their measurements. "Auctairean fashion is too racy to belong anywhere in my house, not that you'd ever dress that way. I always admired you for your discretion. With the way those other Auctaireans dressed…" Rhonda curls her upper lip into a snarl.

Kira holds in a laugh for how unfitting the scowl is for Rhonda's bubbly disposition. "Until now, I never would've believed a Zyandite kept up on Auctairean fashion."

"My mother was mortified when she found out." Rhonda tightly smiles. "How did you do it?"

"What?" Kira asks.

"Become famous in Auctairea without degrading yourself?" Rhonda asks with a hint of skepticism.

"The grace of God is all I can think of. I never once did things like my coworkers." Kira grimaces at the memories. "I had some pretty close calls in the beginning of my career, so close that I almost quit. I couldn't bring myself to compromise my morals."

Rhonda smirks. "I like you even more." She turns her attention to Nadia. "Alright sweetheart, time to get your measurements. Any preference on color?"

"I like purple," Nadia says with a bashful smile.

"The color of royalty," Rhonda grins. "I'm sure I'll find something you'll like. Just one outfit at least, until you can pick out your own clothes. I can't take either of you anywhere, until you're properly dressed."

With how tattered and dirty their clothes are, Kira understands why.

"That sounds great." Nadia is too happy for Kira to decline, even though she doesn't like taking things from strangers.

"Wonderful. There are some clothes in the closet that I took the liberty of picking out for you. I had no idea what size to get, so I purchased the same pajamas in different sizes. I also got a few things you may need to tidy up; soap, toothbrushes, and the like. Unfortunately, nothing is purple. We can fix that later." Rhonda wiggles her nose at Nadia before standing.

Her spine is tight, but Kira has no choice but to accept Rhonda's generosity. She forces herself to smile. "You're so kind, thank you."

"It's an honor to help fellow believers…" Rhonda's eyes momentarily widen. "Oh, before I forget, there's a compact tutor in the closet as well. It's standard for refugees, to help you learn Zyandish, and our culture."

Kira raises a brow. "How soon are we required to learn everything?"

"It takes most immigrants six months to a year before they're able to become citizens."

A year is too long for Kira's liking. She glances at the closet door, determined to master what's required for citizenship, much sooner.

"Dinner will be done in about an hour." With a friendly wave, Rhonda leaves the room.

"I wonder what she got." Nadia runs into the closet and grabs the bag. "It's almost too pretty to open."

"Almost?" Kira smiles.

Nadia takes the cue and unties the plastic ribbon. "I would like to wear this in my hair."

"No, your hair would get tangled in it." Kneeling beside her daughter, Kira feels awful that this is Nadia's first time unwrapping a present.

Nadia pulls out two sets of pajama pants with short sleeve button down shirts made of a silky orange. One is small, and the other, extra small. Kira takes the small and it looks as though it will fit. There are two sets of girl's pajamas, both the same design, but made out of a cotton material donned with a pink flower pattern.

"I love them!" Nadia shouts.

At the bottom of the bag are a couple of unopened toothbrushes, toothpaste, a hairbrush, comb, and an entire set of body care items that are all set in a fancy wicker basket. There's a sparkling golden flower painted on the wrapper, but Kira can't read the name of the scent. Everything is printed in Zyandish. She doesn't like being unable to understand the words that surround her. Opening the wrapper, an unfamiliar, but beautiful floral scent fills the room. "Come on, I want to show you something." Kira carries the toiletries into the bathroom, kneels beside the tub, and turns the water on.

When water starts to pour through the faucet, Nadia covers her mouth and gasps.

Kira smiles, "Running water is such a blessing." She feels the water first to make certain it's not too hot, then takes her daughter's hand and holds it under the stream.

"It's warm!"

"Now, watch this." Kira pours some of the liquid soap under the water and the bathtub fills with bubbles.

Nadia jumps and giggles.

"Why don't you sit down on the window seat while I take a quick shower? By the time I'm done, this tub should be full and you can enjoy a bubble bath." Kira grins widely.

Nadia returns her smile, before bouncing out of the bathroom.

Kira sets the pajamas down on the counter between the sinks. Glancing at her reflection, she frowns. The bruise on her cheek hasn't healed and her hair's a mess. Thinking of how many pictures were taken of her in this state, Kira looks up at the ceiling and sighs. There's nothing she can do about that now, so she searches the cabinets for towels. Kira finds several green towels in the small linen closet. She sets one out for Nadia before hanging the other on the shower door for herself. It's been years since Kira's taken a shower and she intends to take a hot one. When she turns on the faucet, the water is a little too hot. Once she gets the temperature right, Kira relishes in a luxury she once took for granted.

Feeling more refreshed than she has in years, Kira combs her hair at the foot of the bed, while Nadia giggles from the bathtub. Looking around the beautiful room before her, Kira only wishes she had her grandmother's Bible to read.

In order to read anything here, she must learn Zyandish. She eyes the compact tutor Rhonda left, and decides to give herself a day to rest before diving in.

Nadia bounces out of the bathroom in her new pajamas. They're a little big for her, but a better fit than what she was wearing. Nadia's face beams as she jumps onto the bed next to her mom. "I can't believe you used to live like this all the time."

Kira's smile turns into a frown. Nadia should've lived with the bare necessities of running water and electricity. She playfully pinches Nadia's nose. "Do you miss Auctairea?"

Nadia shakes her head vigorously, making Kira laugh.

Wrapping an arm around Nadia, Kira leans back into the large pillows. "We should thank God for being here."

"For sure," Nadia says with a nod.

Kira bows her head to pray. "Dear God, thank you for Ruger. Bless him and protect him as he fights for your people. Thank you for Rhonda. Bless her for her hospitality. Thank you for Zyandite and for bringing us here safely. Help us to be a blessing to the people here and keep Nadia and I safe. Give us victory in all we do, in the name of Jesus, amen."

"Amen. It's so warm here, they don't need that." Nadia points at the fireplace.

Kira giggles. "I think it's more out of comfort than anything else."

"Yeah," Nadia snuggles into her mother's side a little deeper. "I think Rhonda's nice."

"She is." Kira only wishes she could trust that kindness.

"Are we really safe here?"

Kira caresses her hair. "I believe we are, sweetheart."

Nadia closes her eyes and yawns before her breathing deepens into sleep.

Kira looks around this unfamiliar room. She shouldn't be comfortable enough to sleep, but her body is so exhausted, there's no fighting it. Kira silently gives her fears to God before her eyes can no longer stay open.

***

In downtown Brustonite, Wilma Marshal sits in her upscale dressing room, heavily anticipating a download onto her tablet. With thick, brunette hair, she stares at her tablet as images from her protégé finally begin to load. Her sapphire eyes are lined with charcoal shadow and her lips are painted a deep red. The mauve blush makes her appear to have more pronounced cheekbones than her face possesses. As the pixels form into an image, Wilma begins pacing throughout the room. Wearing a black and white polka dot dress, her red heels give her a height that feels like power. "Come on, who is she?" Wilma says through her teeth.

Finally, the first image from the airport is legible. Kira's clothes and hair are tattered, but she smiles for the camera like the celebrity she once was.

The hunger in Wilma's eyes fades into fear. She reaches for the silk cushioned arm of her chair and slowly sits down in front of her vanity. "It can't be…" She looks at her reflection. Already feeling inadequate, she returns her gaze to the screen. Kira Westin was once the most trusted name in news. Admiration is yanked down by jealousy. Wilma glares at Nadia's face. A child complicates her plans, but not nearly so much as the mother's experience. Unlike the women of Zyandite, Kira isn't naïve.

Wilma bites her lip before trying to send a message to her husband, but it doesn't go through. Worried that King Anstone is playing them at their own games, she squares her shoulders, ready to attack.

"Oh, Benson?"

The door behind her opens. Through the mirror she watches Benson step in. The blood disorder keeps him thin and out of battle, right where she wants him. Benson's jawline is pointed below circular glasses that make his youthful blue eyes seem mature. "What do you need?"

Setting her tablet on the vanity, the large oval diamond of her wedding ring causes her eyes to sparkle. "I need you to convince Clark that my evening report must be an emergency broadcast."

Benson raises a brow. "What's the emergency?"

She glances at her tablet. The picture of Kira nearly makes Wilma lose her nerve. "The King's been compromised."

***

Rhonda pulls the roast out of her oven. Deciding it's better to invite her war-torn guests in person, she lightly taps on the bedroom door.

Silence.

She carefully opens the door to find Kira and Nadia asleep.

Rhonda closes the door softly, deciding leftovers are a better option.

She walks downstairs to sit at her table, alone. About to take a bite, Rhonda's tablet chimes. Hoping it's Ruger, she immediately answers it.

Wearing a black sweater, Claudia Anstone's blond hair hangs past her waist, and her blue eyes are bloodshot from crying. "Is it true?"

Rhonda's shoulders tighten. "Yes, mom. It's true."

"What was Ruger thinking?" Claudia sobs and holds her nose with a tissue. "Somewhere along the line, I must have failed him."

"Kira's quite nice, and her little daughter is very sweet." Rhonda shrugs. "I don't think Ruger's decision was that bad…"

Claudia's stops sobbing and her eyes sharpen with a glare. "You didn't hear what Wilma Marshal just said, did you?"

Rhonda drops her fork. "No."

***

CHAPTER 6
ACCUSATIONS

A low sob causes Kira's eyes to open. She immediately feels for Nadia, who sleeps soundly beside her. Figuring it was just a nightmare, Kira should be relieved, but the light above the curtains tinges her heart with guilt. She shouldn't disrespect Rhonda's hospitality by sleeping in so late. Tiptoeing out of bed, Kira draws the curtains and has to cover her mouth in order to contain her gasp. What she assumed was daylight, is the artificial lights of the city. Rows and rows of streetlights, amber lit windows, and sky-rises off in the distance sparkle like yellow diamonds in the night. After living in darkness for so long, she can't help herself and reaches a hand out to caress the glass. "Light," Kira whispers. Her eyes begin to water. "Thank you, God," she says before looking back at Nadia. She almost wants to wake her, but there'll be another night to show off the beautiful sight. Kira closes the curtains and is about to crawl back into bed when she hears another sob. Worried for Rhonda, Kira quietly opens the door and peeps out to find the entire house is dark, except for a crack under a door across the hall. Gently tapping on the door, Kira backs up when Rhonda answers.

Her face is wet from tears and her hair is a mess.

The silence is painful.

"Is everything okay?" Kira asks.

"I didn't mean to wake you." Rhonda looks at the floor and lets out a sigh. "But, no…" Her lips quiver as she brings her eyes back to Kira.

"Everything's far from okay." She motions for Kira to step into her room.

Kira feels silly for assuming the room given to her and Nadia was the master, for this room is twice the size of the guest room. A black canopy bed is showcased in the center with ruffled, emerald bedding. Above the canopy is a chandelier with black crystals that reflect the light, though dimly. Green curtains line the windows with a crinkled fabric that shimmers as it hangs all the way to the dark wooden floors. The walls have tiny string lights that flow down, until meeting up at the center, making them appear like the edge of curtains, giving a comforting glow. The only wall free of stringed lights is crafted entirely of flat, square mirrors, that all have gold speckles on them.

"See for yourself." Rhonda flips a switch to darken a wall before setting her tablet to project Wilma's emergency announcement.

A brunette sits in a lavish studio. Shoulders squared, this woman is calculated and arrogant, but Kira sees through the disguise. Her blue eyes don't hold the confidence of experience, but instead overflow with the hunger of ambition.

"Who is she?" Kira eyes the ridiculous polka dotted dress Wilma dons before glancing at Rhonda.

"Wilma Marshal. She's gives the evening report."

"That's a primetime reporter?" Kira's forehead scrunches at the conniving, but inexperienced face projected on the wall.

"It's a Lineage thing." Rhonda waves at the image dismissively. "She was promoted after marrying King Tidal's only heir."

"I see." Kira reads the Auctrah subtitles and crosses her arms.

"The rumors you've heard, they're true." Wilma places a hand over her heart. "At first I was relieved to hear that our king was alive, and a little proud in my Eve duties that it was a woman who saved him." Wilma's hand slowly falls to her lap. "Unfortunately, my husband heard from a trusted source that right before this Auctairean boarded the plane, she placed her hand on King Anstone's face." Wilma wiggles in her seat, as though such a thing were preposterous.

Kira glances at Rhonda. "Is that a sin here?"

Rhonda shakes her head.

"Now, I admire King Anstone, as does my husband." Though briefly, Wilma's eyes tell a different story. "This woman has an adorable little girl, who deserves all Zyandite has to offer, but it's the Auctairean mother who concerns me. Perhaps, if we had the King's vitals, we'd have proof of his loyalty to the Laws of Chastity, and our God, but considering who this woman is..." Wilma frowns before a graphic appears to her left.

An old image of Kira pops up. Far from the tattered airport photo, in this image, her hair is professionally styled in rolls of curls. Kira's wearing a golden gown and smiles with her signature burgundy lipstick shimmering in the light. Next to her, stands Prime Minister Joplin. It was election night in Auctairea, and he had just won. Shorter than her, Stephen Joplin never has been much to look at. Most eyes were on Kira as she held his hand up in victory.

"Kira Westin..." Wilma practically growls. "Of all the people residing in Auctairea, she's the one who saved our King?" Wilma shakes her head. "I'm not buying it. It's likely King Anstone was set up."

Now the image cuts to Kira standing with George in front of one of Quandii's most luxurious hotels. She's in her wedding gown. Hand on George's chest, the yellow faucets of her 'Roberta,' engagement ring reflected rainbows, even in the distorted gray light of Auctairean skies.

"Widowed to the late Governor of Quandii, could it be that Kira Westin has found herself an upgrade?" Wilma's lips curve into a snarl. "I don't know how she seduced our King, not with Ruger Anstone's reputation, but..." Wilma places a finger on her chin as though just coming up with an idea. "Maybe the years King Anstone spent in Auctairea, made him susceptible to her guiles?" She shrugs. "Hopefully, Lead Pastor Trigon, and our generals will get to the bottom of this. Until then, and as always, pray for Zyandite." Her eyes begin to tear. "If our King sinned..." She sobs, and holds a hand to her nose to contain herself. "May the great I Am have mercy on us all."

Rhonda sobs before turning the projection off.

"That's ridiculous!" Regretful for yelling, Kira closes her eyes and silently prays it won't wake up Nadia.

"It's really not, at least, not without his vitals." Rhonda nurses a headache. "This is hard for me to ask, but I must know." She shakes a little before straightening her shoulders to gather the gumption. "Were you physical with my brother?"

Kira slouches and tells the truth. "We kissed."

Rhonda's bronze complexion turns ghostly white. "On the lips?"

"Yes."

For a moment Rhonda looks like she's going to faint.

"Is kissing some unholy deed here?"

Rhonda's face tightens. "No. It's a sign of commitment. Zyandites only kiss someone on the lips if they intend to marry them."

Kira's heart skips a beat. Auctairean proposals are gaudy and are more about attention than commitment. Ruger's confessed love felt like a proposal, but Kira couldn't believe he fell for her so soon.

Not even after she fell for him.

Even now, the memory warms her heart enough to burn her cheeks. "You know, when Ruger told me he was going to make me his queen, I thought he was being metaphorical."

"My brother's never metaphorical." A storm brews in Rhonda's eyes. "That's all you did?"

"Rhonda, I'm a Christian. I wouldn't betray my God!"

"I believe you, and I can't imagine my brother sinning like..." Rhonda takes in a deep breath. "Well, like that."

"I didn't want this to happen. I didn't even know who your brother was when God told me to save him. I thought he was just a pilot." Kira holds in a tear. "I never imagined it would lead to this."

Rhonda grits her teeth. "A world renowned reporter not knowing her neighboring country's king isn't exactly believable."

"My connection to the world was lost when the electricity was turned off."

"Can you prove it?"

"All anyone has to do is take one look at my house."

Rhonda studies her for a moment. Finally, her shoulders relax. "Well, enough of this. Everyone knows Wilma expected to be queen." Anger crosses her eyes. It's not fitting for her demeanor. "And her husband would've been crowned, if you hadn't saved my brother."

Kira's stomach sinks. Feeling protective of Ruger, she tilts her chin. "Do you think Ruger's crash was an attempted coup?"

Taking a step back, Rhonda's eyes are no longer suspicious. "I couldn't dream of the generals doing that. No Zyandite is that selfish."

"Your brother said something very similar." It's hard for Kira to understand such gullibility. Biting her lip, she shrugs. "I hope you're right."

"Of course, I am." She waves nonchalantly.

Kira's not so confident. Wrapping her arms around herself, she soaks in the memory of the night Ruger held her until she fell asleep. Their love is genuine, and clean. She won't let anyone taint it. "Rhonda," a boulder of fear almost sinks Kira's courage, she silently asks God to help her rise above it. "If I were to address the people of Zyandite, would my words be translated?"

"Yes…" Rhonda nervously looks down.

Kira glances at her reflection in the mirror. Just from one shower her hair is shinier than it's been in years, but the bruise on her cheek still hasn't healed. She caresses it. Ruger saving her is yet another reason why Kira can't let him down. "Can you request an interview for me?"

Rhonda's eyes bulge. "You want to face Wilma Marshal?"

"Your brother and I were pure. I deserve the right to defend that."

"What are you going to say?" Rhonda asks.

"Whatever God leads me to…" Kira takes in a deep breath. "He hasn't let me down yet."

Rhonda's eyes warm to Kira more than she's displayed since they've met. "I'll put in a request for you tomorrow." She glances at her tablet and sighs. "I'm sorry I woke you."

Taking the cue, Kira steps towards the hall. She stops at the doorway as the words boil inside of her. "If it's any consolation, God told me to save Ruger. That's how I know God will bless this." She doesn't look at Rhonda while leaving the room.

Feeling like ants are crawling on her skin, Kira rubs her arms. Checking on Nadia, Kira's relieved she slept through her outburst. Doubt creeps up her spine and fills her mind with hopelessness. She knows there's only one thing that can help her and Ruger now. Silently, Kira lips 1 Peter 5:7:

Give all of your worries and cares to God, for he cares about you.

Eyes adjusting to the glow of amber that frames the edge of the curtains, Kira drops to her knees and whispers a prayer. "Oh Lord, my loving God, I know you brought Ruger into my life for a reason bigger than just us. You've sent Nadia and I to this place to bring you glory. Don't let these accusations detour the plans you have for us. Make these wrongs right and protect us, in the name of Jesus, amen."

Her faith is strong, but the weight of dishonor sinks her hope. The image of her holding up Joplin's hand flashes through her mind, making her cringe. Deep down, Kira knows she doesn't deserve to be a king's wife, not after letting *them* down...

***

CHAPTER 7
PUMPKIN CREAM CAKE AND COFFEE

The morning sun makes Kira feel silly for assuming the artificial lights were the dawn. Never seeing the sun so bright, she sits at the windowsill to watch it rise. Behind her, Nadia stirs before awakening with a smile.

"Are we still in Zyandite?" She rubs her eyes before bouncing to her mother's side.

"Yes, look." Kira points at the cloudless sky.

"I've never seen a sunrise so pretty."

"Me neither." Kira gives Nadia a quick hug before looking at the door. She's been dreading facing Rhonda again after last night. The last thing she wants is for Nadia to feel insecure, but they can't hide in this room forever. "You think Rhonda needs help making breakfast?"

"I sure hope so."

"Let's find out." Kira chuckles before taking Nadia's hand, and braving the walk downstairs.

On the first floor, the only window coverings are white lace, see-through curtains. Even without the drones of Auctairea lurking outside, the openness makes Kira uncomfortable. She shoves it down and steps into the kitchen to find Rhonda's in a better mood.

"Good morning," Rhonda practically sings.

Kira's brow furrows. She can't help but wonder if their conversation last night was only a dream. "*Good* morning?"

Rhonda gives her a wink.

"Good morning," Nadia says before noticing the food. Along Rhonda's countertop are several plates full of scrambled eggs, bacon, toast, orange juice, coffee, and pumpkin cream cakes with white icing drizzled on the top. "This is amazing."

"It's all for you," Rhonda says. "Just so you know, my brother handled Wilma's accusations last night. So far, the people support him."

Relief nearly causes Kira's knees to buckle. She sits next to Nadia to keep from falling. "He did?"

"Yes. Now, Wilma's facing backlash."

"Praise God," Kira whispers.

"You'll have to watch his address after we eat." Rhonda's hair is styled in perfect curls and her shoulders are relaxed, a far cry from the state she was in last night.

Looking down, Kira finally notices the food. "I can't believe you went through the trouble of making all of this. Thank you."

"Actually, I called it in," Rhonda says before taking a sip of coffee.

"Oh," Kira leans back in her chair. "Food delivery was one of the things I missed the most. It took me a couple of years to get over it."

Rhonda's eyes widen. "I can't even imagine. Well, let's pray so we can eat." She bows her head. "The great I Am, thank you for these wonderful ladies, and for the food we're about to eat. Thank you for making my brother so courageous, and please, justify him. In the mighty name of Jesus Christ, amen."

"Amen," Kira and Nadia say in unison before digging in.

"My brother was adamant about you trying pumpkin cream cakes."

Rhonda serves one on Nadia's plate.

"He said they're his favorite." Nadia takes a bite. "This is so good!" She exclaims between bites, making Rhonda grin.

"Yes, and this coffee is amazing," Kira says, remembering the last time she had coffee. Nadia wasn't walking yet, and it was extremely watered down.

Rhonda nods approvingly. "Pumpkin spice is my favorite."

"Pumpkin and coffee…" Kira smiles. "I never would've thought they'd go well together."

"Zyandites have been drinking it for years," Rhonda says with a playful wave.

"Pumpkin is perfect!" Nadia proclaims before gobbling up another cake.

Laughter fills the room like a melody. Kira takes another sip of her coffee and soaks in the sunshine from the window. Slowly, her muscles relax.

In Rhonda's backyard, a wooden swing overlooks a wide, green lawn with a large oak tree in the center. There's a water fountain that several birds have designated as their bathtub. The blue and brown feathers playfully bounce around the gray stone. Kira can't help but compare, for even the birds of Zyandite are innocent, unlike those in Auctairea…

Kira won't let the past taint this moment. "Zyandite is so beautiful."

"Thank you." Rhonda looks down at her tablet. "I was able to schedule you an interview with Wilma. November seventh is the earliest available."

"That's a month away." Kira tries not to frown in front of Nadia, but doesn't understand why Wilma would wait so long. "This should be a top story."

"Well, I called to schedule *after* my brother corrected her." Rhonda blushes. "I think Wilma needs time to nurse her wounds."

"Oh?" Kira raises a brow.

Rhonda turns her attention to Nadia. She watches her take the last two bites from her plate before pointing at the back door. "I have a jar of bird feed under the bench on my porch. If you toss some by the fountain, more birds will come."

Nadia looks at her mom with worry brimming from her eyes. "I can go outside?"

Kira looks at the backyard. It's fenced, but she already feels the perspiration building on the back of her neck. It was so dangerous for Nadia to go outside in Auctairea, Kira wants to say no. The fountain is just five feet from the backdoor. Kira grimaces before she nods.

"Really?" Nadia's face beams as she backs her chair up to stand.

"Yes, but no further than the fountain."

"Okay," Nadia runs outside with a skip. She stops and takes a moment to admire the glow of sunshine on her arm.

Kira leans against the door, ready to rush outside if Nadia needs her.

Rhonda watches from the window as Nadia gathers the bird seeds. "She couldn't go outside?"

Kira doesn't take her eyes off of Nadia and shakes her head. "I wasn't allowed to have her. All children of Auctairea are institutionalized in an Education Center from birth. Nadia would've been raised an atheist. I couldn't do that. When the law came down, I hid her."

Rhonda's heart is so stung she sits back and places a hand over her chest. "My brother mentioned a daily drone patrol. How did you hide her from that?"

"Every day she had to hide in the only room in the house without a window. That's how we survived." Kira's lips curve into a smile upon watching Nadia giggle at the birds. "She's missed out on just about everything. Birthday parties, Christmas, friends. I educated her at home, but resources were limited. At least her soul belongs to God."

"We always knew Auctairea was bad, but to fall that far…" Rhonda shivers. "I'm so sorry."

Kira glances at Rhonda, but only for a second before refocusing on her daughter. "Don't be."

"Well, things are better here, especially after this." Rhonda's eyes soften before she points her tablet at the cleared wall in her living room, and turns the projection on.

Staying in position to maintain an eye on Nadia, Kira's heart melts at just the sight of Ruger. She's never seen him cleaned up, and feels her cheeks flush.

"Good evening, Zyandite, it's come to my attention that my life being saved by a foreigner is somehow an emergency." He grins and straightens his shoulders. "We know the real reason why Wilma Marshal used the emergency broadcast, and it certainly wasn't to follow the instruction given in Jeremiah 7:6, nor was it to better Zyandite. No, Wilma's accusations were nothing more than a ploy to elevate her status. What's worse, she's using a widow and a fatherless child to do it. As your King, I owe it to the people of Zyandite to be transparent, but now is not the time to parade around my personal life. I didn't want to put our soldiers at risk by distracting the Lineage with my relationship with Kira. I'll wait until after this war is won to pursue my own interests. It's too bad Wilma Marshal couldn't do the same. Then again, if I had died, Wilma would be queen..." His chin lowers with a slight glare.

Kira's jaw drops before she looks at Rhonda.

"My brother doesn't beat around the bush," Rhonda says with a smirk.

Rhonda may be right, but Ruger didn't come forward and say he intends to marry her. Unable to hide her frown, Kira looks at the floor. She shouldn't expect him to marry her, even if he did say he'd make her his queen. He was still recovering from kepweed poisoning, and has probably come to his senses by now. After all, they only knew each other for a few days.

Ruger lifts his chest. "Accusations should never be taken likely. To ease your hearts and swiftly prove mine and Kira's innocence, I have put our Satellite Charge Commander on the case of finding my vitals. General Danning had better prove he's worth his salt or I'll replace him with New Blood."

"Non-Lineage," Rhonda explains.

Kira's heart flutters. "That's quite the threat to them?"

Rhonda only nods.

Ruger slowly takes the monitor off and shows it to the camera. "My sensor hasn't changed, and everyone can see it's working now. Once this mystery is solved, mine and Kira's purity will be revealed. Until then, we know the laws of our land are open to Christians all around the world. Kira and Nadia's journey into citizenship shouldn't be scrutinized unless they refuse to assimilate." Ruger's eyes brighten. "From what I've seen of them, the opposite is true. Kira and Nadia were more like foreigners in Auctairea. This widow, and her precious little child, had been reduced to dire poverty in one of the most dangerous places on earth, yet the love they displayed for God was greater than I've seen." He smirks. "I certainly wasn't charmed by Auctairean guiles." Ruger quotes Wilma with a brief shake of his head. "Not only did Kira risk her life to save mine, but she risked it every day just to believe in God. That's something Zyandites should admire, not condemn. I'm certain that once you get the chance to know Kira, you'll see why I sent her home. Until then, no matter what Wilma Marshal, or anyone else with a stake in the crown says, Proverbs 12:19 tells us that, Truthful words stand the test of time, but lies are soon exposed. The great I Am is faithful, and always shows what's true. Now, we must all pray for Zyandite's victory in this war. Ask the great I Am for discernment regarding Kira. I love you all."

The projection fades.

Rhonda's face beams as her fingers scroll along her tablet. "He asked for you to call him after watching." She hand the tablet to Kira.

Kira takes it. The device is larger than the cellphone she used to have, but is thinner and feels smooth in her hands. "Oh, sweet technology," Kira says while waiting for it to ring.

"I can't imagine..." Rhonda says with a sympathetic shake of her head before going to clean up the remains of their breakfast.

Ruger's face appears on screen. He's smiling and appears a thousand times healthier than when she last saw him. "Good morning."

"Hello Ruger," Kira whispers. Her heart races at just the sight of him. Yet he didn't publicly admit to loving her. Her lips press together in disappointment.

"How are you and Nadia doing?"

"Good," Kira holds the tablet up towards the window, so that he can see Nadia playing with the birds.

"She's adjusting well."

"Yes…" Kira frowns. "Apparently, Zyandite is not."

"Not Zyandite, but Wilma's aspirations," Ruger gently corrects.

Kira doubts Wilma's their only opposition. "I didn't know I'd cause you so much trouble by coming here and…" The words get stuck in her throat. She should do everything she can to fight for Nadia's position in this new place, but that would make her worse than Wilma. If she and Ruger are to marry, Kira wants it to be for the love she thought they shared.

Ruger frowns. "I didn't expect this level of scrutiny either, but we're here, and must defeat it."

"You make it sound so simple," Kira whispers.

"It is simple. The great I Am is always on the side of truth," Ruger's tone is resolute.

Rhonda observes Kira's every move.

Kira feels the heat from her stare. The reality is she deserves Rhonda's judgement. Releasing a low breath, Kira knows what must be done. "I take it…" Kira looks at Nadia, and silently begs God for her to have a blessed future, no matter what happens. "You're going to send Nadia and I away?"

"I love you too much to do that."

Kira's face morphs into a scowl "You didn't announce your intention to marry me."

"I know it seems dishonest, but I can't do that yet. At least this way, the Lineage can only guess. You, and my men, will benefit from my delaying the announcement."

"It's okay if you changed your mind." Kira lowers her voice. "Only Rhonda knows that we kissed."

He blushes. "I almost did. I even called the King of Tunaunda. He agreed to welcome you with open arms, but the prophecy only confirms my original decision. Our union is God's will."

"Prophecy?" Kira whispers. Looking up, she finds Rhonda's still staring, but the heat has left her eyes and has been replaced by uncertainty.

"Yes. Zyandite takes that gift of the Spirit very seriously. When I crashed, the Lead Pastor's wife dreamt that our nation didn't need a king, but a queen."

Kira's arms cover with goosebumps. Relief may balm the sting on her heart, but doubt fills her mind. "You believe this?"

"Yes. That's why Wilma's being offensive. In her mind, the prophecy should be about her. It's ambition, pride, arrogance, things of this world, things of the *Lineage* that caused her to attack you. It's not personal. Besides that, the people see through it." Ruger hissed 'Lineage' through his teeth.

"I get Wilma, but a prophecy…" Kira's heart sinks. In Auctairea, before religion was made illegal, prophecies were only lies meant to spin a profit. It doesn't feel right to trust one now. "It's just too much for me to process."

"I know it's a lot to take in," Ruger's tone is firm. "So be strong and courageous," he adds with a spark in his eyes.

The memory of God's confirmation to her fills Kira's heart now. Of all the verses for that bullet to land on, it had to be Psalm 31:24, "all you who put your hope in the LORD!"

"That's my Huntress."

Everything she sees in Ruger's eyes reminds Kira of why she fell in love with him. Cheeks hot, she looks down.

"I wish I could talk for longer, but I must go. Tell Nadia 'hello' for me."

"I will," Kira says before the screen turns black. Slowly, she hands it to Rhonda.

"Psalm thirty?..." Rhonda asks.

"Psalm 31:24." Kira holds in a tear. "Your brother's Bible stopped a bullet from hitting his heart. That bullet just so happened to land on my favorite verse."

Rhonda gasps. "This is bigger than just you and my brother."

Feeling unsure, Kira takes in a deep breath, hoping Rhonda's not so naïve.

"In Auctairea, the power of God displayed in our lives was muted. Here in Zyandite, every gift of the Holy Spirit is active, including the gift of prophecy. Farrah will explain all of this very soon."

Checking to see if Nadia's alright, Kira watches her in the sunshine and should feel joy at the sight. Instead, her stomach is tight. Closing her eyes, she fantasizes that Ruger was coming home to them not as a king, but a pilot. Opening them, Kira knows the reality is simple:

This is a life she doesn't deserve.

Rhonda's voice pulls Kira out of her doubts. "This is God's doing. So we might as well have a little fun."

"Fun?" Kira gasps. To her, now is not the time.

"Yes." Rhonda nods, and this smile reaches her eyes. "We've got to get you and Nadia clothes that fit right." She laughs. "Not only are you Zyandite's future queen, but you can't exactly face Wilma Marshal wearing that."

Future Queen? Kira's knees wobble and she looks at the floor. "I don't know…"

Rhonda leans her back into her chair and lets out an exasperated sigh. "Well, I certainly could use a shopping trip."

"You still have brick and mortar stores?" Kira asks while raising a brow. It's been years since she's stepped inside of a store, and the idea of sharing such an experience with Nadia is tempting.

Rhonda's smile broadens. "Of course we do."

***

Under the dark skies of Auctairea, General Danning sits at a desk in his quarters with a scowl. Three generations of charge commanders run through his DNA. He won't let a New Blood, Preacher King taint his legacy and shame his descendants. Yanking out his tablet from the drawer, he dials Wilma's number.

"General Danning," Wilma greets with reverence. "I'm so sorry."

"You should've consulted with Eleanor before saying anything on air."

Wilma holds her head down and frowns. "I know."

"Now I'm on the hook, me! It'll be my descendants who'll suffer, because we both know why I can't deliver his vitals. This is all your fault."

A lone tear falls down Wilma's cheek. "You've change vitals before…" She looks up, her eyes pleading.

Regret covers General Danning's face. "Never for a king. If I did, not only would King Anstone deny it, but former Satellite Charge members would analyze every second of it, and post their findings all over Chadder, where I can't control a thing." His eyes darken. "They've gotten bolder, and have been investigating everything."

"I understand."

"I'll stall, but we can't reveal their innocence or else Auctairean blood will intermingle with ours." General Danning rubs his hair back in an attempt to calm his nerves.

"We can't let that happen."

General Danning raises a cynical brow. "*We* certainly won't do anything if I end up the sacrificial lamb!"

Shoulders weighed down by defeat, Wilma sighs. "I can't apologize enough."

"You should be sorry," General Danning snarls before puffing out his chest, "For the courage."

"For the purity," Wilma whispers.

"For the memories… For the blood," They say in unison, before General Danning hangs up. Scrolling through ZyanBell, the overwhelming support for King Anstone makes his lips quiver in disgust. "If only he had died!"

CHAPTER 8
CULTURE SHOCK

"Are you sure this is a good idea?" Kira asks. She glances around with invisible fears dripping down her back.

Rhonda is adamant as she opens her front door. "Absolutely," she proclaims before walking to her car, where the driver awaits.

Nervous, Kira holds Nadia's hand and does her best to smile. The purple sweater dress Nadia wears fits her perfectly, but the black flats Rhonda was kind enough to order, are so tight they've already rubbed a line on Nadia's heels.

Kira's black blouse is a comfortable satin, but flows like a tent over her skinny blue jeans. Her flats, though cute with black lace over white leather, are ghastly uncomfortable. Still, Kira refuses to complain.

Rhonda steps into the vehicle first and Kira follows. Kira's palms sweat. It's been years since she's been inside of a store, and the language barrier only adds to her stress.

"Do you think I'll get shoes that really fit me?" Nadia whispers.

"I hope so, sweetheart." Kira half-hugs her, attempting to make this as enjoyable for Nadia as she can.

"I don't want either of you to hold back. I have a generous budget and expect no less than two weeks of clothes for both of you, suitable for every type of weather. Coats, rain boots, cute boots, running shoes, dress shoes, basically everything." Rhonda waves her hand around in a careless circle.

"That's very kind, but we can only accept the minimum." Kira has always been uncomfortable being indebted to anyone. After all, nothing's free.

"Did you save Ruger's life?" Rhonda asks with a knowing grin.

Kira rolls her eyes. "Yes, but he saved ours so we're even."

"Well…" Rhonda's brow scrunches. "What about the medicine you spared for him? Perhaps this could make that even?"

"Thank you, Rhonda, but we can only accept the necessities," Kira reluctantly agrees.

"For every season, right?" Rhonda asks with a grin.

Kira shakes her head.

Rhonda smirks admiringly, folds her arms and looks out the window as they journey downtown. She may have backed off for now, but Kira can see this battle is far from over.

Trying to hide her concern, Kira lets out a slow breath before looking outside. The shops of Brustonite are nestled in the heart of downtown, along both sides of a river that runs through the city. There are ducks and turtles on the riverbank, mere inches before the concrete sidewalk begins. Large oak and pine trees along the river make the air smell fresh. Towering sky-scrapers, hotels, and shops on each side of the river should make it feel urban, but reflect the natural landscape, adding to the charm. You can drive along the back of the shops, but Rhonda explained that to enjoy the river, you must walk on foot.

Their shoes are uncomfortable, and Kira likes the idea of a quick escape to the car if needed, which convinced Rhonda to save their river walk for another day.

As they drive along, a sporadic view of the river peers in-between each building, making Nadia dance in her seat.

The moment they park, Rhonda leads the way to a building with pretty pink and gold animals painted on the front. There's a fawn, a bunny, and two swans before pink and gold writing in Zyandish above the glass door.

"Here we go," Rhonda announces in Auctrah before stepping inside. *"Hello!"* Rhonda greets the young woman behind the counter in Zyandish.

The girl can't be older than eighteen, with straight black hair that flows to the middle of her back, a dark complexion, and friendly brown eyes.

"Hello, Miss Anstone. Oh no, I got the measurements wrong," The girl replies in Zyandish.

"Yes, Izzy, and the shoes don't fit her either," Rhonda says with an exaggerated frown.

Kira and Nadia exchange uncomfortable glances, since they can't understand a word of Zyandish.

"She feels bad for getting the measurements wrong," Rhonda says with a wink at Nadia.

"We'll fix it," Izzy promises before looking at Kira and smiling. *"Is that really her?"*

Rhonda only nods.

"Poor thing is so skinny. Wow, um… I don't believe any of the things Wilma Marshal said. Would you mind telling her thank you for saving our king?" Izzy humbly asks.

Taken off guard, Rhonda's mouth gapes before she turns to Kira, "Izzy just thanked you for saving my brother."

"Oh." Kira blushes before smiling at Izzy. "Tell her that it was God who saved Ruger, not me."

Rhonda's eyes flicker with adoration before translating.

Izzy gasps. *"Wow, an Auctairean talking like that. Do you suppose the prophecy is about her?"*

Rhonda shrugs.

"Well, okay." Izzy smiles before refocusing on Nadia. *"You're a very beautiful little girl. Would you mind stepping on our shoe-size mat?"*

Nadia looks up at her mom in fear, before Rhonda quickly translates, causing Nadia to relax. "Oh, yes. I don't mind."

She follows Izzy without letting go of Kira's hand. On the right side of the store there's an array of adorable girls' shoes and boots on display. Before the shelves of shoes are two pink benches and a long floor mat painted with different sized foot prints.

"It's okay, Nadia," Kira says. "You need to take off your shoe, and place your foot on as many prints that it takes to find your size."

"Okay, mommy," Nadia says before doing so with great concentration.

"Size ten," Izzy tells Rhonda.

Within a couple of minutes, Izzy brings over the same shoes Nadia is wearing, but in the right size.

Nadia puts them on her feet and stands up. Her eyes widen and she runs in circles around her mom. "They fit, mommy! They really fit!" She exclaims before jumping up and down, then squealing with joy.

Rhonda translates Nadia's words to Izzy.

"She's never worn the right sized shoes before?" Izzy asks.

Rhonda's eyes become glassy, but only for a moment. *"No."*

Izzy places a hand on her heart in sympathy for Nadia, before running to the shelf to gather as many size ten shoes that she can carry.

Nadia likes the boots, but loves a pair of purple tennis shoes, even though she needs her mother's help to lace them. She also picks out a pair of red flats and brown hiking boots, as well as fancy white sandals and a pair of black dress shoes.

"Can we get all these, plus some in size eleven, in case she has a sudden growth spurt?" Rhonda asks.

"Of course," Izzy replies, more than happy to help Nadia obtain a true

wardrobe.

"You'll need a good jacket, some tees, and jeans," Kira tells Nadia, trying to keep things practical and ready for the outdoors in case they need to flee on foot.

"Is that all I'm allowed to get?" Nadia's eyes are pleading.

"Of course not, you need dresses for church, pajamas, and cute little summer play outfits to match your new sandals," Rhonda answers.

Nadia beams before rushing to the shelves.

Kira looks back at Izzy to see her carrying out a tall stack of shoe boxes to Rhonda's driver. She finds it pointless to argue that there are twice as many shoes than what her daughter picked out. Rhonda's clearly determined to spoil Nadia, and Kira can't bring herself to stop it.

Nadia notices a white dress and gasps. "Mommy, this is so beautiful. May I have it?"

Kira holds back a cringe. White stains easily and is reflective at night. She wants nothing more than to tell her daughter no, but just can't. "...Yes."

"Really?!" Nadia practically screams.

"We're in Zyandite, not Auctairea. You may wear white if you want to." Kira smiles.

After that, Nadia made sure to get the more practical clothes her mother asked her to pick, before finding a red dress she just had to have.

"You need a good coat." Kira searches through the racks and finds a navy blue twill jacket that's lined with fleece. "This one."

Nadia hates it, but wants to please her mom. Then her eyes fall on a light pink, faux fur coat that is hanging behind Kira. "Oh mommy, have you ever seen anything so pretty in your whole life?"

Kira turns as her daughter reaches for the elaborate coat.

"We'll get both," Rhonda says more to Kira than Nadia. "And Nadia, I saw boots displayed in the front window. They'd match that coat perfectly. There's also a pair of skinny white pants and a shimmering golden shirt over there," Rhonda points to her left, "That would complete the whole outfit."

Nadia gasps out of joy and rushes to the items.

Against her instincts, Kira accepts this experience for her daughter's sake.

"That would be lovely, Rhonda, thank you. Nadia, there's also a tan suede vest on the wall over there which would look adorable over a denim dress I saw around here, somewhere," Kira suggests.

"Thanks mommy!"

As they journey towards the denim dress, a shelf filled with dolls and various stuffed animals capture Nadia's attention. Kira's proud of Nadia for not saying anything, but Rhonda's more observant than she lets on.

"Any little girl as brave as you are, deserves a dolly." Rhonda takes a brunette doll wearing a purple dress and hands it to Nadia.

"Thank you!" Nadia exclaims, hugging the doll tight.

By the time they're done shopping for Nadia, all three walk out carrying large shopping bags.

"Just the bare necessities?" Kira asks.

"Of course!" Rhonda shoots her a smile.

"Thank you," Kira lips as they hand over the bags to Rhonda's driver, who puts them in the trunk. He doesn't seem happy, making her feel a tinge of guilt. Kira hopes he doesn't think she's just using Ruger. Shaking it off, she gets into the car to find Rhonda grinning.

"Now, it's your turn."

Kira winces.

"Clothes are a necessity," Rhonda states before waving Kira's concerns away.

Even though Kira hates being a charity case, she decides not to argue. Kira looks out of her window and distracts herself by soaking in the view. A bank of the river flashes in-between the quaint little shops that make this downtown so unique. At a red light, the gap is large enough for Kira to enjoy the natural scenery. She notices a mother feeding the ducks with her two toddlers. Both of the young children have matching mops of blond curls, and look so happy.

So safe.

Their mother smiles and just enjoys being a mom. In watching her, Kira's eyes water. She's barely able to stop the tears from forming and looks down in regret, wishing she could've raised Nadia in that kind of freedom. Ashamed by the envy she feels, Kira silently repents for coveting another woman's life. She turns to Nadia, who is kicking her feet back and forth while admiring her new doll. Perhaps that freedom belongs to them now?

"This is my favorite store," Rhonda says before they come to a stop.

Kira appreciates Rhonda's enthusiasm, and forces a smile. "We'll mind our manners," she says, making Nadia giggle.

Rhonda laughs and leads the way.

The glass windows have Zyandish painted in gold along the sides of the entry. Inside, the two women at the counter greet Rhonda as though they're friends.

"Hello, Creda and Miriam!"

Miriam has a light complexion, curly red hair, and a narrow face. She returns Rhonda's greeting with a smile. *"It's good to see you, Rhonda."*

"Is she the Auctairean who saved your brother?" Creda asks. Her complexion is dark, under perfectly straight, black hair.

Rhonda gives a knowing smile, *"Yes, and she desperately needs new clothes. Auctairean went full socialism, and the poor thing has been wearing rags for years."*

"That's so sad," Creda says before pressing her lips together to gather the nerve. *"I watched the King's address, and I want you to know that I believe him."*

"Thank you."

THE LINEAGE

"Yeah, it's only by the grace of the great I Am we were spared from Queen Wilma." Miriam shivers in disgust.

"I think she's bitter." Creda adds.

"Most of the Lineage are," Rhonda jokes, making both ladies laugh.

Kira worries they're laughing at her, before Rhonda explains, "They think Wilma's jealous."

"Oh." Kira glances around, feeling uncomfortable in her own skin. If these people knew the Great Cleansing was her fault, they'd never be so accepting of her.

Rhonda eyes Kira with concern, before leading the way through the massive store. "I'm assuming you'll want jeans and tees, maybe a jacket much like the one you picked out for Nadia. What about dresses for church?"

Kira frowns. "I haven't worn a dress in over five years."

"That's terrible," Rhonda says before her face brightens. "How about this?" She grabs a yellow paisley dress.

"Government workers wear yellow scrubs in Auctairea. I'm sorry, I just…"

"Dislike the color. Good to know." Rhonda sets the dress back on the rack. "What colors do you like?"

"She always wears black, but mommy loves burgundy," Nadia says, proudly carrying her doll through the store.

"Thank you, Nadia." Rhonda winks.

From there on, Kira was completely overwhelmed…

After a few try-ons to reveal Kira's size, Rhonda took to the store like a hurricane.

"We should buy everything a size up, since Auctairea starved you," Rhonda says before digging through the nearest rack. It didn't take long for Rhonda to find every piece of black and burgundy garment available in one size up.

"That's too much," Kira hasps, but Rhonda waves her hand dismissively.

Kira's shoulders cave. She decides to let Rhonda have her fun.

In the beautiful displays of this elaborate store, only one item stands out to Kira. Out of all her clothing she lost, her burgundy cardigan was her favorite. The one hanging before her is the same beautiful shade of burgundy, but it's trimmed with chiffon on the bottom in a shark bite hem. Kira knows it's soft just by looking at it. There's a shimmer in the fabric, but not the kind that makes it coarse. She reaches for it, and once her fingertips caress the silky fabric, Kira smiles.

Rhonda grabs it, checks the size and adds it to her bundle. Of course, Rhonda couldn't help herself and found a few things for her own wardrobe, but Kira was the main focus. The shoes were easier, for Kira wanted a reliable pair of black boots.

Rhonda convinced her to get tennis shoes, black sandals, brown cowgirl boots, burgundy flats, and black dress shoes as well.

After they finally left the shoe department, a burgundy suede coat with faux fur lining and trim caught Rhonda's eyes. "You'll match Nadia in this!"

"I already picked out a black coat. I don't need that." Kira crosses her arms in determination.

"Oh, come on, it's your favorite color."

"Yeah, mommy. We'll match," Nadia pleads.

Kira gives them a firm glare. "No."

"I have a brown fur coat. With you wearing this and Nadia in her pink, we'll be the bells of the ball when we walk down the river for the Christmas Festival." Rhonda sticks her bottom lip out.

Nadia copies her.

Kira uncrosses her arms. "Alright!"

Rhonda giggles victoriously. Her shoes tap along the hard wood floors before they reach the pajama section. She makes sure Kira gets several sets of pajamas, a robe, and even house slippers.

"You'll need a purse." Rhonda gives Kira an adamant look before leading the way to the handbag department.

Kira lets out an overwhelmed sigh. She plans to get the cheapest purse, until something catches her eye. It's a tiny purse, no bigger than most wallets, but it's what covers it that draws her attention. The white handbag has an array of buttons sewed on it that vary in size and color. "What do you think?" Kira asks Nadia, as she takes the purse off the rack.

Nadia covers her mouth. "A new button family?"

Kira nods, feeling satisfied in making up for the loss.

"That's um… Cute," Rhonda says with confusion, before picking out a large and expensive looking burgundy purse. "We'll get both." Rhonda's unwavering before heading towards the register.

Kira blushes while following her.

The ladies behind the counter smile as Rhonda carries a handful of clothes to them. *"This too,"* Rhonda says in Zyandish, while grabbing a set of burgundy chenille socks. The ladies begin bagging everything up. They occasionally look at Kira with excitement.

Meanwhile, Rhonda eyes the store like a shark, before noticing a handgun peeping out from Creda's sweater. *"Is that the new Jalder 9mm?"*

"Yes!" Creda grins. *"I just got it last week. It fires like a dream."* She pulls it out to show Rhonda.

Kira's eyes bulge. She looks around as the fear of being arrested fills her. Handguns are illegal in Auctairea. Even rifles can only be carried in the rural areas.

"Really?" Rhonda crosses her arms. *"I was considering a Jalder, and now, I'm convinced."*

Creda laughs before holstering her weapon.

"With as much as I like revolvers, semi-autos are beginning to sway me. This little guy is my fave." Rhonda pulls a .38 revolver from her purse.

Miriam pulls out a gun from its holster under her shirt. Like Rhonda's gun, it too is a revolver.

Kira watches the Zyandites chit chat about their guns, in the same way Auctairean women used to show off jewelry.

"She's holding back. You should see her hand cannon," Creda says.

"Show me!" Rhonda exclaims.

Miriam blushes before lifting up her black suede skirt, where another gun is holstered. *"It only holds two rounds, but I figure if I ever have to use it, they'll count."* She holds up the mini-shotgun.

Rhonda grins before translating for Kira.

Kira's heart flutters and she places an elbow on the counter to brace her head in wonder. "Rhonda, I absolutely love it here."

Rhonda's eyes dance at Kira, before she turns to the Zyandites. *"In wretched Auctairea, this sweet lady had to fend off rapists and murderers with only a bolt action rifle."*

Miriam reaches out a hand to Kira out of sympathy. *"That's so awful."*

Rhonda quickly translates.

Kira takes Miriam's hand for a moment and smiles.

"I for one am so thankful you saved our king," Miriam adds, before returning to her work.

Kira looks to Rhonda for translation.

After translating, Rhonda pats Kira on the back, "I couldn't agree more."

"Like I keep saying, it was God who saved Ruger's life. I was only his instrument."

Rhonda translates Kira's response, which causes Miriam to look at Kira with high esteem.

"I get to teach her how to properly use a handgun," Rhonda announces before putting her revolver away.

"How exciting," Creda says, before winking at Kira.

Rhonda translates, making Kira grin. While this exchange couldn't feel more foreign to her, Kira's never felt more at home.

Once everything is bagged up, the trunk is at capacity. "I don't think we have room for many groceries, so we'll just get a few things," Rhonda states with another wave of her right hand.

"I've never been to a grocery store," Nadia says before hopping in her seat. Her ability to adapt makes Kira proud.

Rhonda's all smiles. "Trust me, you'll love it."

***

"What were you thinking?" General Kentwood's nostrils might as well blow steam as he struggles to keep up with King Anstone through the hallway. Even with a limp, Ruger hasn't lost his stamina.

"This isn't important right now." Freshly changed in a new uniform, Ruger looks at his tablet to check on the status of the formation.

"Of course, it is!" General Kentwood shouts.

Taking a deep breath, Ruger turns to face the Charge Commander. "Last I checked, the King's love life isn't a priority when going into battle."

General Kentwood's eyes turn into slits. "Once the bodies of soldiers start flooding in, you'll see why it matters."

"You mean like the body of General Baxton?" Ruger watches General Kentwood coil inward. "There are many things that could be discussed right now, but they can wait. My priority is winning this war. Once we obtain victory, you, and the rest of the Lineage, can smear your mud all over me, the way you've done since I was crowned. I can take it, but until this war is won, I order you to remain focused on the mission."

Pressing his lips together, General Kentwood holds back his slurs. After a long moment of silence, he agrees to the order with a nod.

King Anstone marches outside to see the formation is complete. On the runway, rows of tanks and soldiers await the order to invade Quandii. Ruger smiles at them before turning towards the front. It won't be long, and he'll be the first in battle…

CHAPTER 9
A THOUSAND GARDENS

Rhonda's vehicle pulls into a busy parking lot in front of a large, one story building.

Nadia presses her nose against the window. "Are we really going to a store filled with food?"

"Oh yes, frozen foods, dairy, produce, and your favorite, meat," Rhonda says, making Nadia chuckle.

"I think after today, pumpkin cream cakes are her favorite." Kira playfully pinches Nadia's nose.

"Oh, yeah." Nadia bounces in her seat.

Rhonda's the first out of the car. "Wait until you try my candied cookies. They're quite healthy if you can believe it."

"No," Kira says with a sarcastic smile before taking Nadia's hand, and holding it tight through the parking lot.

"We'll help ourselves by not getting a cart, that way we don't overload. Consider this a trial run." Rhonda gives a carefree wave to the wind.

Kira and Nadia stay close behind. When walking across the street towards the building, Kira grabs Nadia and runs.

Rhonda stops in the middle of the street and stares at Kira like she's crazy.

Once Kira gets her daughter to the sidewalk, she returns Rhonda's stare. "Don't stand in the middle of the road. You'll get run over!"

"Oh, my..." Rhonda places a hand over her heart. "They really drove like that in Auctairea?"

"Yes, I almost died so many times, especially when I was pregnant. I couldn't exactly run." Kira shivers at the memory.

As Rhonda walks up, a car stops about ten feet from her. There's an elderly man behind the wheel. He waves at Rhonda with a kind smile, which she returns before slowly stepping up to the sidewalk. Much to Kira's surprise, the man drives on with no sign of irritation.

"I couldn't imagine anyone acting like that," Rhonda says.

"The people here are so nice, it feels like a dream," Kira whispers. "Is all of Zyandite like this?"

"Of course. The nightmare was Auctairea. Now, you get to truly live. Praise God!" Rhonda pats Kira on the arm before leading the way into the store. Double glass doors slide open for them.

"Whoa!" Nadia exclaims.

"They're called automatic doors," Kira explains.

"I like them." Nadia giggles before her eyes bulge. "Mommy, look at all the food!"

"They used to have stores like this in Auctairea," Kira whispers, in hopes their Auctrah won't be noticed.

"Really?" Nadia asks.

Kira nods.

Rhonda scans the store, biting her lip. "I should have written a list... We need meat, red potatoes, fresh fruit, and perhaps some candy?"

"What's candy?" Nadia asks.

"Oh, you poor thing," Rhonda pouts before grabbing a bag of gummy bears. "Wait until you taste these," she tells Nadia before proceeding to the meat aisle.

Nadia's completely overwhelmed and doesn't let go of her mother.

"It's alright. People are being kind to us, here. Don't be scared," Kira whispers.

"I'm not scared, I'm amazed," Nadia purrs. "This store is better than a thousand gardens."

Kira can't help but to laugh, admiring her daughter's awe of God's abundance.

Following Rhonda through the large store with dozens of aisles, Kira's surprised to see a book aisle. She stops and can't help but stare.

Rhonda notices and steps back to see what's caught Kira's eye. "Once you learn Zyandish, I'll fill you in on our best-sellers."

Kira chuckles, "It's so much more than that. I had to search to the ends of Auctairea, and spend a fortune just to find books in print." She walks down the aisle and allows her hand to caress the many rows of various sized hardcovers and paperbacks. "When I was a little girl, going to the bookstore with my mom was one of my favorite things. So much was lost when Auctairea forced publishers to go digital."

Rhonda shakes her head. "That'll never happen here."

"Good." The magazine section turns Kira's eyes into slits. There covers aren't of sultry women the way they were in Auctairea, but of guns, and a few old men in polished uniforms. One of them stands out to her the most. The face on this cover is harden and arrogant. She can recognize the number five that in bold print above his head, but the rest of the text is foreign.

"That's General Kentwood, five generations of Zyandite kings runs through his blood," Rhonda informs.

Kira's nose wrinkles at the reverence to the Lineage. "I don't see Ruger's face, anywhere."

"He never goes in for a photo-shoot. Except for the night of his coronation, the only pictures they've got of him are in motion." Rhonda smirks. "I'll have to show you some."

"I'd like that," Kira says, while watching Nadia pick up a book with a cow drawn on the cover.

"Looks like Feisty, doesn't she?" Nadia asks.

Remembering the abundance God gave them through their old cow, Kira smiles. "Yeah, she does."

"We'll buy it." Rhonda lifts her chin with wave towards the end of the aisle.

Kira appreciates her attentiveness to Nadia before stepping away from the books. Glancing back, something in General Kentwood's eyes bothers her. His eyes may not share the hunger Wilma's possess, but there's darkness residing in them. Kira continues to shop without sharing her observation.

While loading groceries in the car, Rhonda's tablet chimes. She rushes to pull it out of her purse. "It's Ruger," Rhonda whispers, her eyes frantically reading his message. "He's going into battle." Rhonda's eyes tear up. "He's barely recovered, but off he goes." Rhonda waves her hand around before bringing it to her nose and sniffling. "I'm so frightened for him."

Fear hits Kira's stomach like a boulder. Ruger's hardly recovered from the kepweed, and isn't in any condition to march into battle.

Rhonda reaches out to her. "Pray with me, please?"

"Of course." Kira bows her head and lets the Holy Spirit move. While she prays in Auctrah, Rhonda prays in Zyandish.

"Dear Lord, hear our prayer. Please God, don't let Ruger be killed or seriously injured. Show Auctairea how you strengthen those who follow you, and give Ruger and his men victory," Kira prays.

"The great I Am, go before my brother. Be his guard and protector. You know he's hurt, but give him the strength he needs to fight. Lay his enemies down before him, in the

mighty name of Jesus Christ..." Rhonda prays.

"In the name of Jesus," Kira prays.

Then, both women say, 'amen.'

Rhonda leans forward and gives Kira a hug. "I'm glad you're here. I never take his going into battle very well." She sniffles.

Peace overwhelms Kira, when it shouldn't. She knows that can only come from God. "He's going to be alright. I can feel it."

Nadia places her thin, little hand on Rhonda's arm. "Yeah, Ruger took down the machines and everything."

"Oh, I just love you two already," Rhonda says, sniffling one last time before holding her head up. "Now, if you don't mind, I'd like to invite Farrah over for dinner tonight. With Ruger in battle, I need her counsel. Besides that, she really wants to meet you."

Kira shouldn't feel afraid of a Pastor's wife, but in Zyandite, this woman is a government official. The jetlag has worn off and her mind is clear. It's been a long time, but Kira knows what this means, she's going to be groomed for the position Ruger needs her to fill. She looks down to find her palms are sweating again.

***

General Marshal finishes a third set of sit-ups as the lower enlisted tally the pieces of broken machines. He couldn't care less about following through with the King's orders, and lets someone else count for him.

The young soldiers occasionally glare at the elitist general, but say nothing. It's an insult for a Charge Commander to be so indifferent towards their mission, yet they maintain respect for his rank.

Rumbling shakes the ground, making General Marshal stand. He looks at the main gate for Saffarion Airbase, to see a convoy is heading for Quandii. Yanking out his tablet to let Wilma know, nothing he types goes through.

Curving his lips at King Anstone playing him at his own game, General Marshal watches the fleet heading to Quandii, with no way to warn Wilma.

***

CHAPTER 10
QUANDII

A new day in Quandii doesn't typically start until dusk, making the afternoon landscape peaceful. It's almost as though the debauchery from the night before never happened. Only a few Auctaireans are awake. They stagger through the streets of Quandii and around the tents surrounding the city's walls. Most aren't in search of food, but for drugs, which their government ensures is in supply to keep them dependent.

The ground rumbles, making the Auctaireans stop in their tracks.

Above them, the gray sky is filled with several jets.

These aren't the typical droned jets Auctaireans are used to, but older aircraft piloted by humans. As the last of their air force leaves to fight Zyandite, the citizens of Auctairea don't cheer for the military that defends them. Instead, they cower and hide.

***

Twenty-five miles away, thousands of Zyandite soldiers march from their occupied territory of Saffarion Airbase, towards the city of Quandii.

They are slow and methodical.

On a road surrounded by pine trees, these tanks and various vehicles move low to the ground on sky-mode, while hundreds of soldiers march on foot. October is the start of winter in Auctairea, making the air colder than their home. Not a single Zyandite is used to seeing their breath. The fog and heavily draped sky is dark in comparison to the warmth of Zyandite sunshine. All these men want is to win this battle and go home.

Marching in formation, each soldier wears a dark green uniform, with his flag sewn on the sleeve like a proud banner. Framed with shimmering gold, the Zyandite flag is red, with a white cross at the center. Gold stands for the strength of God's throne. Red stands for the sacrifice of Christ's blood. White stands for purity. Every Zyandite must discipline their hearts to follow these attributes. Their mission, whether on the battlefield or during peacetime, is to draw closer to God.

Today, they will attack the invaders of their home, to protect the land of milk and honey the great I Am has blessed them with.

However, this frontal assault is merely a diversion.

On the other side of the city, King Anstone leads a secret charge…

***

Fog blankets the forest, as King Anstone leads his men on horseback. The land of Auctairea is eerily quiet, not even the birds sing.

Riding with eight soldiers, Ruger keeps his eyes peeled for kepweed.

He was able to learn what the plant looks like, and doesn't want their horses to step on it.

A sound disturbs the forest. It was only a scuffling, but it came from behind.

Ruger looks back to see a scrawny man, with unkempt, long hair that's filled with pine needles, hunker down behind a tree. To Ruger's left, Sergeant Wright aims his rifle at the Auctairean.

"Let him be," Ruger orders.

THE LINEAGE

The young Sergeant lowers his weapon, though his keen brown eyes remain on target.

"It's just a Vag," Ruger growls.

Jordan raises a brow. "A what?"

Ruger keeps his eyes straight ahead. "Drug pushers these people call vagabonds." Holding in a chuckle, he looks at Jordan. "They think they're tough."

A flicker of amusement crosses Jordan's face. "Clearly." He glances back at the cowering vagabond and shakes his head.

"Without their drones, these people can't report our location," Ruger says before continuing on as though the Vag doesn't exist.

There's a clearing up ahead. Ruger can see the tall, gray fence that surrounds the city. Above the bristling pines, the clouds of Auctairea don't seem to move. The thin air gives Ruger a headache, but he won't let anything distract him.

Pulling on Gildiel's reins, even under Auctairea's dark sky, her golden coat shines.

Looking at his men, Ruger's spirit is full of determination. Eyeing their ready faces, Ruger raises his chin up. "Why are we here?"

"To take down our invaders," Sergeant Groth answers.

"Who do we trust?" Ruger asks.

This time, every soldier answers: "God!"

Gildiel knows the pre-battle drill, and eagerly paces back and forth in front of the small Calvary. Even she is readying her heart for war.

"But those who trust in the LORD will find new strength. They will soar high on wings like eagles. They will run and not grow weary. They will walk and not faint." Ruger quotes Isaiah 40:31 before drawing out his sidearm. "We may be weary from the war in Kaddain, but the great I Am won't let us fall."

Several explosions from the east sound across the landscape.

Knowing the last of Auctairea's air force was just shot down, Ruger smiles. "Our men are almost at the gate."

The spark in the eyes of his most trusted soldiers, prove they are ready to fight.

Screaming from the tent city is followed by the scraping of the machines.

Auctairea's last defense is building to block Zyandite's attack, and within a few moments their machines will be nothing but a useless heap of metal.

Ruger never enters a battle without praying first. Closing his eyes, he lifts his chin to the sky. "The great I Am, thank you for the victories you have bestowed on Zyandite in the past. We are nothing without you. Our land is your gift to us, and has been attacked by the godless." Ruger's voice rises as the sound of approaching Zyandite tanks rattles the forest. "Let Zyandites say, 'My help comes from the LORD, who made heaven and earth.'" Ruger shouts Psalm 121:2 in prayer. "Strengthen our hearts for this battle, and give Zyandite victory, In the mighty name of Jesus Christ, amen!"

"Amen!" His men shout before drawing their weapons.

With his army approaching on the main road, Ruger doesn't have much time to be first in battle. Charging towards the fence, he activates his Quhtarr, and with one blue flash, the concrete disintegrates and nothing but blue ash falls to the ground. The gap in the broken wall is large enough for a tank to fit through.

The first through the now crumbled barrier, Ruger rides Gildiel onto residential streets. There are at least fifty homes constructed with cookie-cutter architect. All have large windows that remove any chance of privacy. It's clear that even the rich of Auctairea must submit to daily drone patrols.

A man watering his yard drops his hose and runs into his mansion, leaving the water on.

Ruger frowns at the hypocrisy. Kira lived under the oppressive lie that basic utilities are a crime against the planet, all while the richest of Auctairea live with abundance.

There are cars parked in every driveway. They're old, but luxurious. None of them have the ability for sky-mode. It's almost like entering into the past. So much of this country has been left behind.

Ruger looks at Jordan and gives a nod.

Without a word, his most trusted general rides to the Quandii Tower, alone.

Focusing on the coordinates Kira gave him for the Hive, Ruger's surprised that Hugh Joplin's house is only two stories tall. Unlike the other homes, this house isn't made out of glass. A row of three small windows in the front this home secures privacy, proving that in Auctairea, being the brother of the Prime Minister has its perks.

Ruger notices a sniper is on the roof. The Auctairean fires at him, but Gildiel obeys Ruger's pull and backs up in time to hide behind another house. His men ride up, and don't need to be told to take cover.

"Sergeant Groth, corner shot," Ruger orders.

The Sergeant dismounts from his horse and gets into position at the block wall, before readying his rifle. The barrel curves. With the digital scope, Sergeant Groth can see his target.

He hits the sniper with just one shot.

Walking back to his horse, Ruger gives him a proud nod. "Good job, Sergeant."

Sergeant Groth's brown eyes flicker a smile at his king.

Leading the charge, the sound of a garage door opening catches Ruger's attention.

Across the street from their target, dozens of mechanical soldiers march out of the garage. At first, Ruger and his men prepare to take cover, but these machines aren't armed with projectiles. They have bladed arms that are dull and covered with dry blood. Skull Smashers, as the locals call them, are no match for Zyandite warriors.

Another garage opens, this one belonging to Hugh Joplin. As the machines pour out of it, Ruger wonders if the enemy was tipped off.

Using his Quhtarr, Ruger fires Karthron Missiles at the enemy. Flashes expand outward, disintegrating the machines into a sparkly, blue whirl of heat.

His men weren't gifted specialized weapons from Tunaunda, but know exactly where to fire.

Within minutes, dozens of machines fall.

Ruger blasts another missile into the machines, before something stings his hip. He recognizes the pain, and knows he's been shot. Turning towards Joplin's house, he sees the replacement sniper. He fires a Karthron Missile. One shot takes down the soldier and half of the roof. Ruger's leg isn't bleeding bad enough to deal with right now. Leaping off Gildiel, he lands on his good leg first. He manages to walk without a limp, so his men won't notice the wound. "Stay," Ruger orders Gildiel, before pulling out a rolled cord from her saddle. Spinning the grappling hook above his head, Ruger swings it towards the roof. Once it's taunt, he ignores the pain radiating from his leg, and climbs up. Reaching the jagged edge of the roof, he peers down the hole made from his Quhtarr. Below him, several machines regain their footing.

Without another thought, Ruger leaps down.

He doesn't feel the pain from the drop. All he focuses on is his aim. There are at least a dozen Skull Smashers, and two Auctairean soldiers. The human troops flee downstairs in fear, while Ruger fires down the machines.

In this loft, there are four doorways, but one is double. It's locked. Ruger fires the Quhtarr to melt the door down.

Dozens of desks are before him, where civilians cower and hide.

Beyond the rows of desks, stands two machines, with a shaking man cowering in-between them.

Ruger wasn't expecting to find Prime Minister Stephen Joplin, but here he stands. Sweat beading down his round face, below gray, balding hair.

With two precise shots, Ruger takes down the last of their machines.

Everyone in the room screams, including the Prime Minister.

Behind Ruger, rushed footsteps approach…

***

CHAPTER 11
PROPHECY AND POLITICS

For someone with no children of her own, Rhonda does well explaining to Nadia every detail of the meal she's making.

Sitting at the bar, Kira clips the last button from her new purse, and sets it inside with the rest. "Here you go, Nadia."

Nadia opens the purse and gasps. "I love my new button family. Thank you!"

Kira smiles at that. "Why don't you take them up to our room and play before dinner?"

Nadia's eyes sparkle before she runs upstairs.

Rhonda looks up from chopping potatoes. "Button family?"

Kira shrugs. "In Auctairea, spare buttons were all she had to play with."

"That's creative, but sad."

Kira hates taking sympathy, and frowns. "Is there anything I can help with?"

"No." Rhonda piles the potatoes in the roasting pan. "It's all pretty much done." She places it in the oven and wipes her hands on her apron before sitting down next to Kira. Opening her tablet, Rhonda's eyes widen. "My mom sent me a message. She said most Zyandites are quite vocal against Wilma's accusations." Rhonda navigates the screen on her tablet to Wilma's profile, and leans over so Kira can see it. It's all in Zyandish, but Kira follows along the words as Rhonda reads them, trying her best to decipher them.

"I remember Kira Westin. She was a warrior for Christ in Auctairea. Just imagine what she'll do for Zyandite. Besides, the truth will reveal itself. After all, the Bible says, 'The first to speak in court sounds right—until the cross-examination begins.'" Rhonda quotes.

"Hmm," Kira lifts her chin. "Proverbs 18:17?"

Rhonda sits back in surprise. "You put my Zyandite reputation to shame. I didn't even know that one!"

Judging by Rhonda's smile, Kira knows she's sincere. "I drank God's word like water. It's how we survived."

Rhonda studies Kira's face. "Yes, I'm starting to see why my brother fell for you."

Kira's cheeks become hot.

With an approving smile, Rhonda continues reading. "We've been so secure in our way of life. We almost lost what it takes to protect it. Kira Westin knows evil, and our King shouldn't be ashamed for sending her to safety. She's God's daughter too." Rhonda scrolls up to read another comment. "King Anstone was right in his retort to such vile accusations. If Wilma didn't have a stake in the crown, it would be easier to believe her. I'll wait to see what Ms. Westin has to say before deciding if these accusations against her and our King are true." Rhonda's lips quiver before she reads the next comment. "Kira Westin is as gracious as she is strong. I've always adored her. Welcome home, my sister in Christ."

Kira holds her face in her hands. She can feel the tears building momentum. "Why would they stand up for me?" Kira bites her lip. She shouldn't have revealed her suspicions.

Instead of getting angry, Rhonda's eyes fill with sympathy. "This isn't Auctairea. Wilma's an abnormality. Most of us genuinely love one another because Christ loves us."

Rhonda's eyes are so genuine, even innocent, Kira wants to believe her. Smiling, she hopes that one day; her heart will be able to trust again.

***

Clark Natorin may have passed his prime, but maintains the same workout routine he held in the military. A retired general, he was activated to save Zyandite from Kaddain, and now commands Zyandite Press. His salt and pepper hair remains in the same high and tight style he donned in service, over bronze skin, and shrewd, blue eyes. Marching down the hallway, his current target is damage control.

"Wilma?" He pounds at her dressing room door.

"Come in," her voice sings through.

Clark steps in to find her styling her hair in front of the lighted mirror. She glances at him and lays on a sweet smile. He's never been one to fall for her antics, and leans against her vanity before crossing his arms. "Have you seen the response to your escapade?"

Wilma frowns. "They're fools."

"I'd hardly call the people of Zyandite fools." Clark laughs. "Just because you're married to King Tidal's heir, doesn't mean I'm obligated to keep you."

"I made a mistake, so what? General Danning will clear it up when he figures out whatever happened with King Anstone's vitals."

Clark's brow furrows. "No, *you'll* clear this up tonight."

Wilma presses her lips together, but can't reign in her tongue. "And do what, apologize?"

"Yes. This is the kind of mistake that happens when there's only one general in a bloodline." He eyes her disapprovingly before leaving the room without formalities.

Feeling slapped in the face, Wilma holds her head in her hands and sobs. Mockery from her childhood sings in her ears now. With only one general in her family tree, she's barely qualified to be a member of the Lineage, and has hated it her whole life. Taking in a deep breath, Wilma focuses on fixing her makeup. She'll prove her worth by becoming queen. Not even Kira Westin can stop that.

***

Nadia takes in a deep whiff as Rhonda pulls the chicken out of the oven. "That smells delicious."

Rhonda grins. "Ruger told me you like rosemary chicken."

Nadia's jaw drops as she watches Rhonda lift the lid. The potatoes and carrots simmer around the bird, creating a cloud of steam. "I've never had rosemary chicken like this."

"It smells amazing." Kira smiles, but inside, foreboding brews. Fear of disapproval collides with self-doubt, making her stomach whirl. She looks away from the food to hide it.

The doorbell rings. Rhonda does a little happy dance. "She's here." In a blur she rushes to the front door.

Nadia sits on her mom's lap. She seems as apprehensive about this guest as Kira feels.

Farrah Trigon steps into the kitchen gracefully. She's wearing a long, gray sweater dress. A large cross necklace, crafted of hammered silver hangs to the middle of her torso. Her strawberry blond hair waves in curls above green eyes, which reflect the light of God. Kira would be able to recognize that Farrah's a Christian, even if she knew nothing about her. She smiles at Kira with such acceptance, it's almost as though they're already friends.

"I am glad to finally meet you, both," Farrah greets in flawless Auctrah.

"She speaks Auctrah too?!" Nadia's mouth widens.

Farrah bends to Nadia's level. "Why yes, sweetheart. My husband and I oversaw the missions in Auctairea. That was well before he became Zyandite's Lead Pastor."

"Her husband is a member of the three pillared government under the king," Kira explains.

Nadia's eyes widen. "Oh."

Farrah straightens her posture. "It's nice that you know so much."

"I'm still learning," Kira admits.

There's nothing malicious in Farrah's eyes as she tries to lighten the mood, "Aren't we all?"

Kira forces a smile.

"So, are you a pastor, too?" Nadia asks.

Rhonda bites her lip before stepping to Farrah's side. "Farrah is a Prophetess."

Nadia gasps. "Like Elijah?"

"Not quite like Elijah, no. My gift is one that means God speaks to me in dreams, to better those around me. It's not on the same level as Elijah, not even close."

"That's still pretty cool," Nadia says.

Farrah's eye light up. "Yes, it's an honor."

Kira's not nearly as trusting. Her brow furrows as the reporter within her automatically questions this. "Does the Lead Pastor always have to marry a prophetess?"

"Goodness, no," Farrah laughs. "There are many prophets in Zyandite. I just happen to be the gal he fell in love with. Brian was doing missionary work in my homeland when we met. He was so compassionate, and full of life." Farrah sits down at the bar next to Kira. "He was nothing like the aloof boys in my village."

"Has being a foreigner brought discrimination upon you?" Kira asks.

Farrah bites her lip and shakes her head. "No. I love Zyandite, and I consider it the greatest gift my God has given me. Second to my husband, that is."

Slowly, Kira's shoulders relax. "So, an immigrant in a position of authority isn't abnormal here?"

"No, well…" Farrah tilts her chin down, her eyes intense. "It's yours and King Anstone's purity we must ask God to reveal. If we had his vitals, your birthplace would be a nonissue, unless of course, you refused to assimilate. For now, the lack of proof for your honor is something the generals and their wives will use against you." Her lips stay straight, but Farrah's eyes smile. "Did Rhonda tell you about the prophecy the great I Am gave to me?"

From the kitchen, Rhonda shakes her head.

Farrah laughs. "That's alright. It's a lot to take in."

"You really believe in prophecy here?" Kira frowns upon realizing how accusing that came off. "How do you know it's not a scam?"

"That's a very wise assessment considering Auctairea's corruption. I wonder what your gift is?" Farrah rests an elbow on the counter and studies Kira's face.

Farrah's kind enough, but the question discomforts Kira enough to squirm in her seat. "I don't know. I've never thought about it. After Zyandite missionaries left Auctairea, the churches stopped focusing on anything other than the tithe."

"The church of cash cow, as it was called." Farrah momentarily cringes. "Like greedy dogs, they are never satisfied. They are ignorant shepherds, all following their own path and intent on personal gain. Isaiah 56:11 describes the lost church of Auctairea to a T, but that's not how things are run here. Tithing is important, sure, but Auctairean churches cared nothing for the hearts of the sheep, which is why they bowed to the government order to outlaw faith. Here, we take matters of the heart very seriously."

"We also take gifts of the Spirit seriously. Mine is to teach." Rhonda holds her chin up before gathering plates.

Farrah smiles before looking back at Kira. "From what I hear, your heart is exceptionally strong."

Kira's never appreciated flattery and only frowns in response.

"Yep. Mommy hunted and cleaned and scared the bad guys away," Nadia says while wiggling in her mother's lap.

"That's impressive." Farrah gives Nadia a kind smile.

"Yeah, and God almost always answers mommy's prayers. I've seen it."

Farrah looks at Kira and straightens her posture. "Perhaps you have the gift of faith?"

This is so foreign to Kira. She only shrugs.

"I understand this must be uncomfortable." Farrah's eyes are kind while she searches Kira's face as though looking for an explanation. "The church you grew up in watered down the gifts of the Spirit, diminishing its power in their lives. Here, parents and pastors pray for the youth, so God leads them to their gifts early, in order to fortify their fruit."

Heart stirred, Kira's lips curve into a genuine smile. "That sounds amazing."

Rhonda takes the rolls out of the oven. "Dinner's ready," she sings.

"Perfect." Farrah relocates to the table, where beautiful green china shines under the wrought iron chandelier. "You really know how to coordinate."

"Thank you," Rhonda says before setting the serving dishes on the center of the table.

As Nadia takes a seat, her eyes widen at all the food before her. Rosemary chicken, red potatoes, carrots, yeast rolls, and a chocolate silk cake are lined up in a feast before her. "Mommy, I can't believe we're going to eat this much, especially after all the food we've already had today."

Kira sits next to her daughter and smiles. "Rhonda's extremely generous, and we must ask God to bless her for it."

Farrah and Rhonda exchange glances. It's not judgmental, but it makes Kira feel uncomfortable, just the same.

"Would you mind doing the honors?" Rhonda asks Farrah.

"Sure." Farrah bows her head.

Kira's thankful Nadia is so quick to follow suit.

"The great I Am, thank you for the good company, and for this bountiful food. We ask for your presence to flood into our hearts, and fill us with your love, your wisdom, your truth, and understanding. Bless this food so that it will nourish and strengthen us, and bless the hands that prepared it with joy, prosperity, and love. In the mighty name of Jesus Christ, amen," Farrah prays.

Everyone says amen before Nadia is served first.

"So, Kira, God told you to save Ruger?" Farrah asks while serving her plate.

Kira's heart skips a beat. She wasn't expecting such a bold question. "Yes. Though at first, I wasn't..."

Rhonda's eyes widen and she almost drops her fork.

Kira grimaces. "I was going to turn him in for the reward."

Rhonda's jaw drops. "You would've done that?"

"Put yourself in her shoes." Farrah gives a reprimanding look. "Ruger was not only a foreigner, but an enemy."

Kira almost doesn't share the full details, but truth is vital. "I thought he was dead and wanted his sidearm. Otherwise I would've just left him. His hands were entangled in his parachute, so when I heard him breathing I knew that he couldn't fight me. I considered turning him in to the Mayor's drone. Then, God spoke." She looks at her plate. "I'm glad I obeyed."

"It was so scary to have a strange man in our house," Nadia says before taking a drink of water. "Mommy said God told her to do it. I didn't like it at first, but Ruger's so nice. I like him now."

"Wow, what a brave and kind girl you are," Farrah says before taking a bite of chicken.

"Of all the places for my brother to crash…" Rhonda sniffles before focusing on her plate. "Thank you, Kira. I was sick with worry for him."

"We all were." Farrah's voice is calm, but a spark ignites in her eyes. "If not for the dream the great I Am graced me with, Brian and I would've been devastated when General Brice informed us that King Anstone was dead."

"Mother and I feared he was." Rhonda carefully sets her fork down to wipe away a tear.

"God had other plans." Farrah looks at Kira and smiles. "And He knows exactly what Zyandite needs."

"What's that?" Nadia asks.

Farrah's eyes are resolute. "A queen…"

Kira's heart skips a beat while Nadia laughs.

"We were shocked when Ruger said he was king," Nadia admits before taking a large bite of chicken.

"Yes, we were," Kira says before looking at Farrah. "Ruger and I have only known each other a few days. To choose me for such a ginormous task is a bit crazy on his part, don't you think?"

Farrah raises a brow. "As crazy as taking an enemy soldier into your home?"

Kira should be happy that Farrah's on her side, but this foreboding in her gut won't go away. She feels like she's playing dress up, readying for an event she's not worthy enough to attend. God put her in a position of authority once, and she blew it. Kira looks down. She wants to ask Farrah to help her convince Ruger to call the whole thing off, but that thought only sinks her stomach.

"You must stop thinking like an Auctairean." Farrah crosses her arms. "In Zyandite, we aren't looking for casual relationships. Every one of us is on alert for our future spouse. Sometimes, the search for that union takes years. Most of the time, it takes weeks. To us, it's not abnormal for a man and woman to fall in love quickly."

"Your divorce rate must be astronomical," Kira whispers.

Rhonda gasps. "Divorce is illegal."

Kira can't eat anymore. She takes her napkin off her lap and tosses it on the table. "Why would Ruger risk so much for me?"

Rhonda has felt the same since he first messaged her with his intentions, but she takes a bite without saying anything.

"This has been God's plan, all along. From what I know about you, Kira, you're exactly what Zyandite needs. We've become too comfortable in our bubble and have forgotten how dangerous the rest of the world is to our faith. You not only overcame that, but your experience with our enemies will give us an advantage. We have no real tact on how to handle the GPU, and they seem to be growing more powerful each day. Zyandite needs you," Farrah states.

Thinking of George, the foreboding in Kira's stomach mixes with a pain that's familiar, the pain of being used. "With a prophecy like that, it's no wonder Ruger sent me here."

Rhonda's eyes bulge. "My brother would never do anything like that."

Farrah places a hand on Kira's. Surprisingly, it comforts her. "When God spoke to me, King Anstone's account was offline. There's no way he could've known about the prophecy while he was with you." Farrah shakes her head. "Besides, I know Ruger, and he would never fall for a woman because he was expected to."

"That's the truth," Rhonda murmurs.

Farrah pulls her hand away. "This must be frightening for you, but Zyandite doesn't want to exploit you or your daughter."

Those words should offer security, but darkness breeds in Kira's mind. Prime Minister Joplin fooled her. George fooled her. Others could, too. The confliction brewing in her heart is agonizing. She has to refocus. "What happened in your dream?"

Farrah straightens her posture. "I saw a woman wearing a silver dress. In one hand was a sword, the other, a rifle. A crown was on her head with the name Anstone engraved across the gold. The sunlight was intense, so the features were distorted, but her hair and eye color was the same as yours."

Goosebumps cover Kira's arms. She hasn't felt a chill once since landing in Zyandite, but in this moment she wishes she had a sweater.

"Did she have a ring?" Rhonda points to her wedding finger that's bare.

Farrah shakes her head. "If there was, I didn't see it."

Nadia taps on Kira's arm. "Does this mean I'll be a princess?"

Farrah and Rhonda laugh at that, but Kira's not amused and doesn't want her to be disappointed. "Zyandite's not a hereditary monarchy."

Nadia pouts before eating more chicken.

"You're a princess to me," Rhonda says with a wink.

Kira's heart is touched. This woman is practically a stranger, yet comforting Nadia is still a priority to her. Perhaps most Zyandites live their faith, and Ruger's affections were as sincere as she believed. Remembering the admiration in his eyes, Kira can almost feel his lips against hers now. She couldn't help falling in love with him, but being in a position of power was never part of the deal. Kira feels a little betrayed that he didn't fill her in on everything his love includes. "And to think, I thought I fell in love with a pilot."

"You really had no idea who Ruger was?" Farrah asks.

"No. He didn't even tell me he spoke Auctrah until hours after I saved him." Kira reaches for her glass, but her hand shakes. She places it in her lap and adjusts her seating. "I thought Sampson Tidal was still King. Ruger didn't fill me in until we were on our way out of Auctairea."

"He probably didn't want you to desire him for his title. He gets enough of that," Rhonda says before taking another bite.

"What do you mean?" Kira asks.

"Oh," Rhonda's shoulders slouch. "Lots of women dream of becoming queen, and then there's the Lineage..."

Farrah rolls her eyes. It's unfitting for her sagely appearance. "Brian's relieved he never had to go through what the generals push on Ruger. Their worship of blood is about to be dealt with by the great I Am." Her eyes are flames before softening on Kira. "I believe that's really what this prophecy is about. You see, idolatry has infected the land. Only with the few, but it's strong enough to harm us all."

"Ruger briefly mentioned the Lineage." Kira's hand stops shaking enough to take a sip of water.

"Purity of blood," Rhonda's lips curve into a snarl. "Something my brother lacks."

Farrah watches Kira's reaction.

Kira sets down her glass in time before her hand begins shaking again. "I don't want anything to do with that."

Farrah laughs. "They wouldn't accept you if you wanted them to."

Worried for what she and Nadia have gotten themselves into, Kira constructs her next question with consideration for Nadia. "What's the worst thing the Lineage can pull?"

Farrah glances at Nadia and smiles. "They don't have the power they think they do. The people proved that during their mock-election."

Kira's convinced that her original fear of Ruger being setup was correct. This subject is too frightening to discuss in front of Nadia. For the rest of the meal, Kira focuses on eating before carrying Nadia upstairs.

Nadia crawls into bed wearing her new pajamas. "Mommy, I've never felt so full."

"I'm glad," Kira whispers before kissing her cheek. "We must thank God for this provision."

Nadia's eyes are closed while she smiles and nods.

"Dear God, thank you for the safety of Zyandite, for Rhonda and her generosity. We have not been this full in a long time, if ever. Thank you for your provision. Please keep Ruger safe, and help us find ways to bless our hostess with your light and love, in the name of Jesus, amen."

"Amen," Nadia says through a yawn.

"Will you be okay up here alone for a while?" Kira asks, but Nadia doesn't respond. She's already asleep.

Closing the door softly, Kira tiptoes downstairs to find Farrah and Rhonda sitting on the emerald couch. Their body language proves they're comfortable with one another, almost like family. Both lean forward as they whisper, eyes intent with devotion.

"Nadia's so full from that wonderful meal you made, she fell asleep as soon as her head hit the pillow." Kira takes a seat next to Farrah.

"Wonderful!" Rhonda exclaims.

"Yes. Now that she's asleep, we can talk." Kira folds her hands and musters up the bravery to be frank in this foreign land. "When Ruger told me he couldn't access ZyanBell, without knowing anything about the Lineage, I suspected he was sabotaged from within. So I need to know, what's the Lineage capable of doing to my daughter?"

Farrah eyes Kira with admiration before raising her chin. "No Zyandite can harm a child, or a widow, and ever be accepted in our society again. The punishment is death. God will stop their plans. He's going to use you to do it. The battle on your end will only be political."

Remembering how the reporters frowned at the sight of Nadia, suddenly makes sense to Kira. If she didn't have a child, she'd be an easier target. "What about Ruger?"

"You can't become queen without him. That's how I know he'll survive whatever the Lineage does to retaliate." Farrah says before staring at the floor.

"Ruger sending you here has put him in danger," Rhonda whispers, but seems ashamed to have spoken her mind.

"It's God's will," Farrah quickly corrects.

"I know. I'm just frightened." Rhonda fans her face to stop herself from crying.

Kira is frightened too, but doesn't show it. She's used to hiding her heart.

Farrah slowly brings her eyes to Kira. "Zyandite was formed on a covenant with God. Our flag bears a cross to remind us of that promise. The Lineage has contaminated that vow with idolatry. They worship the blood God created, instead of the creator." She leans forward. "God is going to use his servant from an unclean land with unclean blood, to destroy their idol and bring our country back to its covenant with Him." Farrah straightens her posture. "That's why Ruger fell in love with you so quickly, and you with him. Your souls were designed for this purpose."

A tear falls down Kira's cheek. "He promised me this."

"Ruger promised you, what?" Rhonda asks.

"No, not Ruger..." Kira doesn't take her eyes off of Farrah. "God promised me that I would be a splendid crown in his hand. At the time, I misunderstood why he led me to read Isaiah 62:3-5." Kira raises her voice as she recites the verses: "The LORD will hold you in his hand for all to see—a splendid crown in the hand of God. Never again will you be called "The Forsaken City" or "The Desolate Land." Your new name will be "The City of God's Delight" and "The Bride of God," for the LORD delights in you and will claim you as his bride. Your children will commit themselves to you, O Jerusalem, just as a young man commits himself to his bride. Then God will rejoice over you as a bridegroom rejoices over his bride." Kira takes in a breath. It's so overwhelming, she laughs through her tears. "I don't deserve this."

"You've been faithful in the little things, Kira. You'll be faithful with larger ones," Farrah says.

"Luke 16:10..." Kira mumbles.

Farrah's face brightens as she glances at Rhonda with surprise.

Rhonda nods. "She knows the Bible better than my mom."

With a chuckle, Farrah reaches into her purse. "Speaking of the Bible..." She pulls one out. "Our church has Bibles printed in every language, so I picked up one that's written in Auctrah."

"Oh, thank you!" Kira takes it and the brown leather feels at home in her hands. Hugging it to her chest, she feels selfish in asking, but must learn their language or she'll never withstand the Lineage. "I would like one that is Zyandish too, in order to help me learn it."

"I have a spare," Rhonda says.

Kira blushes. "Thanks. I feel like I've taken too much already."

"God's restoring everything you've lost. Don't refute the joys of his blessings." Farrah looks up at the wrought iron clock on the wall. "I had better get going."

"Oh, my," Rhonda says upon noticing that it's almost nine.

Kira stands with her. "Thank you Farrah, for everything."

"It was nice to meet you Kira. Now, remember that you are exactly who God created you to be. Not a drop of blood can ever change that," Farrah assures before Rhonda walks her out.

Rhonda's living room is beautiful at night, with several lamps giving off a warm glow as night darkens the scenery beyond the windows. It's surreal to have electricity again. As Kira looks around, she pledges loyalty to this place for more than just the luxuries of utilities, choice food, and clothes. This land belongs to God. She's blessed to be here.

Rhonda walks back into the living room with and grimaces. "I can't believe how late it is."

"Good conversations do that." Kira grins. "I just wish I wasn't so tired."

"Of course, get some sleep," Rhonda says with a playful wave of her hand.

Kira enters her temporary room to find Nadia breathing deeply, and it warms her heart. She changes into burgundy pajamas that are softer than she's used to. Every moment in this land is like living in a dream.

Yet that dream is tainted.

Looking around, the thought of the Lineage twisting the beauty of Zyandite into sin makes Kira's heart ache. She crawls into bed and pulls her knees to her chest. The cords of fear tighten around her heart, and her chest muscles ache. 'God help me,' Kira lips in a silent prayer. 'Please protect Nadia and me, and protect Zyandite.' She bites her lip and caresses Nadia's hair. The life offered to them seemed so beautiful, a life with a man who adores Nadia and loves her, in a Christian nation, warm, and far from Auctairea's horrors. Yet, there is darkness in this land, and she worries they may be in danger. It's like a torrent storm in her heart, swaying her in different directions.

In all the terrors, long nights, and hunger she survived in Auctairea, Kira never once did so on her own. Picking up the Bible Farrah gave her, Kira opens it to Isaiah 51:4-5:

"Listen to me, my people. Hear me, Israel, for my law will be proclaimed and my justice will become a light to the nations. My mercy and justice are coming soon. My salvation is on the way. My strong arm will bring justice to the nations. All distant lands will look to me and wait in hope for my powerful arm.

She smiles before flipping the pages back.

Unless your faith is firm, I cannot make you stand firm. Isaiah 7:9

Strengthen by God's word, Kira will have a firm faith that God will not only protect her and Nadia from the Lineage, but will also help her defeat them.

***

The Marshal's penthouse may have rows of windows facing downtown Brustonite, but it's a far cry from typical Zyandite taste. Modern and sophisticated, these halls are not set up for entertaining, but for comfort. Wilma needs the gray décor in order to feel at home. Looking at her reflection in the bathroom mirror, she slips off the navy heels that match her blazer. Wilma needs a shower to regain her pride. It may have been half-hearted, but the apology stung to say.

Taking her pearl earrings off, Wilma's eyes fill with tears of defeat, since General Danning will never let her mistake be forgotten. Now, even Frank knows it.

Her tablet breaks the silence. Recognizing the tone for General Kentwood, Wilma wipes her eyes and hurries to answer. When her husband's face greets her instead, she gasps.

"He's played me at my own game." General Marshal holds up his tablet to show her he can't get through to ZyanBell.

Wilma can't help but respect Ruger's antics. "He is sly."

General Marshal's eyes harden. "Regardless, this is the first chance I've had to call you. King Anstone has already invaded Quandii."

"When?"

"This afternoon. He's keeping everyone outside of his charge uninformed."

Wilma momentarily closes her eyes. "If only you had called me sooner."

"I'm calling you now, so let your snake charmer know. Perhaps the King will be dead by nightfall?"

"Hush!" Wilma shouts with rage uplifting her shoulders. "You're on General Kentwood's tablet. If he finds out, we'll—"

"I took care of the settings. There's no way this is recorded."

Her skin crawls just from the risk. Wilma wants to hang up on him, but needs Frank's loyalty. "I'm glad you thought of that." She forces her tone to soften.

"Don't lie. Just let him know, while there's still time." Frank Marshal lays a thick glare upon her, and hangs up.

Wilma bares her teeth at the blank screen in her hands before taking her glare to her closet. Ripping her clothes off the hanger, she snarls at the elaborate tapestry on the wall that displays Frank's impressive Lineage, and all hers lacks. Yanking the horrid thing down to reveal a safe, Wilma's heart thuds, making her breaths jagged.

What will he say?

She's already disappointed him enough.

Fighting tears, she types in the code, opens the safe and carefully takes out a smaller device, before making the call.

After five rings, the distinguished face of Thorton Lazeed answers. Though his blue eyes reveal his years, age has yet to tarnish his skin. Darker complexion accentuates his full lips and perfectly straight nose, as Thorton stares at her with an amused grin.

The hunger Kira noticed in Wilma's eyes now seeps a starved adoration for this man. *"Maestro..."* Wilma whispers in Pazmirish.

"Has your husband prepped the Flatiron?"

The words get stuck in her throat. Wilma trembles before she can release them. *"You haven't heard?"*

Thorton's eyes darken. *"Has Joplin's feet become cold?"* He runs his fingers through his hair. *"I've offered him more than any politician, yet he's been most difficult. It's just land, I tell him, but his heart wages war. Is the Pazmirish Republic not good enough for his taste?"* Thorton scoffs with a shake of his head. *"Man's hardly worth his salt."*

The news she's been dreading can no longer remain hidden. Wilma closes her eyes and whispers, *"King Anstone's alive."*

For a moment, the anger on Thorton's face shows his age. *"How can this be?"*

"An Auctairean saved him."

"Fine." Thorton slaps his hand on the chair. *"The plan remains, but with different players. We'll convince King Anstone to Flatiron Auctairea, and the fear will still spread."*

"He refuses to use the Flatiron." She winces before bringing her eyes back to his. *"My husband's tablet was disconnected from ZyanBell, and Frank could only contact me a few minutes ago. Otherwise, I would've served you better, my love. I'm sorry, but Quandii has already been taken."* Her eyes plead for his approval.

Thorton's face twists into a glare. *"You seduced the wrong man."*

Wilma can't hide the tears that fall. *"I tried. I did everything you taught me, but he's heartless."*

"No, Ruger Anstone's smart." Thorton smiles. "Don't cry, my girl. You make want to kill when you do that. I hate it so."

Her eyes fill with hope while she worships his every word. "*Please, forgive my failings. I...*" Desperation causes her to wince. "*I love you.*"

"*I'll always love you, even when you disappoint me. Oh, why can't things be as simple as they were that first summer we met?*"

Wilma's finger caresses the screen above his face. "*If only we could travel back in time.*"

Thorton laughs. "*There's no such thing as going backwards. We move forward to make a better life. That can't happen unless Zyandite belongs to me. Fear, Wilma, fear is how we control. It's how we gather strength. That weapon provides fear while in Zyandite's hands, but will be much more generous in mine. So what do we do?*" He taps his finger on his chin. It's far too playful for their situation. "*I say let Prime Minister Joplin fall. If he hasn't already, that is.*" Thorton laughs but this time it's more a cackle. "*He couldn't even agree on the evacuation plan. Joplin's foolishness far outweighs his worth.*"

"*Joplin's always been a headache to you.*"

"*He was the only one willing to betray his country.*" Thorton shrugs. "*What choice did I have?*"

"*None.*" Wilma holds her chin up and braces her heart for his reaction. "*There's another matter. I thought perhaps you knew, but the woman who saved King Anstone, isn't just a run-of-the-mill Auctairean.*"

"*You behave as though she's the boogeyman,*" Thorton says with a laugh. "*Who is she?*"

Wilma let's out a long sigh. "*Kira Westin.*"

All humor drips off Thorton's face. "*Can't be. She's dead.*"

"*Who told you that?*"

"*Joplin.*"

Wilma raises a brow.

"Yes, lie to one, lie to all." Thorton's the one sighing now. *"Let's not tell Charles, quite yet. He'll want revenge without any foresight. We,"* he points at her, *"Can use this for our advantage."*

"I've been trying, but the people love him. I can only do so much. The window to take him out without suspicion is closing," Wilma hisses.

"No, my dear. The opportunity to kill him has passed us by."

His words cut through her heart. Wilma bends over from the pain of her invisible wound. *"I'll never be queen."*

There's a flicker of compassion in Thorton's eyes. *"You know I love you, but you must swallow your pride and find a woman who can accomplish what you could not. We have to pin Ruger down. Once the young lady is queen, you'll rule her."*

The pain of regret dances across Wilma's eyes. *"King Anstone sent Kira Westin here. The rumor is she's the woman from the prophecy. I believe he intends to marry her."*

"This is perfect. It sets the stage for what must be done in order for that weapon to belong to me. Obviously, King Anstone's lonely. Let the Lineage destroy Kira. She'll step aside, and once King Anstone's bed is made, you'll give her to me. Charles will be so happy." Thorton leans his face closer to whisper, *"We have to be very careful in orchestrating this. Work the Lineage on our behalf. Make them want to help you find a pureblooded queen. After Zyandites are conditioned, you'll be my overseer of the providence. Then, I'll be able to visit you anytime I want."*

"You mean it?"

"Of course, you know you're my favorite."

Wilma bites her lip. *"What about Frank?"*

This time Thorton bellows out laughter. *"When Zyandite's under the GPU, divorce will be legal."*

She smiles. *"I can't wait."*

***

CHAPTER 12
FALLEN

The machines didn't see General Brice in time to stop him, but if he were to dismount off of Wesley now, his horse would be killed. Riding his black stallion up the concrete steps, Jordan can't think of what will happen if they fall. All he can do is reach the top of the tower. The stairs spiral around the tower so tightly, Jordan feels dizzy. Behind them, the scraping of machines gain, but occasionally, they crash into each other. Thanking God these machines aren't graceful, Jordan reaches the doorway at the top.

He doesn't need to go inside. The explosives will take the entire tower down. Attaching the double row of Kadurah grenades onto the door, Jordan's eyes widen. He only has thirty seconds until this tower disintegrates. He makes the time for a silent prayer, before drawing two rifles.

The machines are already reaching the top of the steps. They are ugly, with painted smiles below rows of camera lenses. They look sinister, as the bladed arms reach for his horse.

Jordan digs his heels into Wesley's sides, "Bolt!"

Wesley lifts his front legs off the ground, and after kicking down two machines, the stallion rushes towards the stairs.

Jordan fires on the machines, making them drop before they can harm his horse. Wesley manages to leap over each fallen machine in his path. The spiral downward should give Jordan vertigo, but he's too focused on defeating the enemy.

Jordan continues shooting down the machines and doesn't hear the initial blast behind them, but Wesley picks up his pace.

Now that the tower is falling, Jordan doesn't have to shoot the machines for them to crash.

Relief causes him to smile, before Jordan hears the soft roar gaining from behind. He looks back to see the tower engulfed in a blue flame that melts everything in its path.

Smile gone, Jordan only looks forward.

Wesley leaps over the last curb and lands on solid ground. Jordan digs his heels in tighter. The well-trained stallion obeys his unspoken command.

Charging towards the main entry of the city, Jordan doesn't have to look back to know that Quandii Tower is gone.

Machines begin to drop all over Quandii, including the thousands on the highway. Zyandite tanks roll over the metal remains before reaching the gate.

There are at least thirty Auctairean soldiers on the concrete edge of the wall. They're visibly shaken, but point their rifles at the road. Jordan won't let them fire on his brothers. With his two rifles drawn, he fires each Auctairean down. Reaching the guards at the gate, Jordan needs them to open it, and only fires on their guns.

Both men cower to the ground.

"Open the gate!" Jordan yells in Zyandish.

By the look in their eyes, neither of these scrawny men understood what he said.

"The gate!" Jordan points one of his rifles at it.

One of the men nods, and types something into the keypad with thin, lanky fingers. Gears turn, but the sounds of tanks approaching override their noise. Jordan and Wesley take this moment to catch their breath.

As the faded sun begins to set, the metal gate opens.

Jordan greets his countrymen with a smile.

***

Ruger doesn't need to turn around in order to knock out the man approaching. With one motion of his elbow, Hugh Joplin falls to the floor.

Gasping for air, Hugh slides back in fear.

"Nice try," Ruger says before focusing on the Prime Minister.

"King Anstone," the Prime Minister's voice shakes. *"What a surprise."* Stephen Joplin is not pleasant to look at. His hair is receding and his built is far from fit. Joplin's gray suit matches his eyes, and is spotting from sweat.

Ruger frowns at the cowardice of this so-called leader.

Marching sounds from the stairs. Ruger knows they're his men by their disciplined steps.

"I'll clear the house," Sergeant Wright says, before he and Sergeant Groth check the other rooms.

A woman screams, and runs out from a room in the back. Her blue hair bounces as she is taken to the floor beside Hugh. With an unkempt beard and skinny jeans, Hugh isn't as old as Prime Minister Joplin, but just as chubby. He looks like he wants to hide behind the woman.

Ruger takes a quick glance around at the pictures on the walls to figure out the blue haired woman is Hugh's wife.

Outside, the sound of metal crashing causes Zyandite soldiers to cheer.

Ruger's lips curve while keeping his weapon pointed at the Prime Minister. *"Seems one of my generals took down your tower. Wasn't that thoughtful of him?"*

Joplin swallows hard, before attempting to flatter Zyandite's king. *"Your General is very talented."*

Disgusted by the brownnosing, Ruger glares at him. *"Why did you cross our borders?"*

Joplin's face twists into what could be a scowl, before it sinks back into pitiful fear. *"I was offered a job."*

Ruger's brow creases. *"From who?"*

"Don't tell him!" Hugh yells.

The Prime Minister shakes his head at his brother, while sweat oozes down his round face. *"I wanted your technology."*

"You didn't think of offering trade?" Ruger asks.

"Oh, we both know you wouldn't have traded with me. Our greatest export isn't desired by Christians." Joplin fakes a smile.

Ruger lets out a jagged breath and translates so his men can know how evil this man is.

They know what Auctairea's greatest export is, and it makes them sick. Sneers from the Zyandite soldiers make every Auctairean in the room shudder.

"What made you think you could win a war against Zyandite?" Ruger asks.

"We were told the war with Kaddain had weakened you." By the way the Prime Minster shrugs, Ruger can tell he's lying.

"I hear you had help, Zyandish help." Ruger steps right up to Joplin's face. *"Who was it?"*

Joplin shakes his head violently. *"I could only wish for such assistance, but your men are loyal to your flag."*

Ruger can only hope that's true, but doesn't let his concerns of treason in his own country show. *"Everyone in the world knows attacking Zyandite is a mistake."*

"What are you going to do to me?" Joplin stutters with terror seeping from his eyes.

"To you?" Ruger scoffs. *"Don't you care for your people?"*

"You can have it all. I give you the key to Auctairea, it's yours. Just please, spare me," Joplin pleads by putting his hands together.

Ruger's so disgusted that he would shoot Joplin right now, but there'd be no honor in that. *"I am the King of Zyandite, when another nation attacks my homeland, I wipe them off the face of the earth. It's a message, so everyone will know not to cross our borders. You knew that, yet you sent an army of machines into our land. How could you be so stupid? What did you think you would gain, other than a death sentence?"*

The Prime Minister's eyes widen. He seems to want to speak, but is too frightened to.

"King Anstone?" Captain Hayes shouts from downstairs.

Surprised that he'd be here already, Ruger doesn't take his eyes off of the Prime Minister. "I'm up here."

Lieutenant Coltner steps aside for Captain Hayes. Behind him are five Zyandite soldiers. They all share the same shell-shocked look as the young Captain, who steps up to Ruger's side.

"Sir, we've taken Quandii."

Thinking he misheard, Ruger tilts his chin. "What?"

The young Captain with his light brown hair and wide green eyes above a square, battle harden face, only shrugs with the same disbelief Ruger feels. "Once the machines fell, the Auctaireans surrendered."

"We have control of Auctairea's capital?" Ruger clarifies.

"Yes, sir," Captain Hayes looks at the Prime Minister. Joplin's beady eyes watch as Zyandite soldiers flood into his brother's home. Some round up the civilians from their hiding places, while others check the computers, hacking into Auctairea's central system.

Observing how compliant the civilians are, Ruger's surprised no one puts up a fight. "This doesn't feel right, does it, Captain?"

"No, my King, even the soldiers give up. I've never heard of a society so willing to surrender, have you?" Captain Hayes asks.

"No. Not one," Ruger replies.

Watching the small framed men and heavyset women being led out without so much as a word of discourse, Captain Hayes brow creases. "Do you think they despise themselves?"

Ruger only shrugs.

Eyeing his leader, the Captain gasps. "Sir, you're bleeding!"

Following the Officer's eyes, Ruger had forgotten he was shot. His pant leg is covered in blood. Ruger looks back and smirks. "I'll take care of that later."

The Captain returns the smile with eyes full of admiration before Ruger turns back to Joplin, whose entire clothes are now drenched in sweat.

"Medic!" Captain Hayes shouts down the stairs. No one replies, so he walks up to the front window. On the street, Private Tyler is patching up a stab wound on a Zyandite soldier's arm.

Captain Hayes opens the window. "King Anstone's been shot!"

Private Tyler looks up with eyes wide, before hurrying his treatment of the soldier, and running into the house.

Ruger doesn't pay attention to Captain Hayes. His eyes are set on the Prime Minister. *"What are you hiding?"* Ruger asks in Auctrah.

Joplin's eyes fearfully bulge. *"N-n-nothing."*

Ruger's had enough of Joplin's games. There may be some sort of counterattack lurking, so he holds up the Quhtarr. Ruger arms the barrel, and it begins to spin. As it turns, it heats up to a blue light.

Joplin stares back and forth from the barrel to Ruger, with sweat pouring down his brow.

"Twenty-seven hundred and fifty-five degrees is how hot my Quhtarr can reach without melting. Impressive, isn't it?" Ruger grins as Joplin's face turns pale. *"I need to know you don't have any surprises for my men."* He points the Quhtarr at

Joplin's face. *"I'm asking again, what are you hiding?"*

Private Tyler stumbles into the room, his face flushed from running. With his strawberry blond hair and yellowish brown eyes, he doesn't look a day over eighteen. This is his first time giving the King treatment, and his mouth becomes dry before he pulls out the first aid bag.

Ruger doesn't turn his eyes from Joplin as he watches Private Tyler walk up to him in peripheral view. "Now's not the time, medic," he orders in Zyandish, without even looking at him.

Private Tyler's shoulders drop. "According to Zyandite law, if the king is hurt and a medic doesn't treat him, the punishment is death."

Turning away from the Prime Minister, Ruger pities the medic. "Alright, soldier."

While Private Tyler treats his wound, Ruger disarms his Quhtarr, but remains standing. It's inconvenient to have his wound tended to, but he takes the time to study the civilian prisoners. There are at least thirty, mostly female. The common trait they share is pale skin and unnatural hair color. Every male is too skinny to fight. Ruger finds himself feeling sorry for them.

A commotion scrambles from the loft, before an Auctairean runs into the room. Two Zyandite soldiers chase after him from the hall. He manages to duck below a desk before one of Ruger's men lifts him off the floor by the collar, using only one hand.

"What's this?" Ruger asks as his soldiers arrest the civilian.

"We found him in the supply closet," Sergeant Porter explains. "He threw a keyboard at us before running off."

This civilian has pink streaks in his hair, but is larger than the rest.

"Impressive," Ruger says. He can't help his smirk. At least one Auctairean did something to defend his country. *"Good job,"* he tells the young man in Auctrah.

The thin man gasps and stares at Ruger in terror as Sergeant Porter cuffs him.

Private Tyler yanks the fabric off enough to show the new bullet hole. Blood pumps out of Ruger's skin like a thin, red river.

The man with pink streaks in his hair glances at the wound, and passes out.

Ruger can't process such weakness from a man in his prime, while every Zyandite in the room bellows out in laughter.

There's no threat here. Ruger holsters his Quhtarr. Ready to face Joplin, he's surprised by the firm grip Private Tyler has on his knee.

"Sir, I've almost got it!" Private Tyler shouts.

Ruger notices how badly the young soldier is sweating, and realizes what he's put him through. "Alright." Making sure to stay still as the bullet is dug out from his leg, Ruger puckers his lips to the side as though board. The pain intensifies, but Ruger won't allow his men to see it. "You know, you've got quite a grip there, Medic. Perhaps you'd do well in a hospital."

"Got it!" The Medic screams victoriously, while holding up the bullet pinched between the forceps.

"Good job." Ruger waits for the wound to be bandaged up, so he can finally walk away.

"Done," The Medic says, before nearly collapsing.

"You just earned your stripes, Sergeant Tyler." Ruger winks, causing the young man to smile.

Ruger shifts his focus back to Joplin. *"I couldn't believe a nation would give up their home with hardly a fight,"* Ruger begins in Auctrah, *"Yet, now I see there has never been a youth wasted in society more than here. Auctairean men don't deserve to be called men, and it's because you have failed them as their leader. You've denied them ownership of anything. You took away their right to know God and His precepts, the right to be respected as the head of their households, and the right to enjoy the profit working gives. You stole it, all of it! You created a society full of adults who act like spoiled toddlers. They actually take pride in victimhood! Their dignity, their self-respect, their honor, you took it all from them!"*

"I know I've been a terrible leader, but this all belongs to you now. You can fix what I've done. I'm certain you'll do a wonderful job, King Anstone." The Prime Minister's

face quivers.

Ruger glares at this selfish man, who doesn't deserve to lead animals, let alone men. *"You disgust me."*

Prime Minister Joplin nearly fumbles over himself, before running to the nearest computer. *"Reboot!"* He shouts in Auctrah, over and over.

Two Zyandites rush to grab him, but Ruger holds up a hand. "Stop, let's see what he does."

Joplin reaches under a desk and pulls out a small handgun. He points it at Ruger. *"You're the only thing in our way!"*

Before his men can try to block the shot and get in his way, Ruger draws his weapon. One shot silences the room.

Stephen Joplin's body falls limp in a puddle of his own blood.

The soldiers look at their King with respect.

"Too bad the information died with him." Ruger holsters his sidearm. "Captain Hayes, begin recording."

Captain Hayes pulls out his tablet and points the camera at Ruger, who stares at the dead Prime Minister before looking at the camera. *"I am Ruger Drew Anstone, King of Zyandite. The Prime Minister of Auctairea is dead,"* Ruger begins in Auctrah, while Captain Hayes makes certain the body of Stephen Joplin is in frame.

In typical Zyandite tradition, Ruger begins the Victory Decree, while looking at his men as they gaze at him with adoration and pride. Now, Ruger no longer speaks in Auctrah, but in Zyandish. "This victory belongs to the Lord."

Every Zyandite in the room slams a fist into their chest once and shouts in victory.

Ruger salutes his men before looking up to continue with the Victory Decree. "Only by your power can we push back our enemies; only in your name can we trample our foes. I do not trust in my bow; I do not count on my sword to save me. You are the one who gives us victory over our enemies; you disgrace those who hate us. O God, we give glory to you all day long and constantly praise your name." Ruger quotes Psalm 44:5-8 before looking at his men. "The Godless nation of Auctairea has fallen. THIS IS ZYANDITE NOW!"

His men start cheering, pounding one fist on their chest several times.

Captain Hayes continues filming as Ruger paces the room. "Auctairea is no more! Auctrah is a dead language! And to every survivor in this land that used to be Auctairea, I, Ruger Drew Anstone, am your King!"

The Zyandite soldiers cheer louder, clapping and laughing in victory before Ruger holds up a hand to silence them. "If any nation ever considers harming Zyandite, always remember that God helped us overcome not one, but two nations in just six months' time. Attack Zyandite, and you will end up just like Prime Minister Joplin," Ruger throws a thumb back at the dead Prime Minister on the floor behind him, "You will fall to my hands. Your language, your art, your history, and culture will be destroyed. Let it be known what fate is certain for the enemies of Zyandite, our God assures it!"

Captain Hayes ends the recording and saves it. Soon, it'll be transmitted to every corner of the earth. "That's my King," he says with a grin.

Ruger doesn't let pride take over, "I'm just a man. We all know this victory belongs to God."

His men watch him go, smiling in awe of his humility.

As Ruger steps down the stairs, he makes sure to not limp in front of his men. Within his heart, worry gnaws on him with its bladed teeth.

"You're the only thing in our way."

Taking Joplin's last words as a warning, Ruger knows something nefarious is happening behind the scenes. He only hopes it doesn't involve his countrymen.

CHAPTER 13
THE CALL

'BOOM!'

Kira is torn from sleep, just to hear another explosion.

Leaping out of bed, she's relieved Nadia's sleeping through the commotion, before running to the window.

Outside, Kira hears screaming. The memory of the Great Cleansing seizes her heart. She wants to pull the curtain back, but is afraid of what she'll find. "God, protect us," Kira whispers. Pressing through her fear, she pulls back the curtain.

Expecting of an army of machines marching down this street, Kira's eyes find the opposite.

There are people in the street, but they aren't like the angry mob in Auctairea.

They're cheering.

A burst of fireworks shimmer in the night sky, expanding their obnoxious sound across the air. Kira holds onto her chest in an attempt to calm her racing heart.

Rhonda gently opens the door while tapping on it. She's wearing green pajamas not dissimilar in style from the ones she got for Kira.

"Is it a holiday?" Kira whispers.

"No, come downstairs." Rhonda motions for the hall.

Leaving Nadia asleep, Kira follows Rhonda to her living room and gasps when she sees the image of Ruger projected on the wall.

Ruger's in full uniform, clean shaven, and his stance is fierce. His leg is bleeding, exactly where he was shot when she first found him, causing her stomach to whirl. Kira peels her eyes from his leg and covers her mouth once she sees what's behind him. Someone who looks like the Auctairean Prime Minister is on the floor. Kira grabs her chest. "Is that Stephen Joplin?"

"Yes." Rhonda studies her face, but Kira doesn't notice. Relief fills Kira so rapidly she could cry.

Needing clarification, Kira brings her eyes to Rhonda. "The Prime Minister's dead?"

Rhonda only nods.

Kira lets out a jagged sigh. "He'll never hurt me again." It feels wrong to smile regarding someone's death, but her lips curve anyway. The power that's haunted her all these years has fallen.

She's free.

Bracing her hand on the wall, it takes everything within Kira not to cry. Staring at the still image of Ruger, her heart trembles. It was through this man that God not only saved her and Nadia's life, but has given her freedom. "I can't believe Ruger already took down the Hive."

"Yes, thanks to you." Rhonda sits down and pats the spot beside her.

Kira slowly takes a seat. "His wound is flared up."

"No. He was shot, again." Rhonda grimaces. "I'll rewind it for you."

The image doesn't blur, before a man with a square jawline, blond hair and blue eyes appears on screen. His uniform isn't dissimilar from Ruger's, except below the patch of Zyandite's flag is a red star, with a black horse at the center. Behind him is a plain gray wall, while his muscular form stands at parade rest.

Rhonda's cheeks redden. "That's General Jordan Brice, the King's Charge Commander. We grew up together." By her blushing, Kira would have to be blind to not see there's an attraction there. "He's my brother's right-hand man."

"Ruger appointed him?"

"Yes." Rhonda presses a button on her tablet.

General Jordan Brice has a kind voice, but his eyes are stern. "Today, Zyandite's made history. Before we share with the world our victory, we must show our reason. After we obliterated Kaddain in retaliation for their attack, we didn't expect our northern neighbor to start a fight."

The image pans to Zyandite's border fence along Auctairea, with pines to the north, and nothing but red dirt to the south. Along the fence, there are towers set up about a hundred feet apart. The footage was taken from one of these towers, as Zyandite soldiers patrol the ground.

The familiar scraping fills Kira's ears. In response, her heart begins pounding. "No."

Rhonda glances at her and frowns. She may not know what it's like to live under such tyranny, but sympathizes with Kira, just the same.

Two hundred machines break through the border. Zyandite soldiers fired upon them, but didn't know where to hit. Eventually, they ran out of ammo. While the men went down with a fight, without the proper understanding of the mechanics of the Skull Smashers, they were no match.

Kira can't watch what happens next. It reminds her too much of the Great Cleansing.

A blue light fills the scene. It's much like Ruger's Quktarr, before the light fades, and only blue ash remains.

General Brice's face returns on screen. "We lost twenty-six soldiers that day. Auctairea committed suicide when it took the lives of those men, whose names will never be forgotten." He raises his chin while subtitles of the soldiers' names momentarily fill the screen. "We had what we thought was the key to dismantle every one of these machines, but that information was false. In the process, we almost lost King Anstone. If not for a Christian widow, barely surviving the horrors of socialism, we would've never been given the exact location of the Hive. Thank the great I Am for Kira Westin."

Kira gasps upon reading the honor, before the screen fills with the relic tower in Quandii, with the layers of gray stone swirling up five stories into the sky. In a flash, it's gone.

A new scene covers the wall, as a platoon of Zyandite soldiers break into the Hive. The projection cuts to Quandii's city gate, where hundreds of machines have fallen. Dozens of Zyandite tanks roll in, running over the metal, smashing Auctairea's defense to bits.

The frame returns to General Brice. This time, he's smiling. "No weapon is too big for Zyandite to cut down, because God is with us. We're not sharing this to boast, but to let every nation on earth know what their fate will be if they follow the mistakes of our enemies. Strike Zyandite, and only death awaits you. We follow the true God, the living God, and His victory is with us."

Goosebumps cause Kira to shiver, before the footage becomes gritty. She recognizes the Hive, and gasps once she sees Ruger.

Rhonda pats her arm. "Our king is always the first in battle."

Watching the medic tend to Ruger's wound, causes Kira to wring her hands. Grabbing a nearby pillow instead, Kira squeezes the corners.

Ruger speaks, and his voice is tense. Unable to understand him, Kira's eyes drink in the subtitles. The Zyandite victory decree is just as fierce as its reputation. There's no going back for Auctairea. As Ruger said, it's Zyandite, now.

The image becomes white. Rhonda turns the projection off.

"That's it?" Worried for Ruger, Kira hugs the pillow into her chest.

"Yes. Shocking they gave up so easily, isn't it?"

"Not really. What did they have to fight for?" Kira shakes her head at

Auctairea's decline. "Is Ruger okay?"

Rhonda looks at her tablet. "I keep waiting for his call." She shrugs. "Are you upset?"

"No. I'm relieved," Kira says. "This is what I've been praying for."

"Considering that Auctairea's greatest export is organs harvested from aborted babies, I have no pity for them." Rhonda squares her shoulders. Kira's never seen her so proud.

Knowing the fate of Joplin, and where he is now, Kira shivers. "Auctairea's had this coming."

"Yes, but we still didn't want to do this."

Kira knows that. "How long until Ruger comes home?"

"The Despoliation Process usually lasts a month."

"Despoliation Process?" Kira can't stand being out of the loop on Zyandite's ways.

"It's a little more complex, but Despoliation is basically a plunder expedition. We aren't wasteful, and recover costs by taking everything of worth from a country we invade," Rhonda explains.

"Oh, Rhonda, you have to help me learn Zyandish before Ruger comes home."

Rhonda laughs. "That's hardly enough time to learn Zyandish."

"You heard what Ruger said. Auctrah is dead. My interview is in a month, how can I face Wilma, if I'm breaking the King's law?"

Rhonda's face pales at the challenge. "You have a point, but I'm not a professor or a linguist."

"You teach for a living!" Kira exclaims.

"The violin!" Rhonda grimaces before placing a hand on her heart. "I'll do my best, but no promises."

"Thank you." Kira leans forward. "I feel so out of—"

"Mommy?" Nadia peers from the bottom step of Rhonda's stairs.

"Come here, sweetheart." Kira holds her arms out and catches her daughter with a hug.

"People are being loud outside." Nadia squeezes the doll Rhonda got her, before resting her head on Kira's shoulder. "I'm scared."

"There's no need for you to fear. We're celebrating because my brother defeated Auctairea." Rhonda manages a happy dance from her seat.

Anticipating that Nadia will be upset, Kira bites her lip.

"Really?" Nadia's face beams.

"Mmm hmm..." Rhonda winks.

"That means none of those bad people can hurt us again." Nadia looks up at Kira and smiles.

"That's right." Kira sighs in relief at Nadia's reaction.

Rhonda's eyes fill with a new respect. She opens her mouth, but before she can utter a word, her tablet chimes. "It's Ruger!" Rhonda says in Auctrah, before answering in Zyandish. Her face is worried, and Rhonda speaks so fast, Nadia and Kira exchange uncomfortable glances. Rhonda's shoulders relax before she begins to speak in Auctrah.

"Oh, of course, here she is." Rhonda holds her tablet out to Kira.

"Ruger!" Nadia leans over to better see the screen.

Ruger's harden face melts into a smile. "Hello, Nadia. How's Zyandire treating you?"

Pressing her lips together to hold in a laugh, Rhonda gives the tablet to Nadia, instead.

Nadia's hands encase the tablet, carefully. She's so tiny it makes the screen appear huge. "It's great!"

Both Rhonda's and Ruger's laughter fills the room like music.

Kira's heart swells. This is like a dream she was too afraid to have in

Auctairea.

"I knew you'd like it," Ruger says.

"Yep, and you know what else? We eat three meals a day. Can you believe that?" Nadia's jaw drops dramatically. It's an adorable sight, but the room darkens with pity.

"Never expect less, Nadia. This is the life God has for you now." Ruger's tone is determined.

"God is awesome." Nadia grins before handing the tablet to her mom.

"Yes, he is," Ruger proclaims before his eyes meet Kira's. Sitting at a large desk, Ruger's green eyes study Kira's face. They're filled with the same light that drew her heart. "It's good to see you," he whispers.

Rhonda's eyes widen. She's never heard her brother talk like that before and looks to the floor for a moment. "Nadia," she says with a grin. "How about you and I get a midnight snack?"

Nadia's jaw drops, "More food?"

Rhonda nods.

"Yay!" Nadia skips to Rhonda's side.

Thankful for the privacy, Kira gives Rhonda a bashful smile before walking upstairs. She flips the switch and half-expects the lights to stay off. Smiling at the glow from the wrought iron chandelier above, Kira sits on the top step. The cream carpet is lush and the lighting is romantic enough to fit her mood. "I thought we weren't supposed to speak Auctrah anymore?" A playful smile dances across her face.

Ruger's cheeks redden, and he glances at the desk for a moment. "Yeah, well…" His eyes meet hers, causing butterflies to swirl in Kira's stomach. "If my generals can enact the Slayden Rule, we can speak Auctrah until you're fluent in Zyandish."

"Sounds fair," Kira straightens her shoulders, "By the way, congratulations on your victory."

Ruger frowns. "It doesn't feel like a victory. Have you ever heard of a nation surrendering so fast?"

"No." Kira sighs. "If Joplin's hiding something, it won't be in his name. You'll have to dig."

Ruger slowly nods, his eyes distant, contemplating. "I keep expecting a reboot of the machines, or a hidden brigade of special forces to conduct an insurgency operation. In all my training, not one history lesson taught of a nation giving up like this. I'm treading entirely new waters, and need prayer for direction." His eyes darken, and while he's in better shape than he was under the kepweed poisoning, Kira can see how tired he is.

"I've been praying for you." Kira leans towards the screen. "I hate it that you got shot again. Especially so close to the wounds I tended."

Ruger grins. "My surgeon already took care of that, but thank you. You know, Zyandite is indebted to you. If it weren't for you giving me the correct location of the Hive, we would've had casualties. As it stands right now, we haven't lost a single soldier. For a siege, that's unheard of."

Kira smiles, but her heart fills with worry. "I hope the lie that caused you to crash wasn't from within."

Ruger's eyes become distant. "Before yesterday, I couldn't have imagined such betrayal." He looks at her with eyes that aren't angry, but full of pain. "Joplin's last words haunt me, 'You're the only thing in our way.' I keep telling myself that he meant Zyandite as a nation, but the way he said it…" Ruger lets out a sigh. "It felt personal."

"Joplin was a plant. A Trojan Horse," Kira whispers. "He pretended to be a Christian, he pretended to love Auctairea. Someone put him in that position, the question is, who?"

"Thornton Lazeed," Ruger hisses.

"He's just a puppet." Kira looks up. The lights above her are too pretty for this subject, but it must be said. "I think Charles Miser is out of jail, and back to playing chess with the world."

"That can't be, or you'd be dead," Ruger says with a half-grin.

Kira blushes. "So, when will I see you again?"

"I'm not sure." Ruger grimaces. "Did my sister explain our Despoliation Process?"

"Briefly."

"Okay," Ruger lets out a slow breath. "I'm willing to give the land back to the civilians, so long as they stay put and don't reactivate their military. We're destroying the mechanical soldiers, but I have to make certain the Auctaireans don't have the ability to reboot them before we leave. It shouldn't take too long. That is, if they cooperate. My goal is to get our soldiers home in time for Christmas."

Kira's face lights up. "I'm excited for Nadia to experience her first real Christmas."

"Me too," Ruger whispers, returning her smile, "but there's nothing I want more than to hold you in my arms again."

Kira's cheeks flush. "I was worried that because you're king, our love wouldn't survive."

He leans forward. "I love you, Kira, but we have to be careful. If my crash was an attempted coup, we must explore all of our options. When my surgeon informed me of how suspicious the Lineage has behaved, I called a friend to help, but I'm praying it won't come to that."

Her heart skips a beat. There are not many allies Zyandite has in the world. Kira can only guess he means to send her and Nadia to Tunaunda. Hoping she's wrong, she asks, "What do you mean?"

Ruger sees the pain in her eyes and winces. "The only reason why I'd consider sending you and Nadia away is to protect you."

Kira looks down. "My nationality is causing quite the stir." She scowls at herself for letting that slip.

"You know that's not it. If I were to send you away it would only be temporary."

Heart stung, she can't bring herself to look at him. Every man in her life has lied, how can she expect him to be different?

"Kira," Ruger's tone is sorrowful, making her eyes return to his. "It looks like the Lineage killed one of their own."

She gasps.

"My surgeon wasn't allowed to conduct an autopsy on General Baxton, who was the people's choice for king. If the Lineage did that to him, I worry for what they'd do to an Auctairean."

Kira feels guilty for accusing him. "God has always protected Nadia and I, so I'm not afraid of your generals. However, I have no right to be queen."

While he's slow to speak, admiration covers Ruger's face. "Yet again, you've proven how worthy you are."

She doesn't feel worthy, and looks away.

"Humility is something most of the Lineage lacks." Ruger's words give her the strength to look at him. "I've had so many arrogant women thrown at me. They'd sacrifice nothing for God, or for Zyandite. You on the other hand, would lay your life down in a heartbeat if God told you to. Zyandite needs you." Ruger's eyes plead and become desperate. "I need you."

Hoping she can share his confidence one day, Kira gives an uneasy smile.

"I've hurt you. For that I'm sorry." Ruger slowly shakes his head. "Sending you away is not the answer. Instead, I'm going to order you something that will make us both feel better."

"Oh?" Kira asks, raising a brow.

"I promised you guns, didn't I?" Ruger gives a tired smile. "Expect your first to arrive tomorrow."

"It helps knowing that Rhonda's armed, but I would appreciate having one of my own. How much paperwork do I have to fill out to get it?"

Ruger laughs. It's too much of a melody for her to be offended. "Guns are part of our culture. To make anyone have to apply for one would go against the fabric of our founding."

"That's so foreign to me." Kira chuckles. "It's like a breath of fresh air."

"I knew you'd love that about my home." Ruger takes a moment to enjoy her company in silence. "I had better go. I've got to sleep sometime."

She should laugh, but a realization hits Kira's stomach like a boulder. She can't help the worry that maps her brow like a parched desert. "Have your men gone through the Education Centers, yet?"

"No."

Kira bites her lip. "They admit children from birth. I'm worried about them. It's only getting colder there by the day."

Ruger lets out a sigh. "I'll look into it." He sets the tablet on a built in stand and begins typing on the outdated Auctairean keyboard on his desk. "There are eight Education Centers within a hundred miles of Quandii. I'll lead the first platoon." He raises a brow. "Sleep can wait."

"Please, be careful."

He smirks. "I'll see you tomorrow."

The screen turns black, and Kira's heart sinks. She shouldn't feel this attached to Ruger, not with how little time they've spent together, but she's fallen too deep. Hugging the tablet into her chest, there's no denying that she's helplessly in love with him. Remembering the faces of those she let down in Auctairea, Kira only wishes Ruger weren't king.

"God, I don't deserve this," Kira whispers before wiping a tear and readying herself to face her daughter. If it weren't for Nadia, she would've left on her own. After all, everyone but Ruger knows that he deserves better...

***

In the historic center of Brustonite, General Kentwood's home was once owned by the first four star general of Zyandite. Meeting on a missionary trip before the old country fell; General Heaton and King Slayden became more like brothers than friends. Their bond helped win the war, and this estate showcases their accomplishments with dozens of artifacts and paintings.

THE LINEAGE

As Wilma walks down the dark halls with swirls of black velvet over golden wallpaper, she keeps her chin down in reverence for the elaborate portraits along the walls. Various portraits of the Lineage shine under beams of sunlight. Overhead, three skylights are the only windows that aren't draped by brown, black, and gold jacquard. The darkness adds to the ambiance. In a way, the Kentwood's house is more of a museum than a home.

The woman of the house, Eleanor Kentwood, seems very comfortable in her surroundings. Though she's past the prime of life, her wrinkles don't diminish her beauty. Sharp brown eyes are framed by white hair hanging in large curls above her shoulders. Every step she takes is calculated, and not a word leaves Eleanor's mouth without careful examination.

"I appreciate you allowing me to stop by, especially on such short notice," Wilma says.

"My dear, Wilma, it's a pleasure to have you in my home."

It wasn't always this way. To hide her resentment, Wilma glances around for a moment. "It's unfortunate this visit is in regards to something unpleasant."

"Oh, General Danning already filled me in."

Wilma grimaces. "I made a mistake. I'm hoping to make up for it by destroying Kira's reputation."

Eleanor's face morphs into a scowl. "Now that King Anstone has attributed his outlandish victory to her, there's no way the people will accept Kira as anything short of a hero. Every word you say against her, will only acquire sympathy for them both."

With a confident smirk, Wilma raises a brow. "I have years' worth of fantasies Auctairean men wrote about her. It's enough to make any Zyandite puke."

"Yes, out of sympathy for Kira," Eleanor says with a roll of her eyes.

Wilma's lips press together. "Thankfully, that's not why I came."

Eleanor raises a brow.

"I may have a solution that could turn King Anstone against her."

A spark flickers across Eleanor's eyes, before she opens the double-doors into an elaborate sitting room. Furnished mostly in gold, several chairs surround a table with the Zyandite banner draped across it, but the focal point is the tapestry covering the wall. Dark beige threads intertwine over a gray background, creating two oak trees. It would take an entire afternoon to read each name on every branch, before the last two connect at the bottom. Wilma does well in hiding her jealousy of it.

Eleanor motions towards a chair before taking a seat. "It impresses even me." Eleanor smiles at the remarkable heritage she and her husband have running through their veins. "I never get tired of looking at it."

Wilma knows better than to bring up her own Lineage. With only one general in her family line, she's barely qualified to be a member.

Eleanor distracts Wilma from her thoughts before pressing her right index finger on the flag, and closes her eyes for a moment in reverence. "For the courage… For the purity… For the memories… For the blood…"

Wilma does the same. Typically the moment of silence is supposed to last two seconds, but Wilma always takes four. It makes her seem more sincere. Opening her eyes, she crosses her legs and leans forward. "I have a perfect plan, but there's no way I can execute it without you."

"What do you need?"

"I need you to find every young brunette of the Lineage you can, and school them on Kira's mannerisms. They must adapt to King Anstone's taste, even have them dress like Kira. They need to make onlookers question if they're the prophesized woman from Farrah's dream. Then, on the day of the homecoming ceremony…"

"Oh, that's right," Eleanor laughs. "Kira can't step foot in the castle until she's made a citizen. Simply brilliant."

"If it works, not only will the stain on King Anstone's blood be purified, but the Auctairean will be exiled. In the meantime, I'll make the people question if the prophecy is about one of us."

"Hmm…" Eleanor squares her shoulders, ready for the hunt. "I know just the lady for the job."

THE LINEAGE

***

CHAPTER 14
DEATH OF A NATION

In what used to be Auctairea, the destruction of a society has commenced. Just hours after obtaining victory, thousands of Zyandite soldiers flood in for the Despoliation. Like a swarm, these troops begin to take down everything that resembles this former nation, by first removing its flag.

Once the morale of the people is shattered, the next step is to break down every material that can be melted down, or refurbished.

Ruger leads a small platoon through the thick night air of Auctairea, and smiles at how hard his soldiers are working. With dozens of artificial lights brightening the nightshift, the city of Quandii appears to be under a dome of daylight. Leaving the glow behind, this windy road surrounded by tall pine trees reminds Ruger of the night he crashed. The first memory of Kira should make him smile, but this is hardly the time or place for joy. Keeping himself focused on the mission, Ruger watches the bend of the road curve into darkness. Their convoy consists of four vehicles, but each gunner is on high alert, intently watching the forests that hug the road. Once they reach the coordinates of the nearest Education Center, Ruger expects to see a fully operational school. Instead, there's only a small, single-story building and an empty parking lot. As they get closer, the sound of babies crying fills the air. It's obvious the caregivers are gone.

"They've been abandoned," Ruger says.

"Auctaireans couldn't be *that* bad, could they?" Sergeant Wright asks.

"Yes," Ruger steps out of the vehicle. Opening the double glass doors, only the stench greets him. Coughing, he bends down before pulling out his Quhtarr to use as a flashlight. "Hello?" Ruger says in Auctrah, while a half-dozen soldiers step in behind him.

A tiny figure peers out of the side of a doorway, before disappearing.

"Sergeant Groth, you take a team to where those babies are crying. General Brice and Sergeant Wright, follow me," Ruger orders in Zyandish, before stepping towards where the girl hid.

"We're not here to hurt you," Ruger says in Auctrah. He can't raise his voice too much, or the smell will hit the back of his throat and make him cough again. *"We want to help you."*

Passing a reception area, a yellow sweater for a large adult is draped over the chair. There are no other signs of caregivers. With how dark and cold the center is, Ruger fears these children were abandoned long before the siege.

Slowly, Ruger steps into the room where the child hid.

In the shadows he sees a little girl who can't be older than three, with blond hair knotted up from dirt and sweat. Her eyes are fearful, but Ruger is keen enough to realize she's not afraid of him.

She points down the hallway and motions for him to follow.

Ruger doesn't hesitate, and is about to step into the dark, before General Brice grabs his arm. "It could be a trap."

Ruger understands his friend's concern, but takes his arm back, "They're just little kids." He follows the girl and as they walk down the hallway, there's a muffled sound of children yelling.

The girl stops, and points at a door. It's crafted of steel, with a metal pulldown knob and three pin locks at the top. There's a chair beside it, and the bottom lock is undone.

The little girl stands upon the chair and tries to reach the top locks, but she's too short.

"Very smart," Ruger praises in Auctrah, before reaching to unlock them. He protectively grabs the little girl and steps back, turning to the side to shield her from whatever may come out of that room.

Several children fall onto the floor. They all cry and shout in Auctrah so loudly, it's hard for Ruger to understand them.

"We're starving!" A little girl with freckles shouts.

"How long ago were you abandoned?" Ruger asks.

"Our caregivers left when we ran out of food." A little boy with blond hair answers while wiping his nose with his hand.

Disgusted by the thought of anyone abandoning children being called caregivers, Ruger looks at the freezer. "Find blankets," he orders Sergeant Wright in Zyandish. *"When was that?"* He asks the small boy in Auctrah.

The boy shrugs. *"A few days ago."*

He doesn't want to risk frightening the children by yelling, so Ruger turns to General Brice and translates everything in a whisper, just to keep his heartrate under control.

Even in this poor lighting, the blue in General Brice's eyes flicker with rage. "What do you want us to do?"

"Call for an immediate evacuation for every Education Center." Ruger looks at the group of shivering children. It makes him sick to see the innocent so neglected. For their sake, he forces a smile.

Only the first girl he found smiles back. The rest are far too suspicious. Ruger hopes that one day, their hearts will heal.

"Evacuate them to where?" General Brice pulls out his tablet, ready to type in the coordinates.

"Home," Ruger whispers, knowing the generals will have a fit.

A flicker of nervous admiration crosses General Brice's face, before he calls in the order.

"Don't worry," Ruger assures them in Auctrah, *"I am Zyandite's King, and I*

promise to put you all in homes where you'll never be abandoned again."

The children exchange glances, intermixed with both excitement and disbelief.

Sergeant Wright steps out of a room with a pile of blankets and yellow scrubs in his arms. Ruger helps him distribute them to the children.

"But first," Ruger says, *"I need to know who put you all in the freezer?"*

"We were put in there by the new orderlies," The young boy answers meekly.

"Yeah," The girl with freckles says with a voice too old for her body, proving she's malnourished. *"They said that since they're the oldest, they're in charge."*

To warn his men of potential trouble, Ruger quickly translates.

"Hey, you can't let them out! You're defying Prime Minister Joplin!" The harsh voice of a prepubescent boy yells from behind Ruger.

Ruger turns to see several faces scorned with hatred and false authority. *"Your Prime Minister is dead. I'm your King now."*

The gang of five kids stop, their confidence wanes, but only for a moment. *"Liar!"* The tallest boy shouts.

Ruger smirks. *"I desire to place you in good homes, where you can learn about our God and His precepts. I promise each one of you will live lives better than you can imagine, so long as you assimilate. Or you can fend for yourselves in the woods."* Ruger's tone is commanding, before he turns his focus on the children who obviously reject the new orderlies, as their eyes are ready for change. Ruger smiles at their eagerness, before the tallest boy screams:

"We'll never believe in any god!"

He runs off, and the rest of his gang follows.

"Good, they were going to kill their own," Sergeant Wright whispers, "We don't need their kind in Zyandite."

"They're still children," Ruger says in Zyandish. He looks at the tattered siblings as they hold onto each other, proving the bond of family can't be destroyed. "Come on, let's get you kids something to eat." Leading them outside, Ruger's soldiers give these young ones food and water.

Bracing himself for the smell, Ruger marches back into the Education Center. The sound of babies crying makes the rest of his men easy to discover.

Walking past rows of bassinets, Ruger finds Sergeant Groth bent over. His other two soldiers are distressed, but Sergeant Groth is the only one puking.

Ruger steps between the bassinets, one with a screaming baby, and the other without life. In order to maintain composure, he forces himself to look away from the gruesome sight.

"I'm alright, my King," Sergeant Groth hasps before standing upright.

Ruger pats Sergeant Groth on the back before noticing that these bassinets have wheels. "Let's get these babies out of here."

Every time these soldiers wheel a baby out into the fresh air, the return to the stench becomes more difficult to endure. It takes nearly an hour for Ruger and his men to gather all the babies and load them up onto the convoy, along with the children who choose to go with them.

The sensation of being watched causes Ruger's hair to stand on end. He turns to see the angry eyes of the self-appointed orderlies, glaring at him from the forest. "Last chance," Ruger offers in Auctrah. He makes sure the bassinets are strapped tightly in place, and by the time he looks back, they're gone. "The great I Am, I'm sorry I couldn't save them all," Ruger prays before the convoy leaves on sky-mode. The sound of babies screaming and children whimpering makes it the most difficult mission of these soldiers' lives.

After typing in the command for his own surgeon to fly back with the children, Ruger decides to break the silence. "In four hours, these children will be at Christ Centered Hospital, where twenty pediatricians and forty-five nurses are waiting to give them care, real care."

"So many have diaper rashes," Sergeant Groth whispers, his face still pale. "I tried to change one. It was bleeding so badly, I had to put the soiled diaper back on. I didn't want to hurt the poor baby any worse."

"I know Sergeant, it's despicable. None of their suffering is your fault. Dr. Tanner is going to fly back with them and do everything in her ability to heal them," Ruger says.

Sergeant Groth straightens his posture. "Yes, my King."

Thirty minutes later, Dr. Tanner walks around the full cargo plane, praying over and comforting each baby she passes. She turns to wave goodbye to Ruger, before the hatch closes.

"Good job, men," Ruger says.

As the dawn lightens the cloud cover of Auctairean skies, Ruger and his men watch the takeoff, feeling accomplished that beautiful lives await these little ones.

"What are you sending to Zyandite now?" General Kentwood shouts from behind them.

Sergeant Groth has never glared at a general before today, but his eyes burn with fire hot enough for Ruger to raise a hand for him to stop.

With a smirk, Ruger turns to face General Kentwood. "How dare you question your king?"

General Kentwood steps back in shock, before eying each soldier on the runway to find they're all glaring at him. General Kentwood puffs out his chest. "King of Zyandite, or Auctairea?"

A low roar of disapproval fills the hanger.

The tension is so thick this division could morph into action at any minute. Ruger must keep his oath and maintain peace. "This is Zyandite now. Why don't you get some sleep."

General Kentwood's face turns red. "How can I sleep after what you've done?" Taking a step closer, he hisses through his teeth, "Is your nursemaid not enough? Why must you contaminate more bloodlines with this godless filth?"

Ruger's lips curve into a snarl. "Those children are going to be adopted, loved, and shown how to revere God. I don't care who their parents were, their souls are worth more to me than any bloodline." With a hard glare,

Ruger marches off.

General Kentwood watches him go with murder in his eyes...

***

CHAPTER 15
GREATEST OF THESE

In the quiet of dawn, Rhonda creeps downstairs to make breakfast and watch last night's report.

Wilma's overdoing the purity look in a white dress as she speaks past light mauve lipstick, a shocking change from her signature red. "Look, just like every other Zyandite, I was impressed with how quickly King Anstone conquered Auctairea. Sure, it was the easiest battle he could've fought, but he did it well. And we all know that Kira Westin's tip on the Hive was helpful." She shrugs it off. "The real issue isn't the fallen enemy of the north. We knew that without their machines, Auctaireans were limp noodles from the start." Wilma crosses her arms. "What concerns me is this prophecy." She unfolds her arms and leans forward. "Kira Westin's not a Zyandite citizen. Remember that as you process the real potentiality of our King marrying her. Did he just recently learn of this prophecy? Was this an act of desperation on his part? Instead of focusing on King Anstone, perhaps Zyandites should ask the great I Am, if we're missing the mark? What I mean to say is, General Danning has a wife, General Kentwood has a wife, General Mayes has a wife, and General Fisher also, has a wife. Now I know that as Christians," Wilma squares her shoulders. "We're supposed to remain humble, but even so, I must say that General Marshal," Wilma's innocent smiles transforms into an arrogant smirk, "has a wife." Wilma points at herself and her eyes give the camera a quick up and down. "Either King Anstone is fulfilling the prophecy by bringing a foreign woman into our homeland, or…" Wilma pauses for so long Rhonda has to look at her tablet to make sure the connection wasn't lost. "Since the timing is just too perfect, perhaps the King is trying to force this prophecy to be about him, rather than God's chosen leader?" Wilma slowly places a finger on her chin. "Of course, our true future queen could be out there, whom King Anstone hasn't met. Perhaps Kira's just the counterfeit?" She throws her hands up. "Pray about it Zyandite, because we can't afford to be misled."

Rhonda's jaw drops.

The sound of footsteps causes Rhonda to fumble with her tablet. She turns the projection off before her guests see it. "Good morning, ladies, I have pancakes and orange juice waiting."

Nadia's eyes widen in surprise. "Pancakes?"

"Yes, you need the calories. I've got a busy day planned for you two." Rhonda claps her hands together. "Today, I'm going to help you learn Zyandish."

"Thank goodness," Kira says. "The digital tutor isn't cutting it."

"Well, we'll conquer this together." Rhonda skips to the table before her tablet chimes.

Kira hopes its Ruger, but Rhonda doesn't answer it. Instead, she intensely stares at the tablet.

"My brother is about to address the nation." Rhonda points her tablet at the wall and Wilma's image is quickly replaced with Auctairean gray skies. "Since the take-over, Auctrah is no longer available through the standard settings." She types something on her tablet. "By God's grace, Farrah gave me access into the missionary network, so every language should be there." The subtitles in Auctrah pop up at the bottom of the projection. "Good." Rhonda's shoulders loosen.

There's a navy platform, where four soldiers stand at attention between rows of Zyandite flags that lift periodically in the breeze. The gold frame encases a deep red, with a white cross standing in the center of each banner.

Remembering when she first noticed that flag on Ruger's uniform, makes Kira smile.

A sapphire wool coat with platinum buttons hangs fitted above Ruger's gray pants. Head tall, his chest displays rows of medals. Kira wishes she knew what they represent.

He steps to the center of the podium, and the soldiers behind him salute, before standing at parade rest.

"He hasn't gotten any sleep," Rhonda mumbles before crossing her arms.

Kira's amazed by that. He couldn't look more handsome if he tried.

"Brothers and Sisters in Christ," Ruger's tone is soft, though his eyes are hard. "I address you today not as your King, but as a fellow Christian. What I'm about to ask of you, has nothing to do with our flag, but our faith." He lifts his chin. "Historically, the greatest victim in war has always been the children. Unfortunately, in Auctairea, children were victimized long before this war began. They were either thrown away like garbage, or used for political gain. They've been starved, neglected, and finally, abandoned. First, they were abandoned by their parents. The law of the land forced every child into an Education Center. From birth, they were taught that government is both their parent, and god. Once the government rations ceased, those who survived were abandoned again, this time, by their so-called caregivers. When we entered an Education Center, we discovered the children were left to fend for themselves. We saved as many as we could, but…" He holds his head down for a moment. "Many were lost before we arrived. The soldiers, who discovered this gruesome sight, need your prayers. I doubt any of us will fully recover from what we saw." Ruger does his best to hold in a tear, but sniffles. The men behind him hold their heads down in sorrow for the unnecessary loss. "Sadly, some of the older kids didn't want our help. When I first crashed into this nation, the woman who God charged to save my life had to hide her child from daily drone patrols. Kira Westin risked everything to spare her child, not just from the physical horrors of these indoctrination centers, but from the spiritual death they ensure. Every child in Auctairea is raised an atheist. Kira told me she couldn't risk that happening to her own. At the time, I found that hard to believe. But now, I've seen it. These children need love to introduce them to Christ. They deserve God's salvation, the security of parents who love them, the necessities they've lacked such as food and proper clothing. So…" He lets out a slow breath. "I've sent every child we've rescued to Zyandite."

Rhonda's gasp nearly shakes the house.

Exchanging a concerned glance with Nadia, Kira turns to Rhonda in hopes to offer support, but Rhonda stares at the projection as though they aren't there.

Ruger's lips curve into a smile. "You can apply for adoption, right now. We have stations set up at the hospital with notaries at the ready. The sooner these kids are placed into good homes, the better." His shoulders tighten. "Yes, we've tested them for disease, and haven't sent any contagions home. Yes, it's going to be a challenge to get these kids to assimilate, but I'm asking the people of Zyandite, as your brother in Christ, to lay your bloodlines down at the cross and accept these Auctaireans as our own people. How can we call ourselves a Christian nation, if we don't practice the love of Christ? A love these kids have never known." Ruger's eyes are so full of compassion that Kira feels a rush of heat rise from her chest. "The Bible tells us: Three things will last forever—faith, hope, and love—and the greatest of these is love." Ruger quotes 1st Corinthians 13:13 before placing his hands behind his back and squaring his shoulders. "Zyandite, join me in prayer," he bows his head, and Rhonda follows suit.

Kira looks at Nadia and nods before lowering her head down, just enough to still read the subtitles.

"The great I Am, thank you for leading Kira to me. Without her, I would've never known the exact location of the Hive, and Zyandite wouldn't have gained this swift, miraculous victory. Without you bringing Kira into my life, I wouldn't have discovered these indoctrination centers, and these precious lives wouldn't have been saved. We praise your holy name, great I Am, the maker of the cosmos. Thank you, our God, for directing our steps. Please, comfort these children, uplift them, speak to them, reach their hearts and guide their souls to you. Make them receptive to your love, so they can fully receive it and one day, share it. Rise up the couples whom you have chosen to be their parents, and bless them for taking up such a sacrificial task. I ask that sacrifice will turn into a blessing. Strengthen these parents as they adopt foreign children into their homes. Make the transition of language and culture easy to adjust through. I ask that these children will love their new parents, be loyal to Zyandite, and most of all seek you for the rest of their lives. Send your Holy Spirit on Zyandite and cleanse it from all biases, and discrimination against these tender souls that you created. Thank you, the great and powerful I Am, in the mighty name of Jesus Christ, amen."

"Amen," Rhonda whispers before wiping away a tear.

"Thank you for your time. I love you, and may the great I Am bless each of you with his presence, and unfailing love." Ruger salutes his country by slamming his right fist into his chest. The soldiers behind him do the same, before the projection ends.

"Oh," is all Kira can understand, before Rhonda falls to the floor, crying. She's speaking in Zyandish so frantically, it doesn't sound legible.

Nadia's eyes widen with fear. Kira hates seeing it and wraps an arm around her. "It's okay, Nadia." Kira stares at Rhonda, searching for the right words to say. "What your brother just did was beautiful. Everything will be okay."

"No!" Rhonda shouts in Auctrah. "It's not okay. The Lineage will retaliate." She takes in several jagged breaths before glaring at Kira. "I feel for those children, I really do, but if your bloodline wasn't bad enough, this…" She points at the wall where the projection has faded to white, "Will be the end of him!"

Guilt creeps its ugly face into Kira's heart. Her shoulders slouch before a familiar voice gives her strength.

"Be courageous."

Kira straightens her shoulders and looks at Rhonda with a solid faith. "So be strong and courageous, all you who hope in the LORD." Kira recites Psalm 31:24 with a resolute tone and wraps an arm around Rhonda's shoulders. "Don't fear man. God is behind this. Your brother won't fail." Kira stands and holds a hand out to her future sister-in-law, "We must greet these kids."

"What?" Rhonda's green eyes bulge.

Kira brings herself to smile. "You're a translator. Nadia and I can bring them comfort. This is an opportunity for ministry."

Rhonda shakes her head. "I don't think it'll work."

Kira tilts her chin. "Come on, you bought us all of these beautiful clothes, let's take this as an excuse to wear them."

Her lips quiver, but Rhonda manages to take Kira's hand and rises to her feet. "Alright, but I hate to think of what's going to happen to these kids if Zyandites won't adopt them."

Pressing her lips together, Kira knows this is God's plan, and won't share Rhonda's fear.

***

After a quick change of clothes, the trio barely makes it to the airport in time to watch the plane land.

It's not cold, but Rhonda's shivering. Kira wants to say something to comfort her, but silently prays for her instead. Glancing at the rows of paramedics waiting to take these young refugees to the Children's Hospital, Kira does her best to ignore the reporters who hound them with questions.

Rhonda presses her fingers against her nose and yells something in Zyandish.

The runway is filled with indignant gasps before the reporters leave them alone.

"What did you say?" Kira asks.

"They kept asking me about the Lineage. I told them we should all focus on Christ, instead."

Kira smiles at Rhonda's bravery.

"Look, mommy!" Nadia points up. The white dot only gets bigger, before the plane lands.

Kira places her hands on Nadia's shoulder in anticipation. A breeze waves their hair, reminding her of when they first landed here. Kira hopes the kids onboard that plane have the same wonderful first impression of Zyandite as she did.

The hatch of the cargo plane slowly descends. A lone woman in her mid-fifties waits for the ramp to reach the asphalt. Her graying hair is in a ponytail above kind, brown eyes. She even smiles at Kira, before she shouts orders in Zyandish. Curt as she's being, it's evident she has authority.

"That's Dr. Tanner, my brother's surgeon," Rhonda informs.

Beyond Dr. Tanner, the oldest child Kira sees can't be a day over eight. Most are too young to walk, and are brought to the ambulances in plastic cradles. As they're loaded up into ambulances, Kira realizes that some are old enough to walk, but can't. Knowing Nadia could be like any one of these children, Kira swallows hard in order to keep from crying. "I can't wait to meet her, but right now, we need to comfort these kids."

Rhonda's face is pale. "Yeah, okay."

Kira walks up to a young girl with strawberry blond hair. "Hi, my name is Kira," she greets in Auctrah.

The girl turns away.

"It's okay, my mommy's nice." Nadia bounces up to her. "My name is Nadia, what's yours?"

"Blue14."

"That's… Different." Nadia pulls a blue button from her purse. "Maybe you'll like this. I named him Joshua."

The girl takes the blue button and grins.

Proud of Nadia, Kira's unable to contain her smile.

Once the children are loaded up, they follow the ambulances to the hospital. The scenery is typical of downtown Brustonite, even enchanting, before something unusual catches Kira's eye. Along the sidewalk, dozens, if not hundreds of women stand in a line so long, it wraps around the block.

"What's going on?" Kira asks.

Rhonda leans to look out the window. Her eyes begin to tear. "I think they're here to apply for adoption."

"I love your country," Kira proclaims.

Rhonda covers her mouth with her hands. "This goes beyond Zyandite. This is for His Kingdom."

"They want to keep the kids?" Nadia asks.

Rhonda nods. "Yes."

"That's so sweet," Nadia says as they drive by.

Knowing they have to walk past the women in line, Kira braces herself. "Oh, God, be our strength."

"Amen." Rhonda is the first out of the car. She marches up to the line and begins shaking everyone's hands. Most of these women are young, and have children at their sides.

"Thank you for your love. These kids are so blessed," Rhonda tells them in Zyandish.

Placing a protective arm around Nadia's shoulders, Kira smiles while they walk up to the crowd. Expecting to be greeted by indifference, she's surprised to find nothing but smiles.

Warmth covers Kira's heart, before noticing many of the ladies in line are glancing nervously across the street. Kira follows their gaze to see a large group forming on the street corner. These women vary in age, but are dressed to perfection. The lady at the center of their group stares at Kira like a ravenous wolf. She's older than the rest, but gorgeous. Everything about her displays wealth and class. The ladies surrounding her hold signs Kira wishes she could read.

As though reading her mind, Rhonda leans in to whisper in Kira's ear, "Save our purity." She straightens her posture with a nod towards the signs. "I knew the Lineage would protest."

The women across the street begin chanting. Their faces are no longer calculating and serene, but enraged.

Behind Kira, gasps from the families in line fill the air.

"What are they saying?" Kira asks.

Rhonda glances at Nadia and shakes her head. "Let's just go inside."

Kira watches as one of the women in line for adoption looks down in shame, before walking away. Two more follow. Whatever the Lineage said is intimidating these women to abandon the orphans. Kira knows that if something isn't done, it'll only get worse. She gently places a hand on

Rhonda's arm. "Please, tell me."

Tears brim from Rhonda's eyes and her lips quiver before whispering, "Protect our purity from the cursed Auctairean blood."

Nadia gasps. "Mommy, is that true? Am I cursed?"

Kira bends to Nadia's level. "They're wrong. You're not cursed, sweetheart." Flames rise up within her chest, but this anger isn't her own. It's righteous and powerful. Kira leaves her insecurity behind and defends her daughter. "Translate for me." She gives Rhonda a knowing look before glaring at the Lineage.

Rhonda takes a step back. For a moment Kira fears she might not translate, but she doesn't care. God's word never returns void.

"Acts 11:17 states," Kira's tone is so firm that the Lineage stops chanting. "And since God gave these Gentiles the same gift he gave us when we believed in the Lord Jesus Christ, who was I to stand in God's way?"

Eyes wide, Rhonda translates.

Indignant glares are the response from the Lineage, but Kira doesn't let that intimidate her and even points at them. "Who are you to stand in the way of Auctairea's salvation?"

Letting out a jagged breath, Rhonda translates.

Eleonor Kentwood holds her hand to her chest, while the younger women in her group look to her for direction.

Behind Kira, the people waiting in line begin to cheer.

"Well?" Kira shouts, letting the Holy Spirit within her gives her strength. "Listen to me, you who know right from wrong, you who cherish my law in your hearts. Do not be afraid of people's scorn, nor fear their insults. For the moth will devour them as it devours clothing. The worm will eat at them as it eats wool. But my righteousness will last forever. My salvation will continue from generation to generation." Kira quotes Isaiah 51:7-8 before pointing at the hospital. "This generation deserves a chance to know God." She points back at the Lineage. "And no mortal piece of dust has the right to deny them that!"

The cheering from behind her intensifies, but Kira doesn't care. Relying on God for strength, she knows she just kicked the hornet's nest, but she did it with His word.

Noticing several women in line have taken out their tablets to film the exchange, Eleanor glares at Kira before walking away. The rest of the Lineage slowly follows her.

Looking at Nadia, Kira wipes away her daughter's tears. "Don't ever let anyone discredit your salvation. Because of Jesus, you're not cursed, you're blessed!"

Nadia's lips press together before she nods.

Rhonda whispers the translation for what Kira just said, and the crowd begins to chatter.

Kira looks to Rhonda for translation. Whatever is said has brought her to tears. "Amen," Rhonda whispers. "That's what they're saying." She looks at Nadia with nothing but adoration. "They agree that you're blessed."

Kira's heart is touched by the grins and kind waves these strangers lavish on Nadia.

Cheeks red, Nadia waves back.

With a tight smile, Rhonda leads the way inside of the hospital. "God willing, this will get the Lineage to back off."

The front desk consists of eight employees before a large waiting room. Beyond them are four elevators and two flights of stairs. The color scheme is gold and purple, with specs of vibrant green. Kira feels more like she's entering a fancy hotel rather than a hospital.

In this pretty environment, Nadia holds her head up. Kira can almost see the jeers of the Lineage melt off of her shoulders.

"Dr. Tanner said they're on the third floor." Rhonda leads the way towards the stairs.

"This doesn't smell like a hospital," Kira whispers.

Rhonda glances over her shoulder and grins.

THE LINEAGE

Once they reach the third floor, the sound of babies crying fills their ears. None of the older kids seem to want to talk with them, but they all seem drawn to Nadia. Kira focuses on helping to bottle feed the babies while Rhonda translates for each child's exam. Nadia makes sure to greet every kid, and gives them each a button.

Relieved that each baby is fed, Kira gently lays one down on the crib. The crying has been replaced by peaceful sleep, before a brash woman's voice steals it.

"I can't believe that Auctairean has the nerve to show her face," Wilma Marshal says to her camera man. Knowing Kira can't understand Zyandish, once she sees her, Wilma smiles and waves.

Kira looks her up and down, slowly, before turning away.

Wilma gasps and looks back at Benson with a snarl. "She's going to regret ever coming here."

"Is that so?"

An elevated voice causes Kira to turn. She sees a man wearing black scrubs walk up to Wilma. His salt and pepper hair is combed to the side, over clear rimmed glasses.

He says something to Wilma that Kira wishes she understood.

"Kira Westin is here to help make these poor kids more comfortable, and you are making it about politics."

Wilma squares her shoulders. "I'm a Charge Commander's wife, how dare you speak to me that way!"

"Oh, really? I'm Doctor Kevin Sanchez, the director of this hospital, and you can charge your way out of it, civilian." He points at the stairs.

Rhonda steps out of an exam room with Dr. Tanner. Her eyes are wide, and she covers her mouth. Dr. Tanner smiles before moving on to the next patient.

The color in Wilma's face churns ghostly white, before her and Benson leave.

The man in scrubs looks at Kira, and his eyes soften before he walks away.

"You'll tell me what was said later, right?" Kira whispers in Auctrah.

Holding in a laugh Rhonda nods, "Yes."

Three hours later, all of the children have been taken care of. Dr. Tanner walks up and doesn't say a word, before showing Kira her tablet.

Ruger is on screen. He is speaking in Auctrah, but the subtitles are in Zyandish. "I want you to know how special you are, and how grateful I am to have you in Zyandite. Things are probably a little scary right now, but don't worry. We love you, and will give you happy homes, very soon."

Kira smiles at the prerecorded greeting. "He's wonderful."

Dr. Tanner places a hand on her heart and smiles, before walking away.

"She's very nice," Kira whispers.

"Yeah, and quite the trooper." Rhonda raises her eyebrows. "She's going back for more. They just cleared another Education Center."

"Wow." Kira's heart is touched. "So, what happened with Wilma?"

Rhonda giggles. "I didn't hear all of it, but that Doctor is the director of this hospital and he kicked her out."

Kira's eyes widen. "Really?"

"Yeah. She tried to use her husband's rank on him." Rhonda shakes her head. "You don't make something like this political."

"No." Kira's mouth curves into a smile. God handled Wilma for her, and she didn't even have to do anything.

***

On the way home, Nadia rests her head on Kira's lap. Playing with her last button, she looks up. "Thank you."

"For what?"

"For protecting me from those centers. Some of the kids told me the things they did there." Nadia shivers.

"You're welcome, sweetheart." Kira hugs her. "God certainly saved us, didn't He?"

"Yeah, He did."

Watching them, Rhonda has to wipe away a tear. "Are you two ready for more? The next plane lands in four hours."

Kira nods. "Absolutely."

Nadia looks into her purse. "I'll need more buttons."

Rhonda and Kira laugh.

***

CHAPTER 16
AMMO

Rhonda was smart to order in food. With only a few hours in-between the next round of Auctaireans, the easy meal gives Kira time to go over Zyandish flashcards. After the exchange between Wilma and that Doctor, she wants to learn Zyandish more than ever. Sitting in Rhonda's loft, Kira hears Nadia giggle from the kitchen. Rhonda promised to find her more buttons, and from the sound of it, she was successful.

Kira smiles before the doorbell cuts her Zyandish lesson short.

"It's from Ruger!" Rhonda shouts from downstairs.

"Really?" Nadia asks.

Kira reaches the bottom of the stairs and shakes her head. "He said he was sending a present. Since he's at war, I didn't really believe him."

"It would go against his honor to lie." Rhonda opens the small box and pulls out a large plush elephant with happy brown eyes.

"I love it!" Nadia exclaims before hugging it.

"Oh, how sweet," Kira says, remembering when Ruger showed Nadia an elephant for the very first time.

"And this one," Rhonda struggles to slide the heavy box towards Kira,

"Is for you."

Kira kneels to open it. A black case and several boxes beneath it smells of oil. She smiles and opens the case to discover a gray handgun.

"That's a lot of ammo. You're not going hunting again are you?" Nadia asks.

Kira laughs. "No."

Nadia sighs in relief, before squeezing her elephant.

"Look, there's a note!" Rhonda says before grabbing the envelope stuck in-between the ammo boxes. Kira takes the envelope to find the text is written in Zyandish. "Auctrah is dead now." Kira hands it to Rhonda for translation.

"Oh." Rhonda takes it. "My dearest Kira and sweet Nadia, I'm overjoyed to have you both in my life. I hope these tokens of my affection find you well. Until God grants me the blessing of seeing you again, know that I hold your memory deep within my heart. Love always, Ruger." Rhonda grins as she folds the letter. "I never knew my brother could be so romantic."

Kira blushes. "A gun certainly beats flowers."

"Here in Zyandite, it's a tradition for a man to show his love, by making certain his woman can protect herself. Personally, I think a gun is better than a diamond."

Kira laughs. "I agree."

"I can't wait to take you to the range. Now, let's figure out how to carry all of this ammo up to your room."

Forty minutes later, they arrive at the hospital to find a new group of women are in line to apply for adoption. The line still wraps around the building, making Kira's eyes water.

"Are you ready?" Rhonda asks.

"Yes, in fact, I'm excited," Kira says, with hope filling her heart for the little ones who are blessed to call Zyandite home.

***

Surrounded by elaborate paintings and glass artwork, Eleanor sits on a velvet chair and stews. Not even the beauty of her home can cheer her heart. Kira crossed a line, one the Lineage must recover from quickly, or it never will.

She picks up her tablet and dials Wilma's number.

Wilma answers on the first dial. "Eleanor, is everything okay?"

"That Auctairean witch has gone too far. You need to throw the gauntlet on her."

"Absolutely. Clark will probably fire me, but it'll be worth it."

Eleanor rolls her eyes. "I'll handle Clark. Use everything you can to destroy her."

***

For the evening report, Wilma Marshal sits in her pretty studio with her face smug. "I know many of you are taken by how caring Kira Westin's been with the children. We must remember that those are Auctairean children. Of course, she's going to help them. My concern is for the children of Zyandite. What will their future be if we keep allowing Auctairean influence in?"

She leans forward, the contrast of white stripes over her black dress blur on the screen. "I hate to sound accusing, but was sending those kids here a ploy to make Zyandite tolerant of a foreign queen?" Wilma crosses her arms and shakes her head. "Could this be a desperate attempt to intertwine Auctairean perversion with Zyandite purity, just so King Anstone can keep the crown? It's not like there aren't any options to rule Zyandite with integrity. There are plenty. We need to ask ourselves if we're going to allow our land to be tarnished by such selfish ambition."

A display of the threads for the Modest Beauty projects behind Wilma.

Fantasies written by perverted Auctairean men are translated into Zyandish, while Wilma nods with wide eyes in disgust. "I appreciate King Anstone's service to Zyandite. He's a true hero, but that was before Kira Westin entered his life. If we don't ask ourselves the hard question now, then THIS will be associated with Zyandite's crown. Look at what Kira did to Auctairean men. What DID she do to our King?" Wilma laughs, once. "I don't know what King Anstone was thinking, or why Zyandite women aren't good enough for him, but like many of you, I'm left wondering, what's he going to do next?"

From her couch, Rhonda holds her head into her hands. "I'm so sorry."

"Don't be." Relieved that Nadia is in bed, Kira stares at the filth from her past. In a way, she feels deserving of Wilma's doubt. Lifting up her chin to fight the tears, all Kira can do now is learn Zyandish, so she can face Wilma on her grounds. Whether she's worthy of the crown or not, Kira owes that to Ruger. "I'm going to study."

Rhonda winces.

Kira doesn't appreciate the lack of enthusiasm, and walks to her room. Nadia's sleeping so deep, Kira's not worried about waking her. Finding the electronic tutor where she left it on her nightstand, she presses the green button to project the lesson above the fireplace.

A woman wearing a modest pink dress stands in front of a bookshelf. With Auctrah already programmed in, Kira watches her go over the basics of Zyandish, again. Frustrated that it's not sticking, she silently asks God for help before opening the Bible Farrah gave her.

And may the Lord our God show us his approval and make our efforts successful. Yes, make our efforts successful. Psalm 90:17

"Yes, Lord God, make my effort to learn Zyandish successful, in the name of Jesus, amen." Kira uses her Bible against Rhonda's, and translates the verses the way she did that first night Ruger was in her home. Smiling at the memory, Kira knows that God won't let her down.

***

In Quandii, there were many luxury hotels and penthouse suites Ruger and his men could have reveled themselves in, but Ruger chose to set up their headquarters in the police station. Much to his surprise, even the police surrender to his soldiers. He stands on the tenth floor, staring at Auctairean gloom. They may have won the siege, but are now faced with thousands of Auctaireans who cannot feed themselves, and refuse to work. He has never dealt with people like this, and doesn't know what to do with them.

History has proven over and over that 2 Thessalonians 3:10 is right. Glancing at his open Bible on the desk, Ruger rereads it:

"Those unwilling to work will not get to eat."

He looks out the window and holds his hands behind his back. During the war with Kaddain, crimes against Zyandites were unthinkable. It was out of desperation that he used the Flatiron to destroy them. That was the first decision Ruger made as king, and while necessary, it's haunted him ever since. Now, he faces a different predicament. The people of Auctairea are complying, but are like a bunch of toddlers living in adult bodies, with no ability to care for themselves. It's unlike any other society in history, and he's at a loss. Usually, once starvation hits, its human nature to even eat garbage if necessary, but something in this society has been so deliberately broken that they would rather starve to death than be independent from their government. Needing to find information on the psychological warfare that was waged on these people, his men have searched, but have yet to discover what methods were used. So far, everyone in the city seems to be a lost cause. Only the ones in the rural areas have learned any form of independence, yet he knows that even they are struggling.

For a nation that was once so wealthy, it's hard to fathom how it could collapse from within. He remembers the Auctairea from his childhood, but even that wasn't the degenerate society before him today. Beneath him, crowds of people would rather cry and scream than work for food. It's hard for even a seasoned warrior to take. The harsh tongue of Auctrah can't be ignored by his ears.

"You need to take care of us! If Zyandite's in charge, then it's your responsibility to feed us!"

The entitlement smeared on their newly sober faces is too far below for Ruger to make out, yet he knows they're all the same; envious, demanding, and enraged.

As he stares at the darken streets filled with desperation and scarcity below, Ruger understands the people of Auctairea lost everything there is to fight for. They have no loyalty, not to God, not to their flag, not even to each other. He's just not sure how to deal with them. "The great I Am, give me an answer, guide my steps, lead me with wisdom on what to do with these people," Ruger whispers. "You know that my generals want me to destroy them, but you made their hearts. Help me save the Auctaireans willing to be saved."

A light tapping at the door draws Ruger's attention.

Jordan steps into the room. "Sir, we have an Auctairean here, who knows quite a bit about our society. She demands a Resolution with the King. She claims that took place a hundred years ago."

"The War of Grief, when King Thilock took the nation of Nelvaria. After the siege, he allowed only a handful of citizens to seek a Resolution, because he had no use for their land. Interesting an Auctairean would know that." Ruger raises a brow, hopeful at this opportunity to bridge the cultural gap. "Does she speak Zyandish?"

"Fluently."

"Alright, send her in."

A few moments later a woman staggers into the room. She's so skinny, she's nearly see-through. At first Ruger thinks she's drunk. He then realizes she's starved to the point of hardly being able to function. Pity hits him like a boulder.

"Who are you and what do you want?" Ruger inquires with indifference. He can't show sympathy, or it may be misinterpreted as weakness. He pulls out a chair in front of the desk before sitting across from her, leaving the window and his prior thoughts behind. Now, all he can think of is how horrifying it is to see a woman with cheek bones as sunken in as hers. She used to dye her hair blond, but the roots are showing two inches of brown. Below wide, blue eyes, her lips are painted a bright red, which clashes with her complexion and doesn't improve her appearance in the slightest.

"My name is Brittany Fowler, I was a professor at Quandii University," her Zyandish is perfect. "I only want food. You see, I ran out of rations and don't know how to survive." She overly blinks and moves in ways that remind Ruger of a cat. It takes him a moment to realize she's flirting, which repulses him.

Crossing his arms, Ruger goes through standard procedure. "Do you have any children?"

"That would be illegal." Her brow furrows. "They're in an Education Center, where they belong."

Ruger closes his eyes for a moment to mourn such a tragedy, before gaining his composure. "Do you have any idea what went on in those centers?"

She merely shakes her head.

"We rescued as many as we could, but your kids are more than likely dead."

Her eyes remain locked with his. There's not a flicker of pain. No remorse, no sadness, it's like she's a machine. "Raising kids is hard. I just couldn't do it."

Ruger loses all pity he had for this woman. "Then you shouldn't have had them."

She looks to the floor, visibly shaken. "Birth control doesn't always work." Her eyes meet his again. They're indignant, as though she was the victim instead of her kids.

Folding his hands, Ruger allows his anger to cool before he speaks, "When I first set foot on this wretched country's soil, I met a woman who had been abandoned by her husband. She managed to not only survive, but take care of her daughter for five years, all on her own. Do you know how she did that, Miss Fowler?"

"No."

"God and resiliency."

Miss Fowler laughs, violently. "There's no such thing as a God!"

"No one is beyond His grace, but you've pushed past mine." Ruger stands. "How dare you insult our creator?" He opens the door. "General Brice, get this woman out of my office."

"Wait, please!" She latches her thin hands onto the collar of Ruger's uniform. "I'll do anything, and you'll find I'm real good."

Ruger can't bring himself to swat away someone so frail, and holds his hands out until Jordan removes her from the office.

Once the screaming of the woman fades down the hall, Ruger holds his head in his hands and prays, "The great I Am, I don't want to forsake the widow and the fatherless, but I can't support those who are too arrogant in themselves that they deny your existence! They don't even care for their own children. I want to take them out of their misery. My God, please, show me what I should do? Will you still bless Zyandite if I listen to my generals?" Ruger rubs his brow in frustration. Peace covers his heart. He's never been intimidated by the generals, and he won't start today.

Ruger pulls his Bible out of his cargo pocket, and allows God to lead the pages. His eyes fall on Proverbs 16:7

When people's lives please the LORD, even their enemies are at peace with them.

He looks up and allows the word of God to penetrate his heart. Remembering Sergeant Lopez, and his willingness to come to God, Ruger's heart is filled with hope.

Typing the order in, Ruger will have Carl Lopez minister to these people. He just has to find him…

***

CHAPTER 17
SCHEMES AND TEA

Across town, the Women of Lineage meet at Eleanor's mansion. Tea and biscuits are served by the Young Ladies of the Lineage, so they can sit on the sidelines and learn.

General Fisher's daughter, Lynn, nearly burns her fingers while getting the biscuits off a cookie sheet. It's not every day her family is invited to a top-tier meeting, and she wants nothing more than to impress Mrs. Kentwood. Brown hair up in a tight ponytail above a navy sweater dress, her hazel eyes scan the number of biscuits. She must bring enough for each Woman of Lineage to have two. She needs at least three dozen more, and quickly spoons out another batch.

Her mother's lecture on the way here was well-received. Lynn's father hasn't been included in the meeting on the generals' side for weeks. The stability of their family line depends on the Kentwood's approval.

While Lynn does most of the work in the kitchen, Pricilla Kentwood glosses her lips. Kissing them before the reflection of her golden compact mirror, she brushes her blond hair out of her face in self-worship.

Lynn picks up the platinum tray and with a roll of her eyes carries it down the hall.

The sitting room is filled with colorful, antique chairs, each with a story. With her chin up, Lynn gives her best smile before serving the biscuits.

She's well-received by most of the women, while others take the food and don't even acknowledge her existence.

"While I've never been so insulted, this fight isn't about me," Eleanor says before holding up her tablet. "I couldn't refute the scripture that Auctairean witch quoted, but that doesn't concern me as much as this." She scrolls down a long thread on ZyanBell, where the same keywords are shared. "Last I checked, there were over nine thousand complaints against the Lineage." Gasps and low chatter fills the room. Eleanor may appreciate their sympathy, but doesn't let it deter her. "That's just from today." She pinches the skin above her nose. "It's like a cancer is spreading across our land."

"The people love Kira Westin," Gloria Mayes says with a distraught shrug.

"There's an old adage that speaks true today. Mankind is like a child, and doesn't know what's good for it. All free societies will eventually destroy themselves." Wilma smiles sweetly, leaving out that her words originate from the Pazmirish Republic.

"Exactly. This is what freedom spawns." Eleanor holds up the tablet and presses her lips together. Not even the elegant makeup and clothing can mask her rage. "These words of disrespect will eventually lead to action. It must be stopped, or else the influence of our purity will die."

"I hate to think of what'll happen to Zyandite if the Lineage falls," a young woman with red hair whispers. Her husband may have died in Kaddain, but she still wears her wedding ring. The diamond reflects the light as she hugs herself.

"The Lineage will only die if we let it," Wilma sneers.

"Yes, but sometimes it's the enemies of the Lineage who must die." Eleanor's words silence the room.

"What do you mean?" General Danning's wife asks. With dark hair and mocha skin, Chantel Danning is far too youthful for her husband, but their union fits the agenda of the Lineage so well, no one dares bring it up.

Eleanor eyes each woman in the room before raising a brow. "The W.L. must do whatever it takes to protect the purity of our land. The peasants have made their choice. We can segregate the Lineage from them, but we cannot let Auctairean blood infiltrate our own."

"Maybe if Kira Westin didn't have a child, we could pull that off. It goes against our vow, and the standard of the Lineage, to attack someone so young." Lucille Frankfort says before crossing her arms. She may be the descendant of a king, but her words fall on deaf ears.

"The Lineage only holds a standard for how we treat our own. Everyone else is dispensable."

Eleanor's words shake Lynn's knees. She nearly drops her tray, but catches it in time.

"If we were to do that, the people would never forgive us," Catrina Fisher boldly states.

Lynn has never been more proud of her mom before and knows this is the reason they're excluded from most W.L. meetings.

Their family has heart.

Holding in the tears, Lynn stares at her mom with respect, before a chime sounds from her pocket. Horrified that she forgot to turn the ringer off, Lynn locks eyes with her mother. They're angry enough to make her leave the room.

"Oh, sweet Catrina," Eleanor's eyes are like blue flames before she smiles. "Sometimes, we have to look past popularity to get the job done. If Wilma's plan fails, we will not. King Rankins' fiancé died of pneumonia two weeks before their wedding. Well, at least that's what we're told." Eleanor smirks before opening a leather journal that's so old, it's nearly falling apart. She scans the eyes heavy with anticipation before reading: "From the Handwritten account of General Bayer, Medical Support Charge Commander under the reign of King Rankins." Eleanor lifts her chin. "The responsibility of the Lineage comprises the heavy task of protecting the King from diseases, to include the infection from unclean blood. Perhaps it's ironic that we chose a disease to combat her sickness, but Marcella Rucks must never be queen." Eleanor slams the journal, creating a dust cloud she manages to ignore.

Gasps fill the room.

"You see, my dear pure ones, this isn't the first time our blood has been threatened. Now, I'm certainly not suggesting we use the same measures as General Bayer, not with a child involved." Eleanor's lips quiver at that inconvenience. "However, our purity is too important to lose. If we have to resort to unconventional measures, like what our dear Wilma has suggested, I say we do it. Even at the risk of tainting one of our own, we must do whatever it takes to ensure Kira Westin will never be queen. All in favor?" She raises a hand.

Slowly, the rest of the room follows suit. Head down, not even Catrina Fisher objects.

*****

In the hallway, Lynn holds the tray under her arm and checks to see if it was Mack who messaged her.

Lynn's father is a Charge Commander. She's not supposed to love a Sergeant, but just seeing Mack's profile picture makes her smile.

"Hi Lynn, I've finally been given a moment to breathe. This Auctairean air stinks! I hope you are doing well. If only things were simple. We wouldn't have to hide our love. As it is, all I can think of is when I can catch a glimpse of you when we come home. Love always, Mack."

Her eyes drank up his words too deep to realize she's not alone.

Pricilla glances over her shoulder before Lynn can hide her tablet. "Who's that?" She reaches for it, but Lynn blocks her with an arm. "Oh, this must be good." She wrestles with Lynn until she finally grabs it. "You're in love with a Sergeant?" Pricilla laughs so hard she bends over.

Glancing at the sitting room, Lynn's afraid the W.L. may hear. "That's none of your business."

"We're Lineage. Everything you do is my business." Pricilla's eyes widen mischievously before she runs upstairs.

"Hey! Give that back!" Lynn follows her up.

"Mack, stop messaging me. My blood's too good for you." Pricilla's lips curve before she tosses the tablet down.

Lynn stops where her tablet landed. Pricilla's already in her room by now, but Lynn stays on the steps. Hands shaking, she picks up the tablet, hoping Pricilla didn't actually type those words.

"Message sent."

Letting out a jagged sigh, she feels pieces of her heart leave with her breath. Tears brimming, Lynn's too hurt to face anyone. Searching for solitude, she runs out to her mom's car. With tears wet on her cheeks, Lynn is thankful it's dark before plopping in the backseat. Burying her face into the black leather, she lets her pain go through loud sobs. "Oh, God, I don't even know if you're real anymore. Not with what I've seen." Lynn's barely able to pray through her sobs, "If you are real, please, save us from this evil."

***

CHAPTER 18
ZYANDITE PLEDGE

It's been three weeks since Kira and Nadia began their quest to learn Zyandish. Today, they've obtained victory.

"I can't believe it!" Rhonda laughs. "Now say this, 'I will never leave my faith, or betray my God.'" Rhonda's eyes sparkle in anticipation as Nadia recites those words back.

"No, Nadia. That's not how you pronounce faith, F A I T H," Kira corrects in perfect Zyandish.

"Sorry, mommy," Nadia says back in fluent Zyandish. "I will never leave my *faith*, or betray my God." Nadia smiles as both women clap for her proper pronunciation.

"I think it is safe to say that Zyandish is the only language spoken in this household," Rhonda says while lifting her chin up.

Kira takes her daughter by the cheeks and kisses her forehead. "I'm so proud of you."

"No more Auctrah!" Nadia exclaims in Zyandish, while holding an arm up in victory.

"No more Auctairea," Kira says. Guilt tinges her heart, surprising her enough to frown. She should be happy that nightmare is dying, yet she feels as though her own hands destroyed it long before Zyandite's invasion.

"Great, but in order for you both the become citizens, you must take a history test. Don't worry, I have the study book for it. I also have to film each of you taking the Zyandite Pledge, for a public record of your loyalty." Rhonda pulls out her tablet, "Since you're both speaking Zyandish so beautifully, I don't see any reason why we can't film it now."

"I don't have it memorized," Kira says.

"You're not required to memorize it. You can read it off my tablet as I film." Rhonda points to the wall. "There is a clear place for you to stand."

Nadia grins and jumps into position. She's ready to show off how well she can not only speak Zyandish, but read it. "I believe that Jesus Christ is the one true savior, and Zyandite is a gift from God. As a Zyandite citizen, it is my duty to uphold God's laws in my heart, which I swear to obey." Nadia then reads Mark 3:24, "A kingdom divided by civil war will collapse." She holds her chin up. "The kingdom of Zyandite was birthed in a civil war, and knows the cost of a nation's division. We must never allow an internal conflict to happen again. I vow to be united with my countrymen, and if necessary, pick up my arms and use them to protect Zyandite from anyone who desires to harm it. I will honor the great I Am, and my country, by keeping my body pure. I will love all who love God, and hate all of those who hate our Lord. I will treat my fellow Zyandites with honor, compassion, good will, and respect. I will live the rest of my life as a light in this world, by serving the great I Am, and my country, until the day I die."

"Very good job, Nadia!" Rhonda does a happy dance.

Kira claps before Nadia runs over for a hug. "Thanks. I meant every word of it. I love Zyandite!"

"Me too, sweetheart." Kira looks to Rhonda who points at the wall with a playful smile.

Kira stands in the same place as Nadia and smiles, but that tinge of guilt in her heart becomes a flood of self-doubt. She knows she's not worthy to become a citizen here, let alone their queen.

"Are you okay, mommy?" Nadia asks. Worry has caused her brow to furrow, stinging Kira's heart.

"Yes." Kira forces a smile. "Just nervous." For Nadia's sake, she shoves down her doubts and recites the pledge.

"Yay mommy!" Nadia claps. "Does this mean we're Zyandites now?"

"No, you still have to take a written test and it must be graded by the King himself. After that, he'll sign your citizenship into record and then it'll be official. You'll get your documents so you can drive, work, and get *married*," Rhonda says with a little dance.

Kira blushes.

"Now, I have a special surprise for you." Rhonda winks.

"Uh-oh," Kira mumbles, pretending to be untrusting of a woman she's grown quite attached to.

"I've arranged for us to go to church on Saturday." Rhonda's eyes beam.

"I haven't been to church in over a decade." Kira's surprised by her own hesitancy. "Before they became illegal, churches in Auctairea were overly regulated by the government, with planned that were all about money. It was nothing like the Zyandite services I attended as a child." She shivers. "The last service I attended, I got a stomachache."

Rhonda grimaces. "That was the Holy Spirit prompting you that you were among wolves."

"You're probably right." Kira sighs. "I feel like a coward, but just the thought of going to church scares me."

"You lived under tyranny for too long. The more you go, the more that feeling will fade." Rhonda hands her tablet to Kira. "Tell my brother the good news." With a wave, Rhonda leaves Kira and Nadia alone.

"Are you really going to call Ruger?" It's been so long since they've talked with him, Nadia's eyes brim with excitement.

"Of course, I just hope he's not busy…" Kira dials.

It rings several times before he answers. His hair is a mess and there's a pile of rubble outside of the window behind him. The walls seem familiar, but all Kira can focus on is his face.

"Hello, my darling." He pulls the tablet back to show off the view from the window behind him. "Do you recognize Quandii?"

He must be in the last sky-scraper standing. Most everything else is gone, and soldiers fill large vehicles with what's left of the foundations. "You've taken the steel?" Kira asks.

"Your Zyandish is flawless." Ruger praises, making Kira blush.

"Thank you."

"We only have two buildings left," Ruger explains. "Gathering concrete is the final stage of Despoliation. So far, the Vulton Isles bought most of the lumber. That profit alone doubled the cost of this war."

"I can't believe it," Kira whispers.

"Guess what, Ruger?" Nadia asks, bringing a welcomed change of subject. "We recited the Zyandite Pledge."

"Good job!"

"We're almost official!" Nadia squeals.

Ruger's eyes brighten. "I can't wait to sign you into citizenship."

Nadia smiles before bouncing off to the window seat, where her elephant and doll await her.

Kira sits on the bed. "Are you in a studio?"

"You recognized that?" Ruger's grin widens. "I wanted to look into your past before we finish taking Auctairea apart." He shows the computer on the metal desk before him. Kira squints upon seeing the still shot of a news anchor.

"That's Anton Cove." She snarls her upper lip. "He replaced me." Kira winks at Nadia before stepping out of the room to spare her from Auctairean filth.

"Want to know why Joplin spared you?" Ruger turns the computer on.

"Yes."

Ruger smiles before turning his tablet so Kira can see. On the screen the image of an arrogant young man wearing a tight spandex shirt tucked into skinny jeans, grins from a chair in the studio. His teeth are covered with diamonds and his brown hair is gelled back into a swirl. "Don't worry, Auctairea. I'm not too hung over," he hisses through his teeth. "Seriously, my review of club Knockoutta is this. The booze is cheap, the girls HOT and the music, well…" He shrugs. "I wasn't paying much attention to the music." Laughing, his face twists into shock. "Oh snap! This just in, terrible news! Governor Cantura is dead!" His jaw drops. "No, like for real, he's dead!" Anton cringes. "Wolves. Governor Cantura was killed by wolves. Oh, my… WOLVES!" He spins in his chair. "I wouldn't want to die like that. No way. Well, Prime Minister Joplin gave his condolences. He said Kira Westin is devastated. Shouldn't have moved out of the city, girl!" Anton Cove waves his finger at camera as though scolding rural living. "Prime Minister Joplin said that in her grief, Kira Westin agreed with him on his new law. Religion should be banned. Well done, Kira. Well done!" Anton claps dramatically.

Kira's heart stops. Her knees buckle and she has to take a seat on the stairs.

Anton slides his shoulders back and forth. "Good for you, Modest Beauty. Now, Prime Minister Joplin also said he doesn't want to bother the former First Lady of Quandii, by making her come on the air. That's understandable, right? But she gave her endorsement, so the rest of you Christians, get on board, or else." His face morphs into a heinous glare.

Ruger's eyes replace the image, but Kira can't look at him. She buries her face into her arms and cries. "I never agreed to that."

"Of course not. Not only has your life demonstrated that, but I have proof," Ruger assures her.

Kira looks up to find Rhonda beside her. She pats her on the back, nearly in tears herself.

Ruger shows an email on the computer screen, addressed from Prime Minister Joplin to Miles Gardner, the Producer of A-Rah Studios:

With all she's done for my campaign, I don't have the heart to make Kira work after losing George. Just lie, the people will believe it. We'll get this law passed within a week.

"Oh, my," Rhonda mutters as she and Kira exchange glances.

"I'm going to save all of this. We're taking this building down tonight. Our guys need to get home."

"When?" Rhonda asks.

Ruger sets the Auctairean computer in his backpack and gives a sheepish smile. "A couple of weeks."

Rhonda nearly bursts before tapping her hip into Kira's. "That's something to celebrate!"

***

The next morning, they celebrate by going out for breakfast.

Kira keeps an arm around Nadia as they sit together in the backseat of Rhonda's vehicle. Now that her guests know Zyandish, Rhonda's excited to show off her favorite bakery. Her driver parks in front of the small, red building in the shape of a barn. Nadia presses her nose against the window.

"Somebody's hungry," Rhonda says before leading the way inside. The décor is mostly burgundy and red, making Kira smile. There are fiery orange glass vases on each of the tables, and some green and gold splatters of color on the walls, before the glass counter where an array of pastries are on display.

The young girl with her red hair up in a ponytail grins at Rhonda, before her jaw drops at the sight of Kira anh Nadia. "Oh, my goodness! Is that the woman who saved our king?"

Kira blushes now that she can understand Zyandish and responds carefully, "Ruger Anstone is definitely a man worth saving, but it was God's idea, not mine."

The young girl gasps before looking at Rhonda. "I didn't know Kira Westin spoke Zyandish!"

"I taught her." Rhonda's quick to brag.

"Wow! Well, what can I get for you? I'm sure my parents won't mind it being on the house."

"Oh nonsense, we don't mind paying. That's very kind of you, though." Rhonda playfully waves before looking at Nadia. "What would you like?"

"That one, please." Nadia points at a chocolate covered croissant.

Right then, two teenage girls walk in, giggling.

One has raven black hair and the other is blond. They are happy and carefree as the blond tells her friend, "No way! I'll only share that during my Coalescing."

Both girls giggle again as though that's some sort of revelation or trend in their society. Yet 'Coalescing' is such an odd word in that context. Kira wonders if she misunderstood.

"And for you?" Rhonda asks.

"Pumpkin cream coffee and a slice of vanilla cheesecake," Kira answers.

"Well, I'll have a chocolate croissant and chocolate milk," Rhonda says, making the girl behind the counter smile before ringing up their order.

"Yummy!" Nadia exclaims after taking her first bite of the croissant.

"This is the best bakery in town," Rhonda announces before chewing her own first bite. "And we need the sugar, because I've got plans." Her eyes widen. "Today, we are going to go for a boat ride on the river."

Nadia gasps while Kira playfully cringes.

***

Sweat causes Wilma's hair to stick to her face. Thorton couldn't have called at a worse time. Leaning against the wall in her closet, she's exhausted from her run and would prefer to have taken a shower before he saw her.

"It's like everything I do only makes the people like Kira more," Wilma says in Pazmirish.

Thorton presses his fingers against his lips. *"Have you begun to orchestrate MY plan?"*

"Yes. Eleanor picked a girl. She's training her now."

He laughs. "She needs Pazmirish training. You must take over."

"And insult Eleanor?" Wilma shakes her head. "I don't have the Lineage to do that."

"Not insult her. Help her. Eleanor doesn't have to know."

Wilma grimaces. "I'll do my best."

***

In a posh apartment downtown, Isabella Ordan wears mauve lipstick and the title of Zyandite's fourth king well.

Pacing across purple and teal carpet, she doesn't let the colorful glass artwork on the walls distract her from studying Kira. Maneuvering her shoulders, her hair rests a foot longer than Kira's, but she carries it the same. With hazel eyes and a light complexion, she's the closest the Lineage has to match the prophecy.

This is her only chance to be queen.

A light tap at her door draws Isabella's attention. "Come in." Her voice was too high-pitch and feminine. Isabella bites her lip. Kira never speaks with such a high tone. She must learn to control her voice.

Wilma steps in and gives a nervous smile. Wearing a teal jumpsuit that's a far cry from her workout gear, she takes a seat and brushes aside her curls.

"I didn't expect you." Isabella sits on her couch. Behind her, the sun begins to set, cascading vibrant colors in through her window.

"I'm here on behalf of Eleanor." The lie causes Wilma to glance down. "She requests this meeting be confidential, even from her."

Isabella gasps.

"I know. However, she wants me to share things that make most Zyandites uncomfortable." Wilma banks on Isabella's naivety and smiles.

THE LINEAGE

"You know my family was on a mission in the Pazmirish Republic?"

All color fades from Isabella's complexion. "I've heard."

"Well, it's hard maintaining purity when surrounded by filth." Wilma shivers. It's so dramatic, Kira would see right through it, but Isabella's too trusting to believe a Zyandite could lie. "That said, I learned a few things, through observation, of course. Things that may help you..."

Isabella begins trembling, though she tries to hide it.

Wilma gives a sympathetic smile and takes her by the hand. "What I'm about to teach you, doesn't leave this room."

***

CHAPTER 19
HEARTFELT WORSHIP

Kira nervously stares out of the window as they pull into the parking lot before a single-story building. It's tan and rather plain, nothing like the last church she attended in Auctairea, which was lit up like a casino.

"I've reserved our seats at the front row next to Farrah." Rhonda's lighthearted, but it doesn't calm Kira's nerves. What if the parishioners don't like her? What will that mean for Nadia?

Stepping up to the entry, memories of the Great Cleansing attack Kira's mind. How can she walk into a church, when the people she let down never will? "I just need a moment." Kira forces a playful smile to ease Nadia's mind.

"Are you okay?" Rhonda wraps an arm around Kira's shoulders. "We can go home."

"No." Kira straightens the creases in her teal dress and lifts her chin. "It's just been so long."

Rhonda smiles. "No worries, Kira. You're safe here, I promise." She leads the way into the building, proudly showing off her guests.

The crowd consists mostly of women wearing long skirts and dresses crafted in pastels and floral patterns. Plenty of children run around, while some stay close to their mothers. A few elderly couples greet everyone.

"There's Farrah," Rhonda says.

Farrah turns from the lady she was talking to and immediately smiles at Kira. *"It's good to see you again,"* she says in Auctrah.

Kira grins. "It's nice to see you, too."

"Your Zyandish is beautiful!" Farrah exclaims.

"It's been an exhausting month." Rhonda drops her body dramatically for a moment, making Farrah hold in a laugh.

"I'll bet." Farrah bends to Nadia's level. "And look at you sweetheart, all dressed up like a princess."

Nadia gives a curtsy. "Thank you."

Farrah wiggles her nose and straightens her posture. "Since you speak Zyandish so well, would you mind giving your testimony?"

"Are you certain you want me to do that? I mean, after everything Wilma's said about me…" Kira whispers.

Farrah stops to look Kira deep into her eyes, "Especially because of all the lies Wilma's spewed."

Kira is surprised by Farrah's sudden defense of her. She breaks through her fears and agrees. "Alright, I'll do it."

"That would be wonderful. Kristen is giving the service today, but I doubt anyone would mind staying later to hear your story."

"Today?" Kira clarifies, fighting the overwhelming urge to run.

"If that is alright?" Farrah asks.

"Of course."

"Thank you." Farrah smiles before walking to their seats.

Kira's surprised there's not a store in this sanctuary, like the churches had in Auctairea. In fact, nothing here is for sale. There are only rows and rows of white folding chairs, with three aisles, before a wide stage where several people are busy setting up their instruments. The walls are painted gold, with bright white trim. Dozens of pendant lights hang overhead, filling the room with light.

"It's beautiful!" Nadia exclaims.

"Yes, it really is," Kira agrees as they walk to the first row.

"There are two temples in Zyandite, the official Temple of Brustonite is next to the castle, and the great I Am's Holy Temple is in King Slayden's hometown of Sunrise Sands. Everywhere else we meet are venues willing to offer their space for free." Rhonda waves her hand as though showing off the room. "This is a restaurant during the week."

"Wow," Kira looks around in wonder, "Auctairean churches owned their buildings and always wanted to expand."

Farrah rolls her eyes while taking a seat. "Such a waste of the tithe. We rotate where we meet because we know the importance of the church isn't a building, it's us."

"That's right." Rhonda's eyes brighten before she grins. "I have to get on stage, will you two be alright?"

"Yes, go." Kira waves her off.

Rhonda practically skips to join the other musicians.

A man who must be at least ten years older than Farrah, sits beside her. His dark hair is just starting to gray, giving him a grace of wisdom, contrasting his blue eyes that are youthful and beam with the light of God. "Why hello there," he speaks slowly.

Farrah holds in a laugh. "No worries. They speak perfect Zyandish."

He raises a brow. "Impressive."

"This is Kira and Nadia." Farrah gives Kira a wink. "This is my husband, Brian Trigon, the Lead Pastor of the Church of Zyandite."

"I'm honored to meet you both."

"Likewise, sir," Kira's smile fades as a distraught elderly woman steps up behind Farrah.

"I'm sorry to interrupt, but I need to speak with you."

"Of course, Monica. What's wrong?" Farrah asks.

"It's my son. He aced everything, but was denied a commission."

"Please, excuse me," Farrah says with a touch on Kira's arm before stepping away to speak with Monica in a secluded corner of the room.

Kira watches them pray and hug. Monica's shoulders are raised, and she seems a bit stronger as she walks away. Farrah then walks up to a tall woman with long, blond hair that's curled all the way to her tailbone. Wearing an elegant dress crafted with lavender chiffon, this woman's keen blue eyes turn to Kira.

Kira's too far to understand, but the welcoming light that shines in this stranger's eyes comforts her.

A woman with dark hair cut perfectly along her chin has a guitar strapped over her shoulder as she steps up to the front of the stage. Her lips are painted red against dark skin that showcases her youthful green eyes. "Hello, church!" she greets now that everyone is at their seats.

Various greeting of hellos and good mornings is returned cheerfully.

"We have special guests today." She winks at Kira. "Auctairean Christians, can you all believe it?"

The crowd around them cheers.

Kira's overwhelmed by their applause and looks down at the floor.

"Oh, Pastor Trigon and Farrah are here, too."

The congregation laughs.

Farrah wraps an arm around Kira's shoulder and whispers, "Just because you were born in Auctairea, doesn't change the fact that we are all born from dust. No matter what the Lineage says, as fellow believers in Christ, you and Nadia are family."

Kira nods with gratitude before the worship begins.

"Let's sing praise to the great I Am!"

Most everyone in the congregation stands, Kira and Nadia follow suit as the drums, stringed instruments, and even a harp synchronize together beautifully.

The worship leader begins to sing. *"Holy Spirit, come down to this place. Holy Spirit, reign, reign, reign over our hearts. We need to feel the fire of your presence. Holy Spirit, overflow in our souls. Holy Spirit, reign, reign, reign over our lives. We need an abundance of your presence."*

Kira's taken aback by how hundreds of people are able to sing praise to God so openly and many are even raising their hands! She closes her eyes and thanks God for bringing her and Nadia to this freedom, as the warmth of the Holy Spirit fills her heart.

As the worship leader continues in song, Kira raises her hands in both submission and worship of God.

"Holy Spirit, be our anchor, be our guide, hold our feet to the fire in your direction of our hearts, for there is nothing, nothing you do that is not for the good of our souls. Holy Spirit, come down to this place. Holy Spirit, reign, reign, reign over our hearts. We need to feel the fire of your presence. Holy Spirit, we love you."

Kira is so moved by the presence of God, tears begin to fall down her face. She doesn't care if anyone judges her; she is free to publicly express her love and adoration to God. It's as lovely as it is fulfilling, to praise her Lord without having to hide it.

Nadia's hand on her side takes Kira's attention. She looks down to see her daughter's eyes full of concern.

"Mommy, are you sure this is safe?" Nadia looks back at the door as if expecting mechanical soldiers to burst through and punish their worship.

"I promise it's safe here." Kira picks her daughter up and holds her along her side with one arm. "God brought us to Zyandite, and we should thank him with praise." Kira beams before raising her other hand to God while Nadia smiles and allows her heart to enjoy the worship experience.

As another song begins, Kira does not hear the words, but the spirit fills her and she hums along as though in sync with the beat of the drums.

"Thank you, Jesus!" Nadia exclaims, raising her hands in praise.

Kira's heart is struck with gratitude. She never thought Nadia would ever be able to attend church, let alone praise Jesus in the open.

"Praise you God!" Kira calls out along with the music, before the last songs ends, and a silent reverence fills the room.

"The great I Am, the God of all angels, of heaven and earth, the maker of the cosmos," the worship leader begins with her eyes closed in prayer. "We thank you for your presence. We thank your mighty hand that guides our earthly king and warriors into victory. Thank You for our land. Help us to honor you, not just today, but every day, in everything we do. We love You, great I Am. We love YOU! We love you Jesus! We love your Holy Spirit! In the mighty name of Jesus Christ, amen."

The congregation says, 'amen,' before retaking their seats and the young woman Farrah spoke with earlier, steps onto the stage.

"Hello fellow Zyandites, for those of you who don't know me already," her voice is as sweet as her face. "My name is Kristen Hollows, and while my husband is off in battle, I'm taking care of our three children." She nods toward the other side of the congregation, where two little girls sit, one with a baby boy on her lap. "Bethany, who is eight, Cassy, who is six and my son Rusty, who just turned one." Kristen smiles proudly at her babies while the congregation claps for them.

"The future of Zyandite!" Brian proclaims, making the crowd clap louder.

"God spoke to me about a week ago, and it is a message I believe we all need to hear." Kristen says with a humble smile.

Kira's amazed the church allows a full-time mom to speak. Not only was that life choice despised in Auctairea, but only celebrity pastors were allowed to preach.

"In the book of Revelation, we find an overarching theme of encouragement to be victorious." Kristen continues, with only a small cue card in hand for notes. "In Revelation 2:7 it states: To everyone who is victorious I will give fruit from the tree of life in the paradise of God" Kristen looks around, her brow furrowed. "That's a promise, but before our Founding Fighters claimed victory, Christians cowered in the status of victimhood. We must make certain we never fall to the faithlessness of defeat again. As Christians, we can't receive victory just by carrying on in complacency. True blessings usually come from sacrifice. If we read a little further, in Revelation 21:7-8 it says: All who are victorious will inherit all these blessings and I will be their God, and they will be my children. But cowards, unbelievers, the corrupt, murderers, the immoral, those who practice witchcraft, idol worshipers, and all liars—their fate is in the fiery lake of burning sulfur. This is the second death." Kristen looks around at the congregation. "Sometimes the separation of my family due to war, is enough to break me into feeling like I'm a victim. So when I dig into the word to find my strength, I am greatly comforted by God's promises, because every single day there's something new to gain victory over. Two wars in such a short period of time can be discouraging, but only if we let it. I think of how great a gift from God Zyandite is, and when I feel that evil fog of discouragement creep into my heart, I petition the great I Am for victory. Not just over my own thoughts and emotions, but for my husband and every soldier like him, victory for our king, victory for our borders, and victory for the right of Christianity to reign free. We weren't given this life to cower behind the cover of mundane lives, but to courageously overcome all adversity and evil with our fists raised high in God's victory!"

The congregation claps in agreement.

"In the book of Joshua 1:6-7 it states: ""Be strong and courageous, for you are the one who will lead these people to possess all the land I swore to their ancestors I would give them. Be strong and very courageous."" Kristen looks at the congregation as she lifts her voice. "Notice the message God is giving here, because you can't be courageous, let alone VERY courageous without a threat. We were given this life to follow God's law, but also to fight for it. We can't let our hearts falter when life becomes difficult. We must press harder under pressure, because that's where the true blessing is. There have been many Christian countries before Zyandite, and they fell, why? Because they became cowardly! They compromised on God's law a little more, and then a little more, until there was nothing left to compromise on. They sought to appease people instead of God. The end result is always the same, God's law and the belief in Him eventually becomes illegal. Religion is replaced by socialism, and the genocide of God's people soon follows. We can never let that happen here."

Farrah looks at Kira to observe her reaction; obviously expecting this to offend her, but Kira's heart is in full agreement.

Kristen wipes a tear from her eyes. "The very definition of the word courage, is not deterred, by danger, by loss, by pain. The definition of cowardly, is lacking courage. I for one am greatly encouraged to know that God counts the cowardly as the same as defiled sinners. It keeps my heart in check, to always be courageous, for courage brings strength, but cowardice brings shame. May the mothers of Zyandite, myself included, always teach our children to be courageous for God."

The entire church stands with applause and Kira is so moved, she joins them.

"You can't have victory without courage!" Kristen shouts over the cheering, while Brian walks up to her side.

"Praise God for Zyandite and its dedicated mothers, who take up their Eve duty with such grace and dignity." Brian smiles as the applause continues. "Praise God for Zyandite and our brave fathers, who take up their Adam duty with ferocity, as they fight for the security of our way of life."

The crowd really cheers before Kristen steps of the stage and back to her children and everyone else takes their seats.

"Now," Brian raises a hand to address the church, "my wife Farrah and I, would love to introduce you to a guest, whom has experienced oppression in ways we Zyandites can't fathom. Kira, would you mind coming up here and sharing your story with us?"

Kira smiles at Nadia before slowly walking up to the stage.

"Thank you, Brian," Kira glances at Brian before looking at the congregation.

"No Kira, thank you," he says before retaking his seat.

Kira stares at the crowd. While she has made public speeches in the past, it's been so long that standing to speak in front of this many people makes her knees wobble. Kira silently prays and presses through it. This may be her only chance to give God glory for her life in front of this many people, and she will not waste it. "Back when Auctairea was still free, I was born to a Christian woman. I was baptized by a Zyandite Missionary, and as far as I can remember, I've always loved God. But, much like Kristen said, God's law was already compromised before my time. Every year, it was compromised a little more. My mom told me that it started with the social acceptance of taking our Lord's name in vain. That was justified, for those were just words, after all. Then, the Sabbath was desecrated and after that, wide spread coveting. From there on, every one of God's laws was broken and a new Sodom and Gomorrah was born."

Kristen is taken aback and has to hold in tears for how God has used the message she gave for this very day, because Kira's words confirmed it to be a message that needed to be heard.

"I was a star journalist and a Governor's wife. I had everything any Auctairean could want, but I always felt the need to fight against my own people. Whether I was in-line at the store, walking across a parking lot, driving on the roads, basically, everywhere I went there was such a dog-eat-dog mentality. At the same time, everyone walked on eggshells socially, because Auctaireans were so easily offended. It was beyond hostile, and I stopped feeling free. I don't know how God spared me from the degrading expectations Auctairea held over its women, but He did. As my popularity grew, I thought I was helping people. Spiritually, I bent on God's law. I reasoned that in order to love everybody, I had to praise their sins. I was conditioned to accept the confines on my religion, and in turn, without even realizing it, I sinned myself. Fear of man became my idol, and displayed the essence of cowardice. I said what was wrong was right, and what was right was wrong. At the time, I didn't realize how little I actually loved God." Kira wipes a tear. "I thought I worshiped God, but really, I worshiped the opinion of others. It wasn't until after I became a mother and everyone told me my child was better off raised by strangers that their opinions no longer mattered to me. Their insults still hurt, but I ran away to my country retreat with my daughter, where I hid, like a coward." Kira looks down, amazed at herself for opening up like this to so many strangers. She can feel God's approval over her words, so she continues. "I enjoyed hiding. My neighbors across the street were Christians, and taught me how to hunt. At the time, that was just for sport. I had no idea I'd be using those skills for survival, but it didn't take long until the Auctairean government stole the little freedom we had. They said it was for the sake of the planet that we lost electricity and modern transportation. Then, they said it was for the sake of security that we lost digital communication. A mechanical army was built from the metal of our cars, just to be used against us. Finally, they said it was for the sake of unity that our basic freedom of believing in God was stripped from us. I will…" Kira does not want Nadia to hear this, but perhaps it's time she knew, "Never forget the night everyone who believed in God were murdered for their faith." The tears begin to flow so much that Kira can't hide them. "I want you all to know that before they were slaughtered, they put up a fight." The sound of their screaming fills Kira's mind. She must push it back to continue, and has to ball her fists to do so. "What I didn't know, was why the mechanical army skipped my house. I was waiting for death to strike, but, God spared us. I never knew why until recently. Your King found the correspondence. God used Prime Minister Joplin's guilt to spare us." Kira looks down for a moment, the pain from that night striking her heart, before looking back at the congregation. "After that horrible night, Nadia and I barely survived. All crime, especially crimes against women, was rampant in every form, and there was no one to stop it. In contrast, if my faith, if my motherhood, had been discovered by the daily drone patrol, the consequence would've been death. I learned how to depend on God in ways I never thought possible. In doing so, I fell madly in love with Him. God strengthens me, and loves me, even with my sins. My past is vile. I helped influence the people of Auctairea to vote Stephen Joplin into power, so how could I possibly deserve the love and protection God gives?"

Brian stands and looks at the congregation. "The Atonement of Jesus Christ knows no bloodline or border, which is why we must accept Kira as our Sister in Christ. In fact, she is our very own Abigale."

The crowd stands up and cheers, while Kira covers her mouth with her hands, before finally composing herself enough to speak. "I thank God that I'm here. I'm so grateful for your acceptance. It warms my heart that the people of Zyandite know what to fight for. Thank you." Kira returns to her seat.

"I want to thank the congregation for continuing the faith in our Lord and Savior, Jesus Christ. Before we break, I would like to pray and worship our Lord, with one more song." Brian bows his head and closes his eyes. "The great I Am, our mighty warrior God, please keep our king and soldiers safe as they wage war in your name. Grant us victory, O Lord, against all enemies. Thank you for sparing Kira and her precious daughter Nadia. In Your incredible name Jesus, we ask that you protect our way of life and the ability to worship in public, the way we worship you today. In the mighty name of Jesus Christ, amen."

As the congregation says, "amen," the worship team steps us and plays "Holy Spirit Fire" one more time.

Kira stands next to her daughter and they hold hands up to God together, both in gratitude and worship.

Once the music is done, the crowd disperses, each allowing another to go first with such kind manners, Kira is filled with love for Zyandites all the more. No one in Auctairea would be so considerate to one another, not even in church.

Kristen receives many words of encouragement for her sermon and Kira ended up blushing at how many people smiled at her and patted her shoulder, as though she was now a member of their family. Then again, they really are of the same family, the family of God.

Rhonda catches up to Kira. "You did so good!"

Kira shakes her head, "I only did what God wanted me to do." She caresses Nadia's hair as they walk up to the doors.

"Oh, Kira," Farrah's voice calls from behind her.

Kira turns to see Farrah waving her towards where she and Brian are standing in the corner of the room with the worship leader.

Kira looks to Rhonda who shrugs with anticipation before they walk over with Nadia.

"This is our Worship Leader, Michelle," Farrah introduces.

"Nice to meet you Kira," Michelle smiles.

"You too," Kira says before one of the band members taps Michelle on her shoulder and she walks way to hear his concern.

"We really appreciate your contribution today, Kira," Brian says. "If you don't mind, I'd like to invite you to the great I Am's Holy Temple, to pray over you with the other pastors before your interview with Mrs. Marshal."

Rhonda gasps. "That's next week, isn't it?"

Brian nods, "Wednesday."

"I'd forgotten all about it." Rhonda winces at Kira.

Kira hasn't forgotten, and holds up her chin. "I need all the prayer I can get."

"Does Tuesday afternoon work for you?" Brian asks.

Kira looks to Rhonda for a silent check before agreeing. "Yes."

"Great." Brian grins. "Because you'll be stepping into is a spiritual battle, we'll anoint your head with oil." He pats her arm like an approving father, before walking away.

Kira's jaw drops. She never would've thought of a simple interview as an act of war, but with everything that hinges on her victory, Brian is right.

It's a war she must win...

***

A layer of fog covers the vast acreage of wheat to Ruger's right, as the light of Auctairea gray slowly darkens into black. He lands his armored aircraft at the coordinates Lieutenant Coltner gave him. It's an old farmhouse, with a large red barn to the left.

An old man steps outside from the barn and gasps before running back in. Soon, Carl Lopez struts out. He's healthier than Ruger remembers, making him smile.

"You're certainly a hard man to find," Ruger jokes while taking off his helmet.

"I'm glad you did." Carl smiles before motioning towards the barn.

Ruger doesn't hesitate and follows Carl up to the double doors. "I need you to share your testimony with my generals, so they can see with their own eyes that Auctaireans can be saved."

Carl stops at the door. "My testimony alone could do this?"

"Yes." Ruger avoids sharing the generals' intent to murder every Auctairean, but shows the importance of this mission through his expression.

After studying the worry lines on Ruger's brow, Carl doesn't ask questions. Instead, he smiles. "Imagine what their testimonies could do." He pulls the large red doors open to reveal a large crowd of people studying under the glow of many lanterns. Most look at Ruger with fear until Carl's smile assures them.

Spotting Kira's old Bible, Ruger's mouth gapes open. "You brought them all to the Lord?"

"I've been very busy," Carl says before stepping in and introducing Ruger as their King in Auctrah.

The crowd cheers.

Taken aback by how the one seed of ministering to Carl has become a vast harvest, it's difficult for Ruger to find the words. Finally, he pulls out his tablet and lifts his chin. "Let's record these testimonies, now."

***

CHAPTER 20
HOLY

Kira looks at her reflection in the small mirror hanging next to Rhonda's front door. Her bruise healed a couple of weeks ago, and while her skin and hair glow from proper nutrition, she hardly feels worthy of stepping foot in the great I Am's Holy Temple. Reminding herself of all the times God has spoken to her, Kira's so overwhelmed by his love, she smiles. Adjusting the layers of burgundy chiffon on her modest, crepe sleeve dress, Kira lets out a sigh.

Nadia steps down the stairs wearing a lilac dress. "This is my favorite shade of purple." She twirls in the entryway.

"You look beautiful," Kira praises.

"Thanks."

"Okay, ladies," Rhonda steps down the stairs wearing her signature green. "Are you ready to see the first building that was dedicated to Christ under Zyandite's flag?"

Kira smiles. "Yes."

It takes an hour, even on sky-mode, to arrive at Sunrise Sands.

"So, this building belonged to King Slayden's religion before it was made illegal?" Kira asks.

"Right," Rhonda looks out the window. Mountains are in view. They're snowcapped, but the valley below is still warm enough to not need a sweater. "Like all churches from that time, it was burned. When our side won the war, it was the first church rebuilt under a new covenant."

Nadia bounces in her seat with a grin. "And it's where Zyandite's first King was crowned?"

Rhonda holds her chin up. "That's right. Because of Zyandite tradition, when a king is crowned, the crown must immediately come off. It's symbolic. You'll learn why, very soon."

The town below seems to have been built around the temple. While the temple isn't the tallest building, it's definitely the largest. Constructed out of a steel frame, the walls are a white marble that encase swirls of genuine platinum and gold. Walking up to the double doors, Kira's amazed by the precious gems that adorn the outside of the temple. Rubies, emeralds, pearls, and opals glimmer in the sunshine. Recognizing stories from the Bible, Kira doesn't need to read the plaques to know these artist renditions are from the accounts of Moses, Noah, Elijah, and most of all, Jesus.

"This would all be stolen in Auctairea," Kira declares.

"Don't I know it," Rhonda glances over her shoulder before the automatic doors open. "We don't even guard it." She lowers her voice out of reverence for the temple and adds, "Zyandites fear God too much to rob Him."

Inside, the floor is constructed out of gold. Pearls line the baseboards and crown molding of the same marble as the outside. "This is magnificent," Kira whispers out of reverence.

"It's just a building." Brian's voice quietly sounds from her left. Kira turns to see him standing under an archway. Behind him, a room with a long, rectangular table rests. It's constructed of brown marble and surrounded by men and women who sit on red cushioned chairs. They're dressed in suits and dresses, but nothing matches. Beyond their table is a grand painting on the wall.

Brian pulls a chair out for Nadia. "These are the regional pastors of Zyandite."

Kira steps in. She has to peel her eyes from the artwork in order to smile at each pastor.

"As you can see, our titles don't matter, His does." Brian points at the painting on the wall.

Bringing her eyes back to the elaborate oil painting that's framed in gold, Kira can't sit down before getting a closer look.

The scenery is over this valley. The same snow-capped mountains, the same, bright blue sky, yet leaping from the ground are several men, each in different clothing. One dons a suit, another, a robe. One has a black collar with a white square at the center, while the man beside him wears a white dress shirt with a name tag. Another man wears jeans and a black tee shirt, and the man beside him isn't quite so casual, with a button-down shirt tucked into slacks. Their left hands are dropping crowns, while their right hands reach for the man above them. Directly centered in the sky stands Jesus, he is wearing a white robe, with his face glorious in golden light.

Just seeing this rendition of Jesus brings Kira's eyes to tears.

Rhonda steps beside her. "It tells a story, doesn't it?"

"Yes," Kira agrees.

"That's our history," Brian says. "When Zyandite was born, King Slayden's religion was the strongest during the war, because it was the most prepared. Still, they couldn't have won without the other branches of Christianity. After God gave them victory, the importance of unity was placed on their hearts, so they threw down their titles and earthly crowns, to come together as one church under Jesus Christ. Some traditions stayed, others, disappeared to form a covenant of unity under the great I Am that would never be divided." He points at the men in their different attire. "Each outfit these men wear represents the denominations of Christianity from that time. Bishops, Priests, Reverends, Pastors, Chaplains, Ministers of all denominations set their differences aside and came together to form the Christianity we know today. At any moment, we must be willing to toss our earthly crowns down, and submit to the King of kings."

"It's beautiful," Kira says.

"Yes." Brian gives a tight smile to the other pastors in the room. "But today, we must ask the great I Am for that unity to stand. It's about to be tested, and you're at the center of it."

Kira turns from the painting and lowers her chin, "Because of the Lineage?"

Brian glances at the other pastors, before looking back at Kira. "Yes. This is a political battle, but it's still a battle you must win. It's not just the slander against your purity, we all saw what happened after Ruger crashed."

Kira watches every pastor nod in agreement. She lets out a sigh of relief. At least not every Zyandite is naïve to the possibility of treachery from within.

Brian grins. "Like me, Ruger's a wildcard the Lineage can't control."

Kira's jaw drops. "You're a member of the Lineage?"

"If my destiny revolved around lives of the past instead of my own, I'd be king." Brian eyes glimmer with the independence of being his own man. "During my mandatory service, I was the worst soldier. I slept in, missed formations, even interrupted my Drill Sergeant. Yet they still enrolled me into the Officer's Academy. I made the rank of Captain before I quit, when I should've only been a Private. General Kentwood was disappointed when I joined the Church. He said I was wasting the blood of kings on the sweat of servitude. That was the moment when I realized Zyandite has a cast system, and ministry is at the bottom." His lips quiver in anger for a moment. "For a country that was founded on God's precepts, the spreading of the gospel had become second-rate. It's despicable, but the great I Am has a wonderful sense of humor, and is using their tactics against them." Brian's smile returns. "It was because of my Lineage that King Tidal appointed me as Lead Pastor. No one else would've fought for Ruger to become king. The generals didn't want him, but the people saw him as a ray of hope for their own sons. It's all by God's design."

Kira raises her chin with pride for Brian's outlook. "It's amazing the way He uses the unexpected to bring forth His will."

"Yes, like you," Brian says. "It's your contaminated blood that will break the chain of Lineage, and destroy their idolatrous ways for good." The way he bends his finger while saying 'contaminated' assures Kira he's not being judgmental. "The Lineage knows that. Like a cornered animal, they'll bite. Yours and Ruger's unique situation gave them some leverage, but with God's help, we can send their own weapon back on their heads."

Kira's heart races, making her look down. "I've been under threat before…" She lips Psalm 31:24 and closes her eyes. "With God's help, we'll be victorious."

"Now that's the woman of faith Zyandite needs."

Kira blushes at Brian's compliment.

Brian looks at the painting. "Our earthly titles are nothing compared to His will. This is all in accordance with God's plan, and once you're crowned, you'll have to let Auctairea go."

Bringing her eyes to the display of humility on the wall before her, Kira silently asks God to help her be the queen Zyandite needs. Her determination is struck by the mistakes of her past. She doesn't deserve to be in any place of influence, let alone a queen. The conflict brews inside of her heart, causing Kira's brow to furrow.

"Kira," Brian's voice pulls her out of the battle waging within Kira's heart. "Your interview with Wilma is your last chance to help Ruger keep his rightful place as king. You must convince the people of your purity." He glances at Nadia and hesitates, before looking at Kira with great intensity. "Do you think Ruger's crash will be the last time the Lineage tries to kill him?"

Rhonda and Nadia simultaneously gasp.

"We shouldn't speculate on that without proof," Rhonda proclaims.

Kira watches the other pastors look at her with pity, before Brian speaks.

"We have eyes, Rhonda, my dear. What happened to your brother certainly *looks* suspicious," Brian raises a brow.

A woman with kind, dark eyes and a matching complexion reaches her hand across the table. "The great I Am has protected King Anstone before. We must pray that He continues to do so."

Rhonda offers her hand, appreciating the comfort with a smile.

Kira glances at Nadia. She's handling this conversation with maturity beyond her years. For a moment, Kira can see a glimpse of the woman her daughter will become, and she's as graceful as she is beautiful.

"Yes, Pastor Laurel, prayer is the most important weapon we have." Brian takes a chair and positions it in the middle of the room. "Please, sit down." He looks at Kira and motions at the chair.

Kira squares her shoulders and takes a deep breath before taking a seat. The pastors surround her while Brian takes a small vile of oil from his pocket. Keeping her feet flat to not show that her knees are shaking, Kira looks up at the kind faces around her, utterly amazed that God brought her here. "Thank you."

"Thank the great I Am," Brian says before pouring a few drops of oil on Kira's head. He and the other pastor gently place their hands above her head. They don't physically touch her, but Kira can feel the warmth of the Holy Spirit and bows.

"Before we pray," Brian eyes his pastors with the authority of his position. "I want to give Kira a scripture to hold onto anytime doubt may creep in. Galatians 6:7 states: Don't be misled—you cannot mock the justice of God. You will always harvest what you plant." Brian lets out a low sigh. "The Lineage has planted the seeds of idolatry, by mocking God with their worship of bloodlines, status, and the past. God is using you, a widowed foreigner, to mock them."

This honor is too much to accept. Kira closes her eyes and presses her lips together to keep from crying.

Brian praying the entire chapter of Psalm 23 over her: "The Lord is my shepherd; I shall have all that I need. He lets me rest in green meadows; he leads me beside peaceful streams. He renews my strength. He guides me along right paths, bringing honor to my name. Even when I walk through the darkest valley, I will not be afraid, for you are close beside me. Your rod and your staff protect and comfort me. You prepare a feast for me in the presence of my enemies. You honor me by anointing my head with oil. Surely your goodness and unfailing love will pursue me all the days of my life, and I will live in the house of the LORD forever." With his eyes closed, Brian continues in prayer. "The great I Am, the maker of atoms and the cosmos, the creator of all, we praise and fear your mighty name. Let your presence fall on Zyandite, and on your brave servant, Kira Valeda Westin. Give Kira all that she needs, including rest, peace, and strength. Guide Kira on the right paths for her life and gently lead her. As Kira embarks through the dark valley on the stage of false accusations, help her not to fear. Protect Kira. Comfort Kira, and give her the right words to say. Honor Kira, and prepare a feast for her in the presence of Wilma Marshal and the

Lineage. Don't let Zyandite be punished for their idolatry. Use Kira to expose the Lineage and free Zyandite from their curses. Justify Kira and King Anstone, and may your goodness and love pursue them all the days of their lives, trickling down to Nadia, and their future children. Great I Am, always bless Zyandite with one of your servants on the throne, in the mighty name of Jesus Christ we pray, amen."

The other pastors say 'Amen' in unison.

Their hands are lifted, but it takes Kira a moment to open her eyes. She didn't feel the tears running down her face until now. Wiping them away, she's not met with judgement, but compassion. All of those dark days of hiding her faith in Auctairea replay like a blur. Kira never could've imagined being where she is right now. Silently, she asks God to help her be what Zyandite needs.

***

Before a long table of disgruntled generals, Ruger straightens his back and projects an image on the wall. Satisfied with the footage of Carl's testimony, Ruger filmed four others as well, just for good measure. He doesn't say anything and lets them play. After each tear-filled testimony is said, Ruger pauses the footage and turns. Expecting to find softened hearts, he's met with more agitation than before.

"They're breaking your rule," General Kentwood scoffs with a nod at the projection.

"They haven't had time to learn Zyandish," Ruger snaps. "Have you been paying attention? In a matter of a single month, dozens of Auctaireans have come to the Lord."

General Danning blows a sigh through his lips.

Ruger glares at the mockery.

"That's, well," General Kentwood points at the projection, "Progress." His tone is indifferent. "We'll cut them a plot of our northern lots. These new Christians can settle there, but they can't ever have weapons. Once they're segregated, we can deal with the rest of Auctairea."

Turning the projection off, Ruger straightens his posture. "No. The Auctaireans who refuse Christ, will be sent off to the Pazmirish Republic."

"That would cost a fortune!" General Mayes shouts.

"This Despoliation has surpassed our expectations. We can afford it." Ruger shoots General Mayes a glare before looking at General Kentwood. "This land will become a continuous source of income. The Auctaireans who stay will find employment in lumber and paper mills. We'll build the best the world has seen." Ruger smiles. "And we'll do it all without unnecessary carnage."

"Yes, leave your responsibility of dealing with this enemy for the next king." General Marshal raises a brow with an unspoken expectation that'll be him.

Ruger presses his hands on the table and leans forward. "If the next king forfeits our covenant with God, Zyandite will be lost."

"You mean like in Ezra chapter ten?" General Marshal asks.

"If you're implying that my relationship with Kira, forfeits our covenant with God, you're blind. The women in Ezra ten were—"

"Foreigners," General Danning says. Interrupting the King causes the entire room to look at him in surprise.

"Pagans. Idol worshippers. Not Kira." Ruger glares at General Marshal, who shakes his head and looks away.

"What if they start an insurgency?" General Kentwood asks.

Ruger shakes his head. "With what, sticks?"

The generals glance at each other, but no one responds.

"Even if there was a risk an insurgency, I refuse to Flatiron this place." Ruger marches out of the room.

The generals glare at the back of Ruger's head. Once he's out of earshot, General Kentwood slams his fist onto the table. "He's weak!"

"This is why we should've never allowed New Bloods to vote," General

Danning hisses.

"Never again," General Kentwood agrees, before looking at General Marshal.

"It would be amusing, if it weren't so dangerous." General Marshal stretches his arms, flexing his muscles before cracking his neck. "There must be something we can do?"

"He has too much support." General Danning leans back into his chair, his shoulders slumped with defeat.

General Marshal's lips curve into a smile. "My wife will take care of that. The interview will make Zyandite turn on Kira, and the Preacher King."

***

CHAPTER 21
THE ARENA

Kira stands in front of her bathroom mirror. She's gained her normal weight back and her face looks younger. Straightening her dress, the collar is black and curls up like a mock turtleneck, while the burgundy layers over her shoulders, arms, back, and sides giving it a color-blocked look. The black continues all the way down the front, becoming narrow at the belted waist, before flowing out into a pleated skirt. The dress is longer than those Kira was used to in Auctairea, but it suits her. Her three-inch, black heels are surprisingly comfortable. The only thing she needs now is the makeup. Brown eyeliner, black mascara, rich mocha and shimmering cream eyeshadows, plus her signature burgundy lipstick are all present, but Kira dreads putting them on. Perhaps she should have practiced first, instead of waiting until the day of her interview.

Makeup is such a pain to apply. It needs to be taken off, or it'll run down your face and flake pieces in your eyes. Kira sighs as she reminds herself that she needs to give Zyandites a familiar face, one whom the whole world knew and appreciated five years ago. She only hopes they'll remember.

***

It takes Rhonda's driver fifteen minutes to reach downtown Brustonite. Kira tries her best to stay calm so she won't sweat out the curls in her hair.

Rhonda grins, wearing her signature green in a modest skirt suit. "You're going to do great."

Kira wishes she shared Rhonda's confidence, and looks down blushing. "Thank you for watching Nadia while I do this. I'm so nervous."

"Don't be frightened, mommy," Nadia says while straightening out the white ruffles of her dress.

Kira smiles and hugs her. "I'm so blessed to be your mother."

Finally, the car stops. With a silent prayer, Kira slowly steps out of the car and looks at the enormous sky-scraper that comes to a point at the top.

"Kira Westin!" A man yells from the large entryway made entirely of blue glass. He's at least thirty years older than her, with graying hair, keen eyes, and a perfectly pressed suit.

"My name is Clark Natorin. I'm the Executive Producer of Zyandite Press. When I heard you were here, I had to meet you," he greets without holding a hand to shake or anything physical, which Kira finds refreshing.

"It's nice to meet you, Mr. Natorin," Kira smiles, "This is my daughter, Nadia. I'm sure you already know Rhonda Anstone."

"Of course. Welcome, all of you." Clark starts walking toward the studio. "Nadia and Rhonda will be very comfortable in our Employee's Lounge, where we have every type of beverage and dessert under the sun."

In Auctairea, what is mostly gray and bland, such as waiting rooms and office buildings, are places Zyandites love to fill with color. It is like walking into a modern art exhibit, with blown glass formations in various shades of blue and red hanging from the ceiling, yellow carpet with blue splatters, and colorful paintings on every wall.

Kira looks up to see the elevator is made entirely out of glass, with the keypad the only metal to be seen. It is entirely different than the elevators in Auctairea, but Kira can get used to it. Once they step inside, the doors close and they move up incredibly fast. Both Kira and Nadia would have lost their balance, if Kira had not grabbed the wall with one arm and her daughter with the other.

"Whoa!" Nadia exclaims.

"I'm so sorry. I forgot that Auctairea doesn't have this technology," Rhonda says.

"If you want to reschedule, I completely understand," Clark offers.

"Oh no, don't be silly. We're perfectly fine." Kira gives her best smile as the elevator stops.

Clark takes the lead, passing a sitting area that reminds Kira of a nice airport lounge.

"This is where your daughter and Miss Anstone will be waiting," Clark glances over his shoulder. "Wilma's studio is just down the hall."

Kira turns to Nadia. "Will you be alright?"

Nadia smiles and nods before taking Rhonda's hand.

"Okay, great," Kira winks at Nadia before following Clark down a large hallway with the same yellow and blue carpet, before opening two tall, mahogany doors. This room has sapphire blue carpet and walls, with various pieces of deep ruby artwork. A white trim bordering the very center of each wall makes it feel bigger. Directly in the middle of the room are two blue chairs, and a man holding a tablet.

Kira recognizes Wilma's camera man from the hospital. "Hello."

The cameraman's face is emotionless as he stares at her.

Not allowing his discrimination to gnaw at her, Kira ignores him.

A door opens, and Wilma steps out wearing the colors of the Zyandite flag. A gold belt encases a red dress, with a white cross at the center.

She knows the theatrics are meant to intimidate her, but Kira almost laughs at how silly Wilma looks.

Wilma gives her a smug once over, before taking a seat and motioning for Kira to do the same.

Kira sit across from Wilma with a humble smile.

"I'll leave you two to it," Clark steps out of the room.

"You look, plain." Wilma raises a brow at Kira, and shrugs before turning to Benson. "Are we ready?"

He motions the countdown with his fingers.

Wilma gives a pretty smile. "Good afternoon, my fellow Zyandites. As most of you know, I'm Wilma, General Marshal's wife, and I'm here with a special guest," She beams at the tablet before looking at Kira. "Who is none other than the Auctairean, and late Governor of Quandii's wife, Kira Westin."

Kira silently begs God to see her through before responding. "Thank you so much for the warm welcome, Mrs. Marshal, and thank you, people of Zyandite, for allowing both me and my daughter as guests in your incredible country. It's such an honor to be here."

"Yes, but not everyone has been kind to you," Wilma lifts a brow.

Kira's smile brightens. "If I hadn't forgiven you, I wouldn't be here."

Wilma's smile fades. "Hmmm. Well, at least the weather is better here than in Auctairea, wouldn't you agree?"

Kira hides her annoyance for such a lighthearted subject. "Yes, I do like how warm Zyandite is, for this time of year, especially."

"It is warm here, but perhaps things were too hot in Auctairea?" Wilma's face is playful enough, but Kira didn't expect her to be so vicious this early on.

So, Kira takes the gloves off with a smile. "Without electricity, the summers in Auctairea were excruciatingly hot." Kira pretends to be naïve, all while redirecting the conversation.

"How long were you out of electricity?"

"Five years."

"Five whole years without electricity," Wilma stares into the camera intensely. "Can you all just imagine, five years!" She shivers as though trying to be Kira's friend, but they both know better.

"Prime Minister Joplin even turned our water off," Kira adds.

"No running water!" Wilma's mouth gapes as she looks back and forth between Kira and the camera. "How ever did you survive, for five whole years under those conditions?"

"God. Without Him, I couldn't have done it, any of it, the hunting, surviving the snow and the heat, surviving the crime, all of it. He protected Nadia, my daughter's name is Nadia," Kira explains to the camera briefly before looking back at Wilma. "God protected us both."

Wilma nervously tosses her hair to the side. "Wasn't believing in God, illegal in Auctairea?"

"Yes. I hid my Bible, knowing that if it was found, I would be killed."

"What a terrible way to live." Wilma takes a moment of silence before continuing the interview. "Now, how exactly did you meet our king?" Wilma asks, shifting her legs while her face beams with intrigue.

"I was out hunting one night and only had one round left. The rest all cracked from so many years of reloading the same brass."

"*You* practiced the skill of reloading?" Wilma holds in a laugh.

The insult wasn't lost on Kira, but she keeps her cool. "I had to, or I would've run out of ammo a long time ago."

"An Auctairean, practicing the skill of reloading…" Wilma chuckles.

Kira knows this is a tactic to get the viewers to doubt her claim. She must explain herself to prevent that from happening. "When I moved to the country, my neighbors loved to hunt. I had never shot a gun before meeting them. Once my love for the self-sufficiency of hunting was apparent, they taught me everything they knew."

"What were their names?"

Kira hesitates, uncertain if the mascara she's wearing is waterproof, as those names are nearly impossible for her to say without crying. "I'd hate to dishonor them."

Wilma's brow furrows. "Why would that dishonor them?"

"Because of your accusations against me. I don't want them associated with that. They were good Christians who were murdered for their faith. Please, leave them out of this."

Wilma's obviously taken aback and has a hard time regaining her thoughts. "No one is accusing you of anything. It's just that while King Anstone was in your house, we had no idea what was going on. His vitals were lost. All we knew was that he crashed, and was stricken with a dangerously high fever before his vitals fell off of ZyanBell, which is why the process to elect a new king was in motion."

"Ruger was shot with a poison laced bullet," Kira frowns at the memory. "He was so sick."

"You had no idea he was King of Zyandite when you rescued him?" Wilma presses her lips together in a disbelieving smirk.

"I had no way of knowing that Samson Tidal was no longer Zyandite's king. I didn't have electricity, remember?" Kira let too much of her annoyance show, and could cringe at the mistake.

"Oh, yes. Of course." Wilma's eyes drip with faux sympathy. "So, our King was gallant enough to get you and Nadia out of that terrible place, after only knowing you for a few days..." Wilma's eyes are accusing.

"Yes, he did. Nadia and I are so grateful."

"Oh, I'll bet. Here you are, speaking Zyandish perfectly after being here what, two months?"

"One month," Kira corrects.

"You learned how to speak a whole new language in just one month?" Wilma's eyes harden. "The incredible," She tilts her head to the side. "Winner of the Sistrine award, adored by Auctaireans, and the Pazmirish... You've got quite the experience of charming the elite."

Kira doesn't allow herself to fall into Wilma's trap. "Those things don't matter to me. They're frivolous. Wilma, I know what it is like to lose all of my freedoms, the very freedoms you have here in Zyandite, which is why it was critical for my daughter and I to speak Zyandish," Kira looks at the camera, "I know there are terrible lies being spread about me and King Anstone, but that's all they are, lies. That's why I'm thankful for this chance to have the ear of the Zyandite people."

Wilma's eyes fill with excitement as she expects Kira to be defensive.

"No matter what you believe about mine and even your King's purity, please, don't make the same mistakes I did, by allowing a godless tyrant to take away your freedoms and tax you into poverty. Please, don't ever let anyone bully you, or guilt you into changing your opinions and your beliefs from what you know is right. Please, keep Zyandite just the way it is, for it is such a beautiful society." She looks back at Wilma. "And division is a surefire way to lose it."

Wilma claps her hands a few times as though cheering, causing Kira to stare at her in perplexity.

"Well said, and we Zyandites do love our country, so much so that the people of Zyandite deserve the truth. Were you and King Anstone, physical in any way?"

"Physical?" Kira smirks with a tilt of her head, "Are you too frightened to flat out ask me if we sinned?"

"I'm not frightened, Miss Westin, but it is a touchy subject." Wilma smirks.

Kira rolls her eyes at the pun.

"Several nights of sleeping in a woman's home, and a woman as beautiful as you, none the less, makes anyone have to wonder. If you were both Zyandites, then perhaps we could trust you. Yet, with a woman whose integrity has been compromised, well, it makes us have to question the judgement of our King." Wilma shrugs.

"First of all, Ruger," Kira has to correct herself. "I'm sorry, King Anstone, was a complete gentleman, and frankly, a breath of fresh air in comparison to Auctairean men. In fact, it's not even fair to compare HIM at all, because King Anstone is so far out of their league. What I need for you to explain is what integrity of mine has been compromised?"

Wilma gives Benson a hand signal, and the wall behind them is covered with a projected shot of a male Auctairean reporter, whom Kira recognizes as Brad Macalister. He was the most vocal advocate for Auctairea's rations, so she is not surprised that he made it into a journalist position. As all Auctairean men, his frame is lanky, but his icy blue eyes against his olive tone skin, made him attractive enough to put on camera. The message is on mute, since under the King's order Auctrah is now a dead language, but the subtitles in Zyandish say it all:

"Governor George Cantura is in Hanover now, and has messaged Prime Minister Joplin with a promise from Kira Westin. She will come on air next week to praise the new law against delusional thinking. This has been by far, the greatest win for Auctairea inclusivity, since nothing divides people more than religion."

The scene disappears and all that is left is a blank wall.

"I never agreed…" Air gets stuck in Kira's throat, "To that," she says with a painful sob.

"So Brad Macalister, and Prime Minister Joplin, lied?"

"You're defending Prime Minister Joplin now?"

"No." Wilma is taken aback. "Never."

"Good. Because, when hasn't he lied?" Kira scoffs. "He certainly fooled me into helping him get elected. In fact, he ended up murdering most of the people who voted for him!" Kira bites her lip in order to control her anger. "I've never heard of anyone flipping on their campaigned promises more than Joplin did. That's on record for anyone to see."

"I understand that, but Prime Minister Joplin's integrity isn't in question here. Yours is. Were you ever scheduled for such an interview?" Wilma's tone is calm, but Kira can see the rage in her eyes.

"I'd never agree to such treachery against my God." Kira hates being vulnerable, but she knows the fear of man is a trap, even if it causes her humiliation. Kira knows God will bless her transparency. "My late husband brought me a script." Kira's never allowed herself to cry on camera, but can't fight these tears. "When I told him no, George almost killed me." Kira's face scrunches from the pressure. "I'm sorry for crying, I just haven't told this to anyone besides Ruger, and it's very hard…" Kira sobs and doesn't bother correcting herself for not using Ruger's correct title, as the painful memories flow out.

"Why did you tell King Anstone and not anyone else?" Wilma seems genuinely perturbed by that.

"Because if anyone else knew, I'd be killed for treason. I only told Ruger because he's a Christian. At the time, I thought he'd be the only person I'd ever come across who'd understand."

"How lonely you must have been." Wilma pouts.

Kira lifts up her chin and doesn't allow her blood pressure to rise at the insult. She didn't come here to speak to Wilma, but to the Zyandite people. "I had my God, and my daughter. My relationship with God grew stronger than I ever thought possible. That wouldn't have happened, if I hadn't been in isolation. God's love was always there for me, which is the reason I always had unexpected favor. You see, I didn't behave the way other Auctairean women did, yet I was promoted. Even so, I didn't realize the extent of how much God loves me, until He avenged me from my own husband."

Wilma shifts in her seat a bit.

Kira knows that Nadia is watching, and hates for her to learn the truth about her father this way, but God's presence is beckoning her to tell the whole story. "God had my side even before I became a strong Christian. I refused to turn on my God, even when doing so would have benefited my marriage and my bank account." Kira's no longer sad, but angry as she recounts the memory. "George was on his way to turn me in for refusing to bow to their oppression, which was a crime in Auctairea. I thought I'd be executed for my faith and didn't know what would've happened to my daughter. It was so tormenting! Yet, in the dark midst of my utter loss of hope, God avenged me in a way that is undeniable." Kira sobs for a moment. "While my own husband was on his way to destroy me, my God used wolves to devour him."

Wilma's eyes bulge.

Kira doesn't let Wilma's fear stop her from sharing what the Holy Spirit stirs inside. "The next day, when I heard a knock at my door, I expected to see soldiers, ready to take me to Quandii for public execution for my belief in God. Instead, I was met with pity. Everyone felt sorry for me and no one ever approached me from Quandii again. As time went on and new threats grew, God not only helped me to protect my daughter, but He also provided our every need. When your king crashed into my life, I was on the hunt. Nadia and I were on the brink of starvation. There was a large doe and I shot her, just before I saw a pilot crash near my estate. When I went after him, it wasn't to save him, but to rob him. I was out of ammo and hoped he had a sidearm. I had no idea Ruger was King of Zyandite, how could I, without any link to the world for five years!" Kira glares at Wilma, who remains silent. "When I got to Ruger, he was tangled up in the cords of his parachute and I realized how easy it would've been to turn him in for a reward."

Wilma gasps dramatically.

"But then, I heard God speak."

"You, an Auctairean, heard the great I Am speak?" Wilma scrunches her brow.

Kira doesn't falter at Wilma's disbelief, for she's only a mortal. "I know my Master's voice. I've heard it before, warning me of danger and leading me to food."

"What did he say?"

"Help him." Two tears roll down Kira's cheeks. "While I didn't know who this stranger was, I knew aiding my country's enemy risked not only my life, but my daughter's. It was crazy to even consider such a thing. I almost disobeyed God, but after hearing God's voice, I saw in the moonlight battered pages to a book that was strapped to Ruger's chest. The text was foreign to me, except one word: Psalms."

Wilma's shoulders drop in defeat.

"So, I pulled this out of hiding," Kira briefly caresses the platinum cross necklace she can now wear in the open, "To show him that I too, am a Christian. It was difficult to take him to my home without getting caught by other Auctaireans, but by God's grace, we made it. When I found out Ruger had been shot with a kepweed laced bullet, I thought he would surely die. I almost didn't give him the antidote. You see, my daughter refused to go hunting with me because of what happened to her father. Nadia was terrified of the woods and the wolves that filled them. Having to leave her to hunt for our survival, the only weapon I had to give her was a spray bottle filled with kepweed infused water. To me, giving the only antidote I had to a stranger would risk my daughter's life. I didn't want to do it, but again, God spoke. I obeyed. I've always obeyed my God, and I can assure you that not only was King Anstone faithful to his purity, but I was faithful to mine. How could I not be, when disobeying God hurts Him?" Kira leans forward as her passion is set free on camera for the first time in her life. "We never did anything close to compromising our integrity. I love God too much, and so does your king!"

Wilma's eyes widen but Kira doesn't let that stop her.

"Isaiah 54:17 promises: no weapon turned against you will succeed. You will silence every voice raised up to accuse you. Those words are from my God, and He always keeps His promises. I serve my God, I served him even when the nights were the darkest, most dangerous, and longest of my life. I served my God when it was not popular, and even after it was deemed a crime. I saw with my own eyes the penalty for breaking Auctairean laws, yet even as other Christians were murdered for their faith, I stayed true to my God. I served my God when men threatened me, and when hunger nearly killed me. I even risked my child's life to serve my God, and you know what, Wilma? God has always been faithful to me. My God avenged me by tearing my late husband to bits, and even if He never avenges me like that again, I will not question His will. I'll continue to serve my God, even if it costs me my life. Yet, I believe in this, not only will God avenge me, but he'll also avenge your king from these vile and false accusations. We don't fear man, nor any weapon you can produce, be it lead, blade, or tongue."

Wilma stares at her blankly. "In all my years on air, reporting for the people of Zyandite, I have never been rendered speechless, before now. What a show."

"No, Wilma. Your false accusations have been the show, a complete and utter disgrace. Instead of investigating me, you lied. You know you're lying, but you continue sinning in hopes to become queen."

Wilma grins. "I would never—"

"What? Go against your vow and divide your nation?"

Wilma's smile fades and hatred flickers across her eyes. "Our King divided this nation when he sent a foreigner here to contaminate his bloodline." She crosses her legs. "Not that it was great from the start."

"Foreigner," Kira's the one smiling now, "You mean like your Pazmirish mother?"

"My parents were missionaries."

"That's how your father met your mom, but that's not what they were doing in the Pazmirish Republic when you were a teenager. You see, ZyanBell may be disconnected from the rest of the world, but Auctairea's linked into the GPU…"

Wilma's eyes widen.

"While King Anstone was researching my past, I had him look into you." Kira fights showing the joy budding in her heart at the horror on Wilma's face. "Not only did he find proof that I never agreed to promote Joplin's law against religion, but he also discovered that while you were in the Pazmirish Republic, it wasn't for a mission. It was because your aunt had cancer, and your mother wanted to be with her. Even after your aunt died, your family stayed for two months. Why was that, Wilma?"

Wilma glances at the camera before glaring at Kira. "You know nothing about me."

"Well, I could say you're the foreign influence you've been accusing me of," Kira says. "But Christ himself said in Matthew 15:19: For from the heart come evil thoughts, murder, adultery, all sexual immorality, theft, lying, and slander." Kira's heart fills with a courage that can only come from God. "What a God we serve who lists slander and false testimony as being just as vile as murder! So no, I won't accuse you of anything, not without proof."

Wilma's body shakes. For a moment she looks as though she could cry. "What a God we serve is right…" She takes a moment before bringing her eyes back to Kira. "I apologize for accusing you, and King Anstone."

Surprised by the sudden shift, Kira sits back. "I forgive you."

"Thank you." Wilma smiles, it's pretty, but Kira knows it's fake. "But I must inquire of you, are you absolutely positive that you are a full-blooded Auctairean?"

Kira's never been a sucker for flattery and isn't about to start now. Compliments rarely come without a price. "My mother was a member of the church, so it's possible that she had some lineage from the Zyandite missionaries, but I can't say for certain. Regardless, God's kingdom is not a kingdom of flesh and blood."

"You're an Auctairean abnormality. There's no denying that."

Kira's heart fills with anger, as the memories of those she lost in the cleansing flood her mind. "No, I was not an abnormality in Auctairea and would not have been so popular of a reporter if I was. There were many good, God fearing, God serving people in my country, before…" Kira grits her teeth openly as the torture from the past replays now. "It was called the Great Cleansing. They were all murdered for their faith, and I won't let you or anyone else tarnish their memory."

"I'm so sorry. What a travesty! They deserve better from us, and you know what Kira, so do you. I shouldn't have accused you, or King Anstone, without proof." Wilma holds her chin up with hard eyes before smiling at the camera. "How about you, Zyandite? What are your thoughts on this matter? Won't you tell us through ZyanBell?"

"Yes, but…" Kira stares at the camera. "Before I go, may I please explain to Zyandite how Auctairea fell?"

Wilma shrugs indifferently. "Sure."

Kira stares at the camera, as though she was facing the people of Zyandite directly. "The fall of Auctairea first began with word programming. In changing the way Auctaireans spoke, the government changed the way Auctaireans thought. Certain words had to be eliminated from the people's vocabulary and eventually, so did their meaning. Once speech was altered, the government could go after mere words, by enforcing appropriated speech through social guilt and even intimidation. Then, they banned our holidays. Gift giving was seen as merely feeding corporate greed and the economy suffered massive job loss, which indebted more souls to the government. Once those freedoms were taken and enough people were enslaved, not just in debt, but in thought, the assault on religion commenced. The very fabric of Auctairea was harmed in physical nature, sure, but the true demise of Auctairea happened when the minds and hearts of Auctaireans became controlled. The deliberate attack commenced further, by turning children against their parents, and parents against their children. We were destroyed before a single person was killed, and it can happen to any society, if due diligence is not practiced daily. In Zyandite, love for God, admiration for family, pride for country, and respect for individualism must never change. The moment just one of those pillars falls, is the moment when the minds of this beautiful country dies, and you're left defenseless to whoever seeks your ruin."

"That's very profound. I take it you like Zyandite?" Wilma asks.

Kira doesn't hesitate to show her whole heart. "I more than like Zyandite, I love it! I never truly experienced freedom until coming here."

"Hmm," there's an ornery flicker in Wilma's eyes, "Do you also love our king?"

Kira stops her mouth from dropping completely and has to be careful not to stutter in her discomfort. "I um…" she looks down for a moment in fear that no matter what she says, it may ruin hers and Nadia's chance in being accepted by Zyandites, but she won't lie. Gathering her courage, Kira boldly looks at Wilma. "King Anstone reverently loves God. After hiding my faith for so many years, it was refreshing to fellowship with another adult, who not only knows God's word, but puts it into practice. Ruger…" She closes her eyes for a moment in disappointment for misspeaking yet again. "King Anstone is strong, yet remains kind and has more integrity than anyone I've met. I respect him." Kira fights off a tear. "With who King Anstone is, admirable, honest, and just, how could I not love him?" Kira looks at the camera to address the people of Zyandite once more. "He saved my daughter's life and mine, before I knew he was your King. After being exposed to Auctairean men all my life, I thought a man as stouthearted and handsome as your king is, had to have a wife at home. It was difficult for me to imagine otherwise. Once Ruger told me he was the King of Zyandite, I knew that any chance of us being more than friends was impossible."

"Why's that?"

Kira turns back to Wilma with surprise at such a question, since she of all people should know better. "Because, I'm only an Auctairean, with a past filled with pain. King Anstone deserves so much better."

"So, you haven't heard of the prophecy?" Wilma's eyes are almost accusing again.

"Yes. I don't think prophecy is always exact. Besides that, if Ruger and I were to marry, I wouldn't want it to be over a crown."

Wilma shifts her weight. "So how do you feel about the Trigon's deeming you as a modern Abigale?"

Kira blushes. "They are so encouraging and kind, but I'm nothing compared to Abigale."

Wilma half-smiles before the light flashes on Benson's tablet to signal they are out of time. "Aren't you humble, Miss Westin, thanks again for coming on the air."

"Anytime, Wilma. Thanks for having me, so that I can recount what really happened to the people of Zyandite. They deserve to know the truth."

"The camera is off," Benson announces before putting his tablet away.

Wilma's eyes Kira with a demeaning glare. "How dare you bring up the worst time of my life."

"You really thought I wouldn't look into your past?" Kira scowls. "You smeared an award winning journalist, what did you expect?"

Wilma wags her finger at Kira. "I promise I'll show the people of Zyandite exactly what you are."

"After you just apologized for accusing me?" Kira crosses her arms. "That's kind of forked tongued."

"I know my audience, and only apologized because it's the Christian thing to do." Wilma rolls her eyes and huffs out of the studio.

This interview may have been a victory, but Kira knows the battle with Wilma has just begun.

Clark Natorin steps into the room. "That was touching."

"I fear I may have said too much, and don't want there to be any harsh feelings with King Anstone. Do you think he could watch the interview before it's aired?" Kira asks.

"That was live."

"Oh," Kira's feels all color flush from her face, but smiles anyways. "Okay."

Clark opens the door to show Kira out of the studio and back to the lounge, where a woman runs up to hug her. "God bless you, you brave girl, and thank you for saving our king," she hasps before walking away, leaving Kira perplexed.

"Well, that was nice," Clark mumbles with an uncomfortable smile before Nadia and Rhonda spot Kira.

"Mommy, you were wonderful!" Nadia greets and Kira realizes they had been watching from the screens in the lounge.

Kira's relieved to know that the recount of what happened to her father didn't traumatized Nadia, and hugs her. "Thank you, sweetheart. It's a good thing too, because I didn't know I was live."

"You did a fantastic job!" Rhonda wipes away a tear before hugging Kira. "Thank you so much, first saving my brother's life, and now, defending his honor."

"I only did what God led me to do, and don't deserve your thanks, I…" Kira can't find the words and Rhonda does not seem to mind as she continues to hug her, sobbing quietly.

"Sorry," Rhonda says, pulling away and wiping a tear.

"No don't be, I have been crying too." Kira looks around to find a mirror, any mirror, to see if her mascara is running. There's a mirror reflecting from the bar, it's too far for any real detail, but close enough for her to know she doesn't have black lines running down her face.

"To Kira Westin, the woman of integrity who saved our king!" A man yells while holding up a wine glass at the lounge.

"To Kira!" Everyone shouts in unison, causing Kira's heart to quake. She should be happy, but their praise only reminds Kira of her past.

"No, not to me, to our God," Kira holds her head down. She can't get out of here fast enough. She's failed fellow Kingdom Members once, and can't risk doing so again.

***

From their modest living room, done up with tan and white furnishings, Brian and Farrah watch the interview smiling and holding hands, they immediately thank God for their modern day Abigale, while asking Him to soften the hearts of Zyandite to her.

***

Once they finally make it outside the building, Kira just wants to get her daughter and herself into the car, but Rhonda isn't helping. Her emotional whirlwind only slows them down.

"I still can't believe how much you risked for my brother," Rhonda says with another sob.

Before Kira can respond, a woman from across the street begins yelling, "That's her! That's Kira Westin, the woman who saved our king!"

Kira's quick to get her daughter and Rhonda shoved into the car and closes the door before anyone else can recognize her. "Rhonda, I'm never leaving your house again," Kira jokes.

Rhonda only laughs, while still crying in gratitude. The odd combination causes Nadia to giggle.

"I mean it," Kira hasps, only making them laugh more. "And thank you for getting waterproof mascara. I'd be humiliated to the grave if you hadn't."

Rhonda gives an all knowing smile. "There are three events a woman must never attend without waterproof mascara: church, a wedding, and finally, being interviewed by a major news network."

Kira is the one laughing now, causing Rhonda to wink at her.

***

The generals sit at a round table in front of the projection of Wilma's interview with Kira. Once the image turns black, General Kentwood glares at General Marshal. "She failed."

General Marshal's eyes flicker with rage before downplaying the concern with a smile. "Believe me, Wilma knows what she's doing. This isn't over yet."

"You'd better hope so." General Kentwood points his finger at Marshal, before storming off.

***

CHAPTER 22
REACTIONS

"You've got to see this!" Jordan doesn't bother knocking.

Ruger looks up from the final draft of his guide for Auctaireans. Now that the Despoliation is complete, it's time for him to give them the choice: They can follow Christ and stay in the land as assimilated Zyandites, or be sent to the GPU as refugees. A pamphlet with all of the details just needs to be handed out.

"Come on," Jordan motions a hand towards the hall.

The last thing Ruger needs is bad news. He wants his men home, and hopes whatever Jordan has to show him, doesn't cause a delay. Following Jordan downstairs, he can hear his men cheering from their makeshift rec room. Ruger picks up his pace to see Kira's interview projected on the wall. He doesn't like the makeup on her face, as she smiles at Wilma Marshal.

"Is that really true, King Anstone?" Captain Hiledal asks. "That tiny woman saved you?"

Ruger sits down beside the young Captain. "Yes, she did."

"She learned Zyandish in a month, who does that?" Sergeant Wright asks with a grin.

"Kira Westin, obviously," Ruger returns the grin.

"She's quite a woman," Jordan proclaims.

"Would someone please rewind it?" Ruger asks and as he watches the entire interview, his heart swells at Kira's bravery.

Once the interview is done, not only is the rec room twice as full, but everyone cheers for Kira, the God fearing woman who saved their king.

With a smirk, Ruger posts the evidence he found in Kira's favor on ZyanBell, proving she never agreed to outlaw Christianity. He also posts the damaging proof of Wilma's time in the Pazmirish Republic. Now that the information is public, with a satisfied fold of his arms Ruger leans back in his chair and awaits Zyandite's response...

***

"The feedback is amazing!" Rhonda shouts before running up to Kira's side in the kitchen, with her tablet in hand.

Kira chops carrots, while Nadia draws pictures at the bar. Both look at Rhonda's tablet to see why she's extra bubbly.

"Look, look, look!" Rhonda shouts and Kira reads the response. Almost everyone on ZyanBell praises her interview with Wilma. The amount of prayers being said for her and Ruger's union, really touch Kira's heart.

"I can't believe it," Kira whispers in awe.

"Praise God!" Rhonda exclaims.

Nadia peers over to read the screen. "Wow, mommy. Zyandites really like you."

Kira humbly nods, before resuming her work. Overwhelmed, she sets the knife down. "I can't believe how much God loves me."

Rhonda can't contain herself and gives Kira a hug.

***

Wilma sits on the floor of her closet, sipping wine. She tries to call Thorton Lazeed for the ninth time in a row, still, no answer. She hangs her head down and sobs.

***

Eleanor Kentwood answers her tablet with sophistication and grace. It's not often her husband calls her from outside of their borders. She knows the reason can't be good, and tries to keep her voice calm. "Hello, dear."

"Have you seen the interview?"

She rolls her eyes. "Yes."

"How can you be so indifferent?" General Kentwood's face turns beat red. "He's even going to let the heathens live!"

"For now, yes…" Eleanor beams a confident smile. "Sometimes, it takes the women to fix things. We have a plan."

Her husband's confusion dances across his brow.

Eleanor hides her irritation before she explains, "We've found the girl from the prophecy. She'll greet King Anstone when he comes home."

"He'll never fall for it."

"That's why you have to stay out of it. Make King Anstone think it's orchestrated by the great I Am. Once they're married, she'll talk sense into him. You'll see." Eleanor lifts a shoulder to her chin with a flirtatious wink.

"Who is it?" General Kentwood asks with a doubting huff.

Eleanor sticks her nose up with pride. "Isabella Ordan."

"Impressive…" General Kentwood's eyes soften. "Isabella can't mess this up. It's our last chance to stop him without risking a revolt."

"Oh, she won't." Eleanor blinks long and hard in order to hide her fear.

***

THE LINEAGE

Ruger walks with the evening patrol. The sun is just beginning to set in Auctairea, and already the people are carrying out their strange rituals.

A group of naked women dance together around a bonfire. Their dance is uncoordinated and sloppy. If his soldiers hadn't confiscated all of their drugs, he'd think they were intoxicated.

Tired of Auctairean filth, Ruger speeds up to pass along the information to these pathetic leaches, which have no hope to be self-sustaining. The pamphlets are ready: It's either leave for the GPU or convert to Christianity.

Most Auctaireans are thrilled by the chance to live under the umbrella of the GPU. It makes Ruger feel sick for their souls, but it's better than the alternative. These people aren't a threat anymore, not with their machines dismantled.

Flatironing them would be murder.

An armored vehicle pulls up nearby. Ruger watches his soldiers escort the so-called orderlies from that first Education Center out, to join the controlled group of Auctaireans. "I knew you'd find them," Ruger praises Sergeant Groth, who gives a slight bow of his chin.

Relieved that those young men will soon be on their way to the GPU, the man Ruger was hoping to see walks up with a healthier group of Auctaireans.

"My King," Carl slightly bows his chin. "I've prayed about your offer." He glances back at the crowd of mostly elderly people around him. Their eyes show the light of Christ. "I'm honored, but..." Carl glances at the crazed women behind Ruger and his eyes morph from disgust into pity before he brings them back to Ruger. "I can't take it. We both know I don't deserve to be in a leadership position. Besides, God wants me to go with them." Pulling out Kira's Bible from his coat, Carl lifts it up. "I've got work to do."

"The Pazmirish Republic outlawed religion years ago. You could be killed." Ruger nods at the Bible.

Carl's smile widens. "I know."

Proud of him, Ruger pats Carl's arm. "I'll be praying for you."

"Thanks."

Watching the crowd follow Carl, Ruger's not surprised to see them go straight to the farmland the drones once plowed. He knows they'll learn to be self-sufficient, and Zyandite won't have to coddle them. Cold air stings Ruger's skin and the stench of raw sewage fill his nostrils. Looking around at his men, their eyes are just as homesick as his.

Once the wicked are forced to flee from this land, it'll be time for his soldiers to return home…

***

After dinner, the sound of Nadia's occasional giggle plays like a song while Kira sits on Rhonda's back porch. The wooden swing she's on is beautifully carved with a few hearts on the back. Kira enjoys its relaxing sway.

Rhonda shows Nadia the various fish in her elaborate water fountain, with its four layers of pools that pour down in calming rhythm. The water fountain is a dark gray and while it would be gothic in any other setting, here it stands with a sophisticated presence. However, Kira's surprised the fountain is not green, since most everything Rhonda owns is.

Sipping her ice tea, Kira watches the large blue sky change colors as the sun sets. It's as though the sky is catching fire, with beautiful arrays of gold, rich orange, and deep pinks, all across the rows of light clouds that are too thin to block the sun's rays, but are thick enough to reflect God's masterpiece in the sky. "Nadia, look!" Kira points at the colorful lace patterns in the sky.

Nadia looks up and smiles. "Wow!"

Kira's overwhelmed with gratitude in this moment, for here they are, able to enjoy the sunset without fear. 'Oh God, thank you!' She silently prays before walking over to her daughter and hugging her under this free sky.

Rhonda's so blessed by the joy of freedom lived out before her, she

THE LINEAGE

pulls out her tablet. "Mind if I take a picture?"

Kira and Nadia turn to face her.

"What do I do?" Nadia asks since no one has ever taken her picture before.

"You just stand still, and be your beautiful self," Kira says, which causes Nadia to smile brightly.

The flash captures the beauty of their smiles. Satisfied, Rhonda sends it to Ruger.

***

Ruger's tablet chimes while a crazed Auctairean woman reacts to the news by running off screaming.

"We're going to the GPU!" She shouts.

Ruger shakes head while the gloom of the Auctairea sunset turns from light gray to a smoky black.

Opening his tablet, the picture of Kira and Nadia makes him smile. Ruger decides it's time to let them know the good news…

***

"Can I see the picture?" Nadia asks.

"Sure, here." Rhonda holds out her tablet and watches Nadia's eyes fill with wonder.

"Wow! How does it do that?" Nadia asks before handing the tablet back.

"I really don't know," Rhonda admits before laughing. "When I push a button, it captures the moment." Rhonda playfully shrugs, causing Nadia to giggle.

Kira retakes her seat and enjoys the rocking sensation. A soft breeze brings the fragrance of the river that intermixes with Rhonda's honeysuckles. Kira breathes it in with the sensation of peace covering her heart. This is how life should, be and she can't help her smile. In Zyandite, there are no Vagabonds lurking, and no jealous, strung out drug addicts watching their every move in hopes to find a weakness. There aren't even the stalking birds with their creepy eyes hoping to feed on death.

Not here.

Even the birds of Zyandite are pretty. Sparrows, red robins, colorful pigeons, and even a few blue birds fill the sky with splendor. The occasional hummingbird zips about in a blur and once in a while a hawk soars above. The mixture of oak trees, cacti, and hills, with clear skies, and fresh air makes Zyandite a place Kira could adore for the rest of her life.

"My goodness," Rhonda plops down on the bench, next to Kira. "Your little girl makes me want to be a mother."

"Will you settle for auntie?"

"Yes," Rhonda's tone is pleasant, but Kira can tell her mind is elsewhere.

"Is there a suiter on your mind?" Kira probes.

Rhonda looks at Kira with her green eyes concerned. "Actually, there is." Rhonda looks down before leaning forward to whisper, "But you see, it's very complicated. He thinks marrying me would upset my brother." Rhonda's face turns red. "We still message each other all the time."

"That's very sweet. I take it your mystery man is a soldier?" Kira asks.

Rhonda tries to hold in her laughter, as she waves a hand at Kira before nodding. "Yes. We've been courting for a very long time."

"How long?"

"A little over a year, but I think he's liked me for a lot longer than that."

Kira's smile fades. "Is that normal here? I mean, for a courtship."

Rhonda shrugs. "Everyone is different, but for us it's complicated. My brother is King, and Ruger has always been very protective of me."

"I understand complicated." Kira's finally comfortable enough to let Nadia play in Rhonda's backyard without constantly keeping an eye on her. "I worry I may be doing Ruger more harm than good."

"Not at all! The great I Am prepared us all for this with the prophecy." Rhonda's childlike carelessness sparkles in her eyes, making Kira smile.

"He did, didn't He?" Kira relaxes her arms as the sky blends between lavender and navy blue as the sun sets on Brustonite completely. "God will also help you and your secret love blossom too."

"I hope so. You know, we wanted to get married after the war, but we don't want to add to Ruger's stress."

Rhonda's selflessness swells Kira's heart, but she cannot help but to interject. "You are so thoughtful, but you also have to live your life. Ruger's mature and compassionate enough to understand."

Rhonda blushes again. "You're right."

Kira decides to teach Nadia the names of the constellations, but as she stands, she places a hand on Rhonda's shoulder. "Give it to God."

Rhonda pats Kira's hand. "Thanks."

Kira walks up to Nadia. There are only three constellations in sight behind the lacy clouds, but it's a start. They weren't able to enjoy the stars in Auctairea. Now, even with the breeze it's still warm out, and there's not a hint of threats anywhere around. Kira can enjoy being outside without fear. "Nadia, come see the Little Dipper."

Nadia rushes to her mom with her eyes full of wonder, as the stars glisten above Zyandite.

Rhonda's tablet chimes. "Hello, brother." She walks over to Kira. "It's for you."

Kira takes it and smiles.

"I will treasure this picture forever." Much to Kira's relief, Ruger looks healthier. He's standing outside of a tent, with only artificial lights giving her a glimpse of him. "I watched your interview."

"Really…" Kira bites her lip.

"I'm so proud of you."

All of Kira's muscles relax. "Good. I was worried you'd be mad."

Ruger holds in a laugh. "I can't imagine why."

The light in his eyes eases Kira's fears. "Good."

Ruger turns the camera to show the large field of dirt behind him. "Recognize Quandii, now?"

Her jaw drops as Kira tries to process what she's seeing. "You're kidding?"

"No." Ruger gives a sheepish grin. "My men have been working around the clock to recover the costs of this war. Now, we've just got to evacuate the civilians who are unwilling to assimilate."

"I'll bet that's most of them." Kira gives a knowing look.

The light in Ruger's eyes fades. "Unfortunately, you're right. Most are happy to be owned by the GPU."

"Hi, Ruger, look, we're learning about the stars," Nadia says while pointing at the sky.

Joy returns to Ruger's eyes. "I'm glad to hear that sweetheart, but guess what? We're coming home."

Kira gasps while Nadia begins jumping up and down.

"Ruger's coming home!" Nadia shouts loud enough for the whole neighborhood to hear.

"What?!" Rhonda runs over from the patio. "When?"

He smiles at her. "A few days."

"Yay!" Rhonda shouts before swooping Nadia in her arms and spinning her in a big circle.

At first Kira's heart rejoices, but fear creeps in. She can't help but worry that once Ruger comes home, everything will change.

***

CHAPTER 23
WORTHY ENOUGH?

Under the fog laced night, Auctaireans crowd the docks. These stragglers anxiously await their transport across the sea, to the tyrannical arms of the GPU.

Eyes hungry, they watch dozens of small, unmanned ships pull up to shore. Pre-programmed for their destination, once they board, there's no turning back. No one seems to mind being kicked off their land, in fact, most Auctaireans are thrilled to be sent under the umbrella of the GPU. In a frenzy, they almost sink the ships in the process of boarding.

A few Auctaireans fall overboard.

"Hey!" Carl shouts before trying to regain order. It's useless. After almost being pushed into the water himself, he steps back until everyone else is onboard, before rejoining the group.

From his vantage point at the edge of a cliff, Sergeant Desoto watches the spectacle through the scope of his rifle. Two Auctaireans get caught in a rip tide and bob away into the darkness, until their screaming can no longer be heard. It's an unnecessary loss, due to the dog-eat-dog bullying. With plenty of seats for everyone, there's no excuse to behave like wild animals.

Sergeant Desoto's stomach curls at their inhumanity.

Without oversight, these adults are worse than feral children. They're not just primal, but predators.

Sergeant Desoto's comfortable with taking them out, but the King's order gnaws at his heart.

Last night he went from packing in his room, happily readying to leave this place. Anna was on the line, with their newly born son cooing in the background. Sergeant Desoto just wants to meet his boy in person, but couldn't even enjoy the privilege of video call.

Not with General Kentwood at his door.

It was so shocking to be visited by a Charge Commander; Sergeant Desoto didn't hang up the call. He muted it, dropped it in his pocket and opened the door.

"Son, Zyandite needs you to purify the waters." General Kentwood's brow was furrowed. Eyes heavy with concern, he laced Sergeant Desoto's record with pride, 'The best sniper in Zyandite,' before giving a verbal death blow. "I know our King believes these people deserve life, but his bloodline has inclusions. He isn't pure enough to make sound decisions regarding the pagans. They can't share how we operate with the Pazmirish Republic, and let's face it; these despicable individuals don't deserve to breed." He lifted his chin. "I can assure that you won't get caught. If successful in your mission, you'll ride home with me." He placed a hand on Sergeant Desoto's shoulder. "I heard that you have a son. Think of what this can do for him."

Sergeant Desoto never agreed to the plan. He didn't have to. General Kentwood left the room without giving him a chance to say no.

To disobey the King means certain death, but something else burns in Sergeant Desoto's chest. All of his life, he's dealt with the discrimination against his blood. General Kentwood's words against King Anstone's purity, felt personal to his own. They're words Sergeant Desoto has heard, many times. Since the lines are drawn, this sniper chooses a side. Letting out a cold breath, he knows the generals are close enough to listen for the shots. He's been in this position a thousand times, yet it's never felt like murder, until now.

Anna had a clearer head, and managed to record the conversation from her end. Even that could be considered blackmail of a Charge Commander, an offense for which could also equal death. They agreed to keep the recording secret, but Sergeant Desoto can't imagine betraying King Anstone, not after all he's done for New Bloods.

"The great I Am, please, make them silent. Make it seem like I did what the General wants." Sergeant Desoto knows exactly where to shoot to make these boats sink. The recoil against his shoulder is familiar, but the splashes on the water are not. He's never missed a living target, and can only keep shooting by imagining he's shooting fish.

The Auctaireans scream. They can, until he stops shooting. If they don't stop, he'll have to reload and make this real.

After hundreds of shots, Sergeant Desoto removes his finger from the trigger and watches the Auctaireans sail away in shock.

The great I Am answered his prayer, for their shock is silent.

***

Since they took down the police station, Ruger and his men have been staying in their own tent city. While these are Zyandite built, military grade shelters, they don't entirely block out the chill. The last few nights, it's snowed. A white dusting on the ground only adds to their discomfort. Gathering up what's left of his paperwork, Ruger's excited to take down his tent. It's their last day in Auctairea, and he can't leave fast enough. A light waving at the entrance causes Ruger to look up, just as General Kentwood steps in.

"Are the enlisted in route?" Ruger asks, barely glancing at the general as he packs.

"Yes." The seasoned general zips up the nylon door. His eyes are troubled, sad even. "But that's not why I'm here."

Ruger raises a brow, but doesn't stop packing.

"There's a rift between two pillars of Zyandite's stability. It goes against the oath we both took against division. I know a big part of that is the untimely death of General Baxton."

Silence fills the tent as Ruger stops packing and folds his arms. "You wouldn't let my surgeon perform an autopsy. If that's not suspicious, nothing is. Not even this…" Ruger taps the sensor behind his ear.

"I have no explanation for that." General Kentwood briefly raises his hands. "However, I can go against my word to a dear friend, if it means saving my country. Zyandite is worth my honor." His eyes glisten, surprising Ruger. He never thought General Kentwood capable of crying. "Amanda Baxton has impeccable Lineage. She's the reason her husband was chosen for Command. She deeply cares about the Lineage, including the Lineage of her son. Detrick is a fine soldier. He proved that in Kaddain."

"Yes," Ruger says, "I remember awarding the young Lieutenant with a Golden Sphere. Why would his Lineage be tainted?"

"Because his father had a dirty secret. You see, after General Baxton's brother died in battle, the loss was detrimental. General Baxton didn't come out of retirement just to serve, but to run from the pain. Zyandite wine isn't strong enough to kill anyone, it would take gallons. Auctairean booze on the other hand, was too much for him." General Kentwood wipes a tear. "I couldn't let his cause of death be on record, or Lieutenant Baxton would've been disgraced."

Relief causes Ruger's shoulders to drop. "I wish you would've told me."

"I'm telling you now." The General's chest lifts in pride.

"I understand why you did it, but a lie is still a lie."

"Amanda begged me to keep it secret. How could I scorn a widow?"

"The way you've scorned Kira?" Ruger yells louder than he meant to.

"You're right," General Kentwood lowers his chin. "To my disgrace, I've been closed minded to your decision. And while there's not a law to stop you from marrying her, at least consider the long term affects such a union could have on our country. Think of the men and what they've seen here. Will they project that on Kira?"

Ruger frowns. "I'm sure they respect individualism enough to not categorize her in a group. Besides, the prophecy is rather convincing, isn't it?"

"The great I Am may have a different path?" General Kentwood shrugs. "Look, I went back on my word to a widow, in order to maintain my oath against division. I have to live with that, but some things are more important than pride. In our positions, we aren't free. All I'm asking is for you to reconsider the engagement. Not for the Lineage, but for Zyandite. For unity. Ezra chapter ten shows how the great I Am deals with his people marrying pagans."

"Kira's not a pagan, General," Ruger says while letting out a sigh.

"I know Kira's faith is what attracted you to her, but she's still born of a pagan race. Think of the implications that can have on Zyandite. Imagine, if King Tidal had survived and brought home a Kaddainese woman for his bride?" General Kentwood shivers at the thought. "Just think about it. Pray about it. Kira and Nadia can have beautiful lives with the other Auctaireans. She'll be compensated for her bravery, and given a large plot of land up here. We'll even build her a mansion, whatever she wants, Kira will have. Her life will be a thousand times better than it was before she met you. Regardless, it's your choice. I just want the pillars of government to heal, and won't press this matter any further."

Ruger tilts his head, contemplating. "What does this healing involve?"

General Kentwood holds up a weary hand. "Keeping our oaths. Nothing more, nothing less."

"Unity?"

"Unity."

"Alright." Ruger brings himself to smile. "I appreciate you clearing up this loose end."

"Will you at least consider my suggestion?"

Ruger's eyes become distant. It's the last thing he wants, but his General is right. He can't imagine having a queen born from Kaddain, and hadn't looked at from that angle. The Kaddainese were so barbaric, it isn't right comparing Kira to them. The argument has merit, but it hurts his heart. A feeling of dread builds in his core. Ruger knows this feeling. It only comes from God. "I'll pray about it."

"Good. And don't worry my King, General Danning will find your vitals." General Kentwood smiles before saluting Ruger.

Ruger returns it. "May the great I Am bless your travels."

"Thank you, I can't wait to get home."

Both men smile before General Kentwood leaves Ruger with a rekindled trust.

Outside, the General smirks. Pulling out his tablet, he presses the icon for his wife and begins typing.

You had better get Isabella ready. The King's ready to heel.

General Kentwood's eyes sparkle at his clever pun. He then squares his shoulders with the confidence of victory.

***

Kira sits on a window seat, watching the planes fly in. Descending on the same flight path, one after another, they land in Brustonite.

"He won't be on any of those," Rhonda says, pulling Kira from sky-watching.

"The king is always the last one home," Kira recites.

"Yes, it's his duty to his men."

"It's admirable, but I'd prefer he was first, the way he is in battle," Kira admits.

"Me too," Rhonda peaks out to watch the planes and smiles. "Well, I'm going to get ready. I'm so sorry you can't join the homecoming ceremony."

"It's alright. We'd only be able to greet him from the street anyhow."

"True, but it's better than nothing." Rhonda steps out of the room to get changed before the doorbell rings. "Who could that be?" She furrows her brow.

Kira steps to the loft and listens as Rhonda opens the door.

"Shouldn't you be with Brian?" Rhonda asks.

Kira steps down the stairs to see Farrah's in the entryway. She's wearing a mint ball gown with two simple rows of rhinestones that fall from her shoulders, all the way to the floor. "I caught wind of something and came here as fast as I could." Her eyes meet Kira's. "You have to go tonight."

"I can't even step on the castle grounds. It would be silly for me to go," Kira says.

"I know, but the Lineage has a new battle plan." Farrah nurses a headache. "Sandra overheard Chantel Danning bragging about their trap."

Rhonda grimaces. "Trap?"

"No matter what Ruger does, they have a hook. They're trying to manipulate the prophecy by making it about a Zyandite instead of Kira." Farrah throws her hands at her sides. "They even found one that looks like her."

"How audacious! I must warn him." Rhonda pulls out her tablet to message Ruger.

"Brian already tried. Message failed," Farrah says, just as Rhonda receives that exact text on her screen. "This is just another account of the Lineage trying to play God."

Since her tablet is useless for warning her brother, Rhonda sets it down. "I'm so sick of it."

"As am I." Farrah turns to Kira. "General Kentwood has a leadership role and a mansion planned out in Auctairea, just for you. If Ruger complies, the Lineage will own the throne, and you'll be bribed into silence."

"Nadia would be safe?" Kira asks.

With a roll of her eyes Farrah places her hands on her hips. "Nadia's always safe, here. This isn't just about you and her, but the integrity of a nation. The idolatrous hearts of the Lineage can no longer rule Zyandite."

"Who are they going to thrust on him this time?" Rhonda asks.

"Isabella Ordan." Farrah presses her lips together as Rhonda's color fades.

"I thought she was engaged?" Rhonda practically screams.

Farrah shrugs. "I don't know, but apparently, they've used Ezra chapter ten to manipulate your brother. It sounds like surefire victory, but the great I Am gave the prophecy to me. I would've recognized Isabella Ordan."

"Is she King Ordan's descendant?" Kira asks.

"You know our history," Rhonda mumbles.

Kira should be outraged, or at the very least emotionally stung. Yet, the weight of inadequacy is too heavy for anything else to get through. "A pure born Zyandite with Lineage like that would certainly help Ruger..." Kira whispers without realizing she said her thoughts aloud.

"What?" Rhonda shouts while Farrah presses her fingers to her lips in silent prayer.

"It was a nice fantasy while it lasted, but we all know I don't deserve your brother." Feeling a tear roll down her cheek, Kira wipes it away to find both her cheeks are wet. How she could cry while feeling this numb is beyond her. "All marrying me will do is cause him trouble." She looks away. "Just like I caused *them* trouble."

"So, you're going to take the generals' offer and run?" Farrah asks.

Dreading how Nadia will react causes Kira's lips to tremble. "Yes."

Farrah kneels to be at eye level. "You're talking like a coward."

Kira shakes her head. "I'm sparing Zyandite from my weaknesses."

"Weaknesses? You've fought for your faith in the land of the godless, and rose up in victory!" Farrah's jaw drops at the defeat in Kira's eyes. "How can you give up on the great I Am?"

"I'm not, but it's because of me His people died. Can't you see that? I got Joplin elected. How dare I waltz into a Christian Kingdom thinking I have a right to rule it?!" Kira didn't mean to shout and bites her lip.

"If Peter could deny Christ three times yet still lead ministry, certainly the great I Am can redeem you." Farrah says.

"This isn't about ministry, it's about politics. Both Ruger and Zyandite would be better off if I step aside." The weight on Kira's heart crushes her shoulders.

"I thought you loved my brother." Rhonda asks so lowly, Kira hardly heard her.

"I love him enough to leave him."

Farrah closes her eyes for a moment. "Holy Spirit, please guide me," She whispers before opening her eyes. "You love justice and hate evil. Therefore God, your God, has anointed you, pouring out the oil of joy on you more than anyone else. Myrrh, aloes, and cassia perfume your robes. In ivory palaces the music of strings entertains you. Kings' daughters are among your noble women. At your right hand stands the queen wearing jewelry of the finest gold from Ophir! Listen to me, O royal daughter; take to heart what I say. Forget your people and your family far away. For your royal husband delights in your beauty; honor him, for he is your lord." Farrah quotes Psalm 45:7-11 before standing. "Do you think God made a mistake when he sent Ruger crashing into your life?"

The verses cut through Kira's spirit to where she can't even speak. God's love is so undeserved, only her tears can flow.

"The Lineage will use and abuse Ruger. They'll enrich themselves and leave the rest of Zyandite in the dirt. The great I Am gave me a dream to prepare the people for you." Farrah leans over. "By the way, the woman in my dream had brown eyes, your eyes. Isabella Ordan's eyes are hazel. You see, this isn't about you. It's about God." She straightens her posture and awaits Kira's response.

Kira still doesn't believe she's worthy of the crown, but Farrah's words have pierced her heart. She can't bring herself to say no. "I'll go."

"Praise the great I Am!" Farrah exclaims before looking at Rhonda. "I've got to get back, or it'll raise suspicions." She looks at Kira once more. "I'll see *you* there."

Kira doesn't say a word. The conflict within her wages on. She doesn't deserve this honor, and knows it would be easier to strike a deal with the generals'. Nadia's life would be safe, but God promised her something more. Kira brings herself to speak, "Forgive me for my doubts." After praying, she looks up at Rhonda. Her brow is creased with worry, making Kira smile to ease her stress. "I need your help picking out a dress."

Rhonda's shoulders drop in relief, "Of course."

***

CHAPTER 24
HOMECOMING

Ruger's heart aches from the fatigue of these wars, until the bright lights of Brustonite catch his eye. The burden of Auctairea lifts off of his chest and he straightens his posture, ready to land.

The soldiers around him smile and begin to talk about their families, before the wheels of this plane finally touch the ground.

Closing his eyes, Ruger whispers a prayer of praise to God, because now, he's home.

They taxi down the runway, before the plane comes to a complete stop.

"Finally!" Jordan exclaims with a smile.

Ruger rises to his position at the door. Once it's opened, the lowest ranking is the first to venture off the plane. As their king, it is Ruger's honor to shake hands with each one of his men, until finally, only General Brice remains. Ruger motions his hand towards the steps.

With a slight bow of his head, the Charge Commander walks away from King Anstone, breathing the moist air of Brustonite in deeply.

Now that the plane is empty, Ruger runs down the steps, before marching onto the pavement of the dark runway. He doesn't follow Jordan and the rest of his men. Instead, Ruger steps off of the pavement, and

THE LINEAGE

kneels onto the bare ground.

"The great I Am, thank you for Zyandite," Ruger praises, before taking a fistful of dirt and pounding it against his chest, in a symbolic salute to his home.

After standing up, even in this poor lighting, Ruger can see the perplexity on General Brice's face. "Must you do that every time we return?"

Ruger exhales deeply. "Yes."

On the bus ride to the castle, Ruger smiles once the tower and main chapel come into view. Following tradition, hundreds of retired soldiers and their families gather on the sidewalk, cheering the troops as they come home. Once he's in their view, Ruger will have to smile. He doesn't know how he can do that, not with the turmoil in his heart. He shouldn't consider the General's option, but he did take an oath. Holding his head down, he silently asks the great I Am for peace...

***

Wilma Marshal stands before the castle as Benson, steadily holds his tablet up to film her. Her gown is a deep sapphire that appears black under the artificial lights. The sun set hours ago, and the last plane from Auctairea just landed. Behind her, rows of soldiers enter the open gates into the courtyard of the castle, where their families and the ceremony await them.

"This is so exciting," Wilma beams. "Our troops are finally home!" She glances at the road as a new bus pulls up to the sidewalk. "Just one more to go and the King will be here." Wilma motions her hand at the crowd. "What a greeting he'll receive." She walks towards the crowd of joyful Zyandites. "I love seeing our flag everywhere." Wilma adds before abruptly stopping. "Oh, my..." She points at a woman standing on the sidewalk. Isabella made sure to wear the golden necklace Wilma gave her, over the silver gown that Eleanor picked out. Nervous, she scans the street for the last bus.

"Could that be the woman from the prophecy?" Wilma looks at the camera and dramatically covers her mouth. "The resemblance is undeniable. I mean, wow."

Isabella follows instructions, and pretends to not know Wilma, even as she gets closer.

"Who is she?" Wilma asks Benson who not only shakes his head, but the tablet.

"Her dress, her hair, everything is exactly what Farrah described." Wilma's smile broadens. "All that's missing is the crown…"

***

Kira sits in Rhonda's car, staring out the window. She'll never get tired of the city lights, and soaks in the view that sparkles like a million diamonds. Wearing a beautiful cream dress that's crafted in velvet and lace, she still feels naked. The only thing keeping her chin up is God's promise. After the plans Farrah shared with her, Kira feels like she's going up against an army." fearing people is a dangerous trap, but trusting the LORD means safety." Kira whispers Proverbs 29:25.

"Hey," Rhonda reaches a hand out to Kira. "Don't cry. It might mess up your makeup"

Kira laughs before taking Rhonda's hand. "I love you, and no matter what happens, I hope we can remain friends?"

"You're the sister I've always dreamed of having." Rhonda squeezes Kira's hand. "And my sister you will be."

"I hope so," Kira let's go of Rhonda's hand and looks out the window.

"Why can't we go into the castle?" Nadia asks.

"Oh sweetie, I already told you. We're not Zyandites yet, and only citizens are allowed inside."

"It's not fair, we'll miss the party." Nadia may be sitting like a perfect little lady in her green dress, but masters grumbling just the same.

"It's the rules, Nadia. Whether we like it or not, we must respect them," Kira says. "Don't you want to thank Ruger for bringing us to his home?"

THE LINEAGE

"Yeah, and I want to thank him for my elephant and new clothes, too!" Nadia exclaims.

Kira forces a smile. "Then relax, sweetheart."

"It's really not a big deal missing the formalities, they'd probably bore you," Rhonda says with a wave.

"You don't have to stay with us. Your driver knows the way back." Kira forces a smile. "Enjoy the ceremony."

"No." Rhonda's kind face is determined. "I'd rather be with you two." She does a happy dance in her seat. "We're almost there!"

The sky is dark, but beautiful. Thousands of artificial lights cause the night air to glow. The sidewalk that leads up the castle's private road is only a short walk from the car, but Kira knows once they turn that bend, there'll be a crowd waiting.

Rhonda intertwines her arm with Kira's, and practically drags her along.

Nadia takes her mother's other arm, causing Kira to smile. It's November, Kira should feel the crunching of ice underfoot, yet all she feels is the heat. "Is it always this warm in November?" Kira whispers.

Rhonda turns with a frown. "Are you kidding, it's freezing!"

Holding in a laugh, Kira rests her head on Rhonda's shoulder for a moment. The honesty of this innocent, yet fierce woman has been a blessing in Kira's life. Straightening her posture, Kira frowns. In just a few moments, the hope of being securely attached to Ruger and his sister, will either be affirmed, or die.

***

Ruger manages to smile for the people. It may be nightfall, but the artificial lights are bright enough to showcase their faces. Even during a huge event like this, people keep a large gap in-between each other. In Zyandite, it's courtesy to not crowd on your neighbor. With Jordan by his side, they walk towards the castle grounds. Ruger should feel excitement for the ceremony. His troops deserve the recognition, but all his heart yearns for, is to sign Kira and Nadia into citizenship. If anything, he can at least give them that.

Out of the corner of his eye, a familiar face draws him. At first, he thinks it's Kira standing on the sidewalk. Blushing, Ruger worries how he'll conduct damage control for the broken rule. Walking up to her, he looks for Nadia, but she's not there. Once he gets closer, he sees the woman in silver, isn't Kira at all. Arrogance fills this woman's hazel eyes, making Ruger frown. He can't be rude and tilts his chin at her, before turning away.

"King Anstone?"

Ruger pretends he didn't hear her.

"I desperately need help with settling a family dispute. It's a complete injustice against me, and no one else can settle this matter, but you," Isabella pleads.

Smile faded, Ruger can't ignore her appeal and turns to face her.

***

Farrah steps out on the castle balcony. Silently, she prays for King Anstone's protection from the trap the Lineage has set. Searching for Ruger, the crowd below Farrah is full of a joy she wishes she shared. Finally, she catches sight of him, and her heart nearly stops once she sees who he's talking to.

Just the sight of Isabella makes Farrah scowl. "No, the great I Am, please, not her."

***

"Would you look at that?" Wilma points at Ruger's close proximity to Isabella. "I think we're about to see the great I Am move." She looks at the camera, teary eyed.

Their plan seems to be working.

THE LINEAGE

***

"I know it's rude to approach you after just coming home, but it's a matter of life or death for me." Isabella's nearly in tears. "You see, my brothers came home tonight, and told me they're going to keep the boundaries of our father's property for themselves. I'll be left with nothing."

"That goes against their honor." Ruger pulls out his tablet. "What's the address?"

"7141 Kantura Drive."

Ruger's brow furrows. "It's not coming up."

Isabella's shoulders slouch. "I was afraid of that. You see, it's been in my family for generations. I would've searched for it in the castle archives, but I couldn't get through."

Everything in Ruger screams this is another ploy of the Lineage. Usually one of his generals or their wives will be standing by, watching like a bird of prey, hoping he'll take the bait. Scanning the crowd of happy faces, other than Wilma, there's not a single member of the Lineage in sight. Suspicions eased, Ruger makes the choice to help this woman himself. "You're not Lineage?"

She looks down. "My bloodline isn't important."

"That's an injustice all on its own, don't you think, miss?"

"Isabella." She gives an innocent smile.

"I'll tell you what. After the ceremony, I'll—"

"Ruger!" Rhonda's voice sounds above the cheering.

He turns towards the street, where his sister stands with Kira and Nadia. Ruger can't help his smile, and nearly forgets about Isabella.

"King Anstone?" Isabella taps his arm. "Will you help me?"

Ruger looks at her. "Of course. General Brice?" He shouts before smiling. "I'll have my Charge Commander look into this for you, right away."

The innocence on Isabella's face drips into stung egotism. "Oh, okay." She looks at the ground. "Thank you."

General Brice steps up beside Ruger. "What do you need?"

"Take this woman into the records hall, and help her establish the boundary lines of her inheritance." Ruger glances at Isabella. "Goodbye, miss." He walks away, leaving her shaking.

***

Wilma's lips snarl at the defeat, before she remembers the camera is on her. She bares her teeth with a smile. "Looks like the King's sister's here. Too bad she showed up with a foreigner, otherwise she could join us real Zyandites in the castle."

Benson follows King Anstone's every step with his tablet. Once the King reaches the edge of the castle grounds, he steps onto the street, causing the crowd to stop cheering as they watch his interaction with Kira in silence.

***

CHAPTER 25
MILITARY TRADITIONS AND CHANGE

Kira can't take her eyes off Ruger. Expecting a wave or perhaps a hello in return, she's surprised to see him step away from the castle to be near her.

With hundreds of Zyandites watching, this is where Ruger's intentions and her future collide.

Ruger stops only a few inches before her.

Everyone and everything seems still. Kira can't find the words. She can't do anything but breathe. He's Zyandite's King, she's merely an Auctairean. The only thing that keeps Kira from succumbing to her doubts is God's promise.

His lips move, but instead of saying a word, Ruger takes her by the waist and spins her in the air once, before kissing her.

The crowd cheers, but Kira can hardly hear them. His lips are softer than the velvet. She's too lost in their kiss to notice anything else. Ruger pulls his lips away just to smile, before he kisses her again. This time, she hears the crowd.

"Hooray for King Anstone and our future queen!"

Kira doesn't care about titles. She just wants to soak Ruger in, and could kiss him forever.

Slowly, he pulls away. "It's so good to see you." Ruger says before directing his eyes to Nadia. He lets go of Kira and bends to Nadia's level. "Hello, sweetheart. How's Zyandite treating you?" Ruger asks with the same kindness that won Kira's heart.

"Great!" Nadia wraps her little arms around Ruger's neck. "Thank you for bringing us here."

"You're welcome, sweetheart," Ruger says before Nadia pulls away from their embrace.

The people are obviously touched by Nadia's adoration for Ruger. The whispered words of kindness makes Kira smile.

Ruger gives Rhonda a tight hug. "Thank you, Sis."

"It's my pleasure."

Ruger looks back at Kira. "I want nothing more than to invite you in, but I can't make you a citizen just yet. I have to lead our formalities, first."

"It's alright. I got to see you. That's enough," Kira says.

Ruger kisses her once more. It's too short for Kira's liking. His eyes stare at her with longing, before he rushes into the castle.

As the crowd begins to follow their King, many Zyandites pay their respects to Kira. She stands there in a daze, hardly hearing anything they say, while Nadia stands beside her and waves.

It only takes a few moments before everyone else is inside, except the trio of ladies. As traditional Zyandite songs begin to play, they turn to leave.

***

From the edge of a balcony in the front of the castle, Farrah watches the exchange between Ruger and Kira with a smile. Voices in the hall behind her cause Farrah to turn around.

"Look at that! My brothers have agreed to the plot of land I requested after all." Isabella holds up her tablet and lies with a smile. "I'm sorry to have bothered you."

"No worries. It's perfect timing, actually. Now, you can enjoy the ceremony," General Brice says before walking away, leaving Isabella alone in the hall.

Isabella's eyes meet with Farrah's with a mixture of guilt and defeat, before she runs off.

"Cover their faces with shame, LORD, so that they will seek your face." Farrah quotes Psalm 83:16 before praying, "Be with her, but convict her so she'll repent." Letting out a sigh of relief, Farrah pulls out her tablet to message Brian:

Praise the great I Am. Their plan failed.

***

Directly centered on the sapphire stage rests a mahogany podium, where Brian waits for everyone to take their seats. Rows of red, white, and gold stringed lights hang above the ballroom named Cathleen, in honor of King Widorsa's wife. The carpet spirals like long sapphires over silver clouds, while the tables are spread out enough to leave room for formations. Every detail is significant, but not so much as the joy of the families reunited with their loved ones.

King Anstone walks in, causing the room to erupt with cheering.

Brian grins more at the message from Farrah, than the return of his King. Discreetly putting his tablet away, Brian waits for the crowd to stop clapping before he speaks. "Two wars, two victories," Brian's voice echoes through the room. "Zyandite, this is a time of celebration and praise." He opens his Bible to Psalm 54:6-7: "I will praise your name, O LORD, for it is good. For you have rescued me from my troubles and helped me to triumph over my enemies."

Ruger takes a seat at the round table in front. Behind him, the generals glare from their polished brass at his flight uniform. Ruger still has the dirt of Auctairea on him and chose not to waste time on changing. Ignoring their scowls, Ruger holds his chin up.

Chantel Danning's dark hair is twisted into a dramatic bun. Lips painted with gold, she can't hide her nervous frown. Leaning towards her husband, she whispers in his ear, "Better unlock his account."

General Danning frowns before looking around for Isabella. She's nowhere in sight. He carefully pulls out his tablet and takes the shadow off Ruger's account. Exchanging glances with his wife, they silently share the agony of defeat, before focusing on Brian.

Ruger feels his tablet rumble from his pocket. Worried it's Rhonda, he pulls it out to see the messages Brian and Rhonda sent earlier, warning of Isabella. The disappointment in one of his own lying about her bloodline doesn't even phase him. Not now, when the treachery of his generals' is apparent. Ruger puts his tablet away, knowing General Danning prevented him from both receiving messages, and looking up Isabella's address. If his Satellite Charge Commander lacks the integrity to do that, he's also capable of masquerading Ruger's vitals. Silently thanking the great I Am for protecting him thus far, Ruger seeks guidance on how to address it.

***

Isabella steps into the ballroom and her eyes lock with Eleanor. She shakes her head, making Eleanor press her red lips together.

Dressed in a black gown etched with real pearls, Eleanor exhibits grace, even when she's angry. She can't get up to ask Isabella what happened, not until after the King speaks. After exchanging a disappointed glance with Wilma, Eleanor frowns.

Ruger doesn't notice the exchange while he focuses on his responsibilities. Waiting for his cue, Ruger allows his concerns to melt away as Brian leads in prayer.

"The great I Am, we cannot praise your holy name enough. These wars have battered our hearts, but you've strengthened them with victory. Each time we felt the desire to quit, you lifted us to our feet. When our King seemed lost, you saved him with the unexpected. That blessing, like so many you give, was multifaceted, and ended up giving us a swift and painless victory over our invader. This victory, like the victory over

THE LINEAGE

Kaddain, belongs to you. We're humbled by your love, and ask that you cover us in peacetime the way you covered us in battle. Fill us with your wisdom and purify our land of anything that could make us fall into sin. Be with Zyandite, always, and never let our hearts be harden towards you. In the mighty name of Jesus Christ we pray, amen."

After the room murmurs with 'amen," Brian motions his hand towards Ruger. "And now I'd like to introduce, the people's King!"

Most of the Lineage in the room rolls their eyes at that title.

Ruger ignores them as he walks to the podium. Before speaking, he scans the eyes of each soldier in the room. Zyandite belongs to them, and it's his job to make sure they know they're appreciated and protected. Following peace, Ruger is strengthened by God to do what can no longer be put off.

"My fellow Zyandites, I dedicate these victories to the great I Am. We've fought hard, and I'm so proud of you." He ignores his generals while looking at every other set of eyes in the room. "It's through faith in the great I Am, and your patriotism, that Zyandite stands free. The things we saw in both Kaddain and Auctairea were only confirmation that our laws and society are just, righteous, and pure. We must protect that. Yes, we have many foreign souls who are now a part of our homeland, but our culture must remain what our founders created: a society based on godly precepts in constant pursuit of holiness and courage. This is why we fight. This is why we must remain united." He now eyes each Lineage general, slowly. "We can't allow enemy forces to invade the land God has given us, nor can we allow the discrimination of bloodlines to separate us."

Gasps fill the room as the non-lineage smile, while every member of the Lineage squirms.

"Tonight is supposed to be a night of festivity, but as we celebrate our dual victories, why not also make this a night of change?" Ruger says while relaxing his shoulders.

General Kentwood's so angry he nearly stands, but Eleanor places a hand on his shoulder to stop him.

Ruger smirks at General Kentwood. "I took an oath to never divide my country, but unfortunately, it was divided long before I was born. That ends tonight." He looks directly into the eyes of his Charge Commanders. "From now on, any form of discrimination against Zyandites, to include every child adopted from Auctairea, and our future queen, is hereby illegal."

Every enlisted soldier and their families rise up to cheer.

Rage in the senior generals' eyes is replaced with alarm. They're far outnumbered to protest the King's decree, let alone stop it.

"I may be your King, but you're all my brothers and sisters in Christ," Ruger proclaims.

The cheering only gets louder.

"Holiness, purity, honor, and integrity are spiritual, and come directly from the great I Am. No one, no matter who their ancestors were, can be righteous without Him. We were all reborn with purity, the day we were baptized. Segregating New Bloods from the Lineage, has crushed the opportunities, dreams, and relationships of our countrymen. Enough. We've all had enough. Tomorrow, I'll officially announce my engagement to Kira, which will seal the end of this discrimination for good." Ruger says with a grin. Most of the soldiers in the room cheer, uplifting his heart. "Now, let's celebrate!" Ruger claps once before stepping off the stage. Per tradition, the singing of Zyandite's National Anthem fills the room.

"This is a travesty," General Danning whispers to General Fisher, who only shakes his head.

"We knew this would happen when a New Blood was crowned. There's no use in trying to stop it," General Fisher says before looking at his wife and daughter. Catrina's age allows her to hide defeat with grace, but it's the hope in sixteen year old Lynn's face that he must address. "Please, excuse me," General Fisher says before leaving the table.

"He's wrong," General Kentwood tells his wife, before standing to join in the singing.

Eleanor can't take it. With tears in her eyes, she rushes over to where Isabella sits. "What happened?" She hasps, making the other women at the table stop singing to exchange glances.

Isabella nearly breaks into tears. "I'm sorry, I couldn't pull it off." She hands Eleanor Wilma's necklace and runs out of the room.

THE LINEAGE

Looking at the locket in her hand, Eleanor's brow furrows. She opens it to discover the hidden camera, and all color drains from her face.

***

CHAPTER 26
BREAKDOWN

Isabella runs through the hallway, passing a young couple in distress. She's too upset to notice the woman is crying, before leaving the castle and her dreams of being queen, forever.

"How could he?" Stella Wagnor sobs into her husband's chest. Impeccable curls wave down to the small of her back, but no matter how much work she put into looking presentable for this event, the puffiness from her tears made it all for naught.

"Shhh," Lieutenant Wagnor rubs her neck. "We'll just play along until the generals' figure something out."

Stella leans into him and closes her eyes. "Lying goes against purity."

"If lying preserves purity, than we must." He kisses the top of her head. "Enough of this… Celebration. Let's go home." Lieutenant Wagnor wraps an arm around Stella's shoulders.

On the way to the parking lot she locks eyes with a young Captain's wife, whose face shares the horror Stella feels. "This isn't over," she declares as her husband opens the door to her car.

Lieutenant Wagnor's eyes harden. "No, it's not."

***

"You kicked the hornet's nest," Brian says as Ruger sits at the table beside him.

Ruger shrugs. "They tried to use my oath against me." He takes his tablet out and shows Brian the delayed messages. "All while manipulating my account... Again?" He gives Brian a knowing look before putting his tablet away.

Brian adjusts his seating. "You'll need more proof than that."

Several soldiers make way to speak with their King. "It's out there. The great I Am will lead me to it," Ruger says before standing to shake their hands.

Behind him, General Fisher steps up to a table of enlisted soldiers. Eyes set on a handsome young man with a few bars of medals on his uniform, the old General puffs out his chest. "One of the benefits of being a Charge Commander is I have access to conversations most would rather keep secret."

Sergeant Mack Bazin's spine tightens, but he doesn't say a word.

General Fisher watches his every move. "I've known about you and Lynn since we came home from Kaddain, and," His tone softens. "I know how much you love her. Go, ask her to dance."

The young Sergeant's shoulders relax before he rises to his feet, and shakes General Fisher's hand.

Across the room, Lynn watches with heavy anticipation. Before Sergeant Bazin can ask her to dance, she embraces her father. "Thank you, daddy."

"The Lineage can't control us anymore," he says before letting her go to dance with the man she loves. He looks at Catrina, who allows her disappointment to morph into acceptance. Ignoring the disapproval on Chantel Danning's face, Catrina takes her husband's hand and joins him on the dance floor.

Eleanor walks over to General Danning and shows him Wilma's necklace. "What is this?" She asks before looking at Wilma.

Wilma smiles before noticing what Eleanor's holding. Her smile fades. Immediately, Wilma turns to General Danning.

General Danning glances at the necklace and his eyes darken. "That's not your concern."

Eleanor gasps. "On your honor, tell me. Did Wilma use—"

"Yes," General Danning interrupts her with rage flickering in his eyes like a flame.

"What's going on?" General Kentwood asks.

"Have the Satellite Charge Commander show you Frank Marshal's vitals." Eleanor leans over to whisper in her husband's ear, "from *before* he was married."

General Kentwood glares at General Danning, who won't even look at him.

Wilma gets up and reaches a hand out to Eleanor. "Seems you found my necklace."

Eleanor clutches it to her chest. "You little—"

"Don't make a scene," General Kentwood warns while glancing around the room.

Wilma's eyes are smug. "May I have it back?"

Slamming the necklace into her hand, Eleanor straightens her spine. "You've tainted your Lineage. I disown you."

"That's illegal now." Wilma smirks before pulling the necklace away. "Frank, it's time to go."

Eleanor watches General Marshal stand. His eyes are broken, almost dead. The realization that Wilma's owned him this entire time, strikes Eleanor's heart. Upon seeing the torment in his eyes, Eleanor's anger turns to pity. "How could you?"

General Kentwood steps between them. "This isn't the time. Let them go."

Wilma locks arms with her husband and laughs right in Eleanor's face, before leaving.

From the King's table, Ruger watches the exchange. Eyes locked with General Kentwood, Ruger knows there's more to be discovered than his lost vitals.

***

Wilma sways her hips as she leads Frank down the hall to their apartment. Frank Marshal stares at the floor. They step into their colorless suite and Wilma slips off her shoes.

"You haven't said a word." Wilma's eyes mock him.

"What should I say?" Frank sits on the couch. When home, it's the only place where he's slept since they got married. "It's over?"

Grabbing a bottle of wine from the fridge, Wilma doesn't bother with a glass. "Nothing's ever over."

"Well…" Frank unbuttons the brass on his jacket and lets it fall on the floor. "Any hope for divorce is done now." He kicks the uniform and the medals he never truly deserved, aside. "Along with my chance to be king."

"No." Wilma takes a swig. "You'll be king."

Frank turns to shoot a glare at her. "The Lineage know!" He looks down in shame. "They'll disgrace King Tidal's line." He winces. "I've disgraced him."

"If they do that they'll have to disgrace themselves. General Danning won't fall alone, you can bet on that," Wilma snickers

"He won't have a choice. Without direction from your puppet master, you're nothing." Franks eyes turn to slits. "Face it, Wilma, it's over. You've ruined our plans, the way you've ruined me."

Frank may just be despondent enough to hurt her. Fear crosses Wilma's face before she locks herself in the bedroom.

Thorton's been ignoring her call, but in desperation, she decides to message him. Thrashing her closet to open the safe, Wilma takes out her precious link to the Pazmirish Republic, and contrives the words most likely to gain a response.

The Lineage knows.

Expecting Thorton to ignore her, Wilma's about to lock the tablet up when it chimes. Gasping, her eyes scan the screen.

Know what?

Why Frank married me.

That's your mistake.

Wilma ferociously types.

King Anstone may have made his intention to marry Kira Westin public, but don't tell me there's no hope in this. I need your guidance.

There's hope, but not for you. I have to tell Charles. You know what he'll say...

She reads his words a second time, then a third. "Plan B." Wilma whispers. Anguish bubbles inside of her, until it turns into rage. She tosses the wine bottle against the wall. Red splatters color in the room.

On the other side of the door, Frank listens to her sobbing, and smiles.

***

CHAPTER 27
A LIGHT IN DARKNESS

So many hours upon the sea has made most of the passengers sick, as the Auctaireans make their way towards land.

Silently praising God for being alive, Carl doesn't know what to expect once they reach the GPU. He's heard of their demands from migrants, but everything's been so fuzzy these last five years, he doesn't know what to believe.

A spotlight shines in the darkness, before its dot of light fades. The light reaches their eyes again, before fading.

It must be a lighthouse.

Auctaireans begin to fidget, making Carl worry they'll sink this boat before it can ever reach the shore.

The light becomes bigger, and their descent slows. Now, Carl knows they've reached their preprogrammed destination.

With Kira's Bible hidden in a pocket over his chest, Carl let's out several slow breaths.

They're almost to shore.

The light they saw wasn't from a lighthouse, but a ginormous spotlight.

As they get closer, Carl sees there are towers and large projectors set up above a fence line. The silhouettes of soldiers stand in front of the barbed wire fencing along the beach. It's nothing like the vacation destination Carl remembers being advertised when he was young.

This setup is a preparation for war.

Skin crawling, Carl silently asks God for courage as he watches the first ship take shore. The panicked Auctaireans fight each other to reach the armed soldiers. A few fall at the wayside, and one ends up being pulled away in a current. Carl fights the urge to help them.

Screaming ensues in different languages, as the soldiers try to make sense of their pleas.

Finally, a Pazmirish soldier yells something Carl understands, "Auctrah!"

The screens along the fence change from white, to a picture of Prime Minister Joplin shaking Thorton Lazeed's hand.

A recording over the loudspeakers fills the air. "Welcome, Auctaireans."

Carl's surprised they had this prerecorded, as he braces himself for the fight to reach shore.

God's presence fills him and the sudden urge to stay still, keeps him in place.

While his fellow passengers beat each other and snarl for who makes it to shore first, Carl sits still, under the warmth of God's direction.

Once everyone is off ship, Carl slowly steps onto the sand.

Tugged to the right, he strays away from the center of the group. These people need the most attention, as they beg the soldiers to take care of them.

"We are overjoyed that you're here," The recording continues. "The GPU will take care of your every need, with only one thing to ask of you…"

Now that the group Carl road in with is promised lifetime dependency, their violence turns to cheering.

He doesn't want to hate them. After all, Carl was once one of them, but this moment makes him sick to his stomach. A flash of light draws his eyes. He turns to the right and in an area of darkness two beams of light meet together, forming a golden cross.

Soon as the light appears, it fades, but Carl trusts the warmth in his heart.

That cross was just for him.

The recording is loud enough to be heard over the cheering:

"Pledge yourselves worthy, by bowing to the GPU, and you'll always be taken care of."

While the rest of the Auctaireans fall to their knees, Carl slips through a narrow opening of the fence.

On this dark road, Carl knows that God will guide him to those who can be saved...

***

CHAPTER 28
CONFIRMED

"Do you think we'll see the castle today?" Nadia asks while brushing her teeth.

Kira's dressed in an elegant, rust colored, peplum sweater that rests flawlessly over a long, tan suede skirt. She pulls on light brown boots, keeping her balance with one arm along the doorway. "We can't be presumptuous about anything. There're still too many customs and laws we don't know."

"Okay." Nadia positions the red bow in her hair that matches her sweater dress.

"Nadia?" Rhonda calls from downstairs.

"I'll be right down." Nadia straps on black boots and skips out the door.

Kira perfects her hair that waves past her shoulders. After applying burgundy lipstick, she goes downstairs to find Nadia, digging through Christmas decorations.

"Look at all of these beautiful things!" Nadia exclaims.

"Decorations." Rhonda winks.

"Yes, decorations. Rhonda wants me to help her put them up." Nadia doesn't look away from the pretty little treasures.

"Can she?" Rhonda fakes a pout.

The joy that her daughter can finally celebrate Christmas makes Kira smile. "Yes."

"Good." Rhonda carefully unpacks a golden star ornament. "I'm decorating late this year. Then again, so is everyone in Zyandite. Usually, we start in October, but with most the men gone, it felt wrong to do so. We're just, sentimental like that."

"I love it," Kira says.

Nadia pulls out a red and gold cross ornament. "So do I!"

There's a knock on the door, before Ruger sees himself in. "Rhonda?" He's striking in a black, long sleeve satin shirt that hangs loosely over dark jeans.

Rhonda stands to give him a kiss on the cheek. "I'm so proud of you, no matter what happens."

Kira's heart flutters with fear. Questions spin through her mind, but the peace in Ruger's eyes assure her.

He briefly hugs his sister, before noticing the wonder on Nadia's face while she unpacks Christmas decorations. "I take it she doesn't want to leave?"

Rhonda gives a knowing look before rejoining Nadia in unpacking the festive treasures.

"Hi, Ruger," Nadia says while playing with an oversized reindeer ornament.

"Hello, precious," Ruger whispers, before giving Rhonda a wink.

Kira steps up to his side. "Is everything okay?"

"Yes." Ruger looks at Kira and smiles. "I'd love for Nadia and Rhonda to be there today, but I really need to talk with you, alone."

Kira turns to Rhonda, but before she can speak, Rhonda waves her off.

"We've got work to do. It's going to take all day. Go, get out of here," Rhonda shoos.

Nervous for Nadia, Kira hesitates. "Will you be alright?"

Nadia grins. "Yeah."

"All Rhonda has to do is call. I can get you back here within fifteen minutes," Ruger whispers, giving Kira the assurance she needs.

"Alright," Kira says before waving goodbye.

"Bye, mom!" Nadia exclaims.

Ruger holds out his arm, Kira takes it in her own. For a moment, everything feels casual.

"I'm surprised you're not in your uniform," Kira teases.

With a bashful smile, Ruger looks down. "I've ordered a week long break for every soldier not on patrol. We've had enough uniforms to last a lifetime."

Kira laughs while Ruger opens the passenger door to his vehicle. Out of the corner of her eye, Kira watches the woman next door wave from underneath a fancy, blue hat. Kira waves back as she sits down on the comfortable, tan leather seat. Her heart skips a beat once the neighbor walks towards them.

Ruger closes Kira's door and greets the woman. They are friendly enough, but Kira notices a stiffness in him that could almost be defensive. Although Kira can't hear what is said, Ruger's muscles seem to relax. He bows his head in humility, before walking back to take the driver's seat.

"What was that all about?"

"That's Maryann, she just wanted to assure me of her support." Ruger lightly blushes before turning the engine on.

The radio fills the car with Clark Natorin's voice: "If Kira's as fierce a matriarch for Zyandite as she is for her daughter, we're in good hands."

"I agree," a woman's voice rings through the speakers.

Ruger turns it off. "I don't like listening to anyone else but God. Talking heads have decimated societies in the past. Even when they say something I agree with, I'm skeptical."

"At least they're friendly." Kira shrugs.

Ruger's eyes harden. "Friendly as a two-headed snake."

"You think they're lying?"

Ruger glances at her with a smile. It's tense, but at least his eyes have softened. "Last night, I made the superiority of the Lineage illegal. This is Clark's way of keeping his position."

Kira's brow furrows. "Lying goes against purity, doesn't it?"

With a chuckle, Ruger shakes his head at the hypocrisy. "Their conniving has tarnished anything pure within the Lineage for a long time. I should've made their bias illegal when I was first crowned." All laughter in his eyes fades. Ruger may be staring at the road, but his mind is elsewhere, nestled deep within the past. "In a way, I was intimidated by them. When I was growing up, these men were my heroes. After believing a lie your whole life, it's hard to see the truth. It's the façade I didn't want to touch, but that curtain is drawn now. All of Zyandite sees them for what they really are."

"How sad. You must be so disappointed."

Ruger winces. "Yes, but enough about that," he says before glancing at her with a grin. "I have something to give you." Ruger reaches for the glove box and pulls out a tablet. The electronic screen is framed with a hard burgundy shell.

It's been so long since she's held a digital link to the world, Kira could cry. "Oh, thank you!"

"I'll get you networked on ZyanBell soon, but it takes a retina scan. I'd prefer to wait until you're queen to get that done. Otherwise you'll have to wait in line twice, just to change your maiden name."

"A retina scan?"

"Of course. We vote through ZyanBell and cannot risk any fraud. We'll set up an account for Nadia, too, once she turns twenty."

"That's the voting age here? Wow." Kira squirms a little. "The voting age in Auctairea was fifteen."

"No wonder." Ruger smirks.

Kira can't help but laugh.

His smile widens, before he puts his vehicle into sky-mode.

Kira's never been this far away from Nadia. Looking out the window, her stomach sinks.

Glancing at her, Ruger seems to read her mind. "Nadia's safe, I promise."

"I know." Kira returns her eyes to Ruger. She allows herself to soak in the view. There's more color on his face than she's ever seen, proving his wounds are healed. His green eyes are the same as she remembered. Compassionate, yet dutiful. She's surprised to see a flicker of a smile at the corner of his lips.

Ruger glances at her. "Keep that up, you'll make me blush."

"Sorry for staring." Kira grins before looking down. "It's just I've never seen you in Zyandite sunshine."

He laughs. "I hope you'll never see me under Auctairean gloom again." Ruger's smile fades. "If only that had been our last battle..." He sighs. "I owe you transparency. Our bond will not be without scrutiny."

"You don't say?" Kira says with a laugh. She's been under scrutiny since she landed. "It's nothing I can't handle."

"I'm well aware of that." Ruger doesn't return her smile. "The Lineage may have lost their power and seem to be infighting, but that doesn't mean they'll let go of their influence. It would be wise to get married as soon as possible. Once you're queen, you'll be protected from them."

Kira glances back towards Rhonda's neighborhood, and her brow creases with worry. "What about Nadia?"

"Nadia's protected now. No one in Zyandite would dare harm a child. We'd destroy them." He glances at her with concern brewing across his brow. "Formally, my title requires it, but more than that, I would like to adopt her. I consider it a blessing to be the earthly father she's never had."

Joy extinguishes the worry on Kira's heart. She looks at Ruger, amazed by his willingness to tackle such a responsibility head-on. "You really are God's gift to us."

Ruger's shoulders relax before he smiles. "I'm excited to make ours an official family. December 14th is the earliest I can take the time needed for our Coalescing."

Kira remembers overhearing that word. It struck her as foreign then, and doesn't make sense to her now. "Coalescing?"

Ruger's face becomes pale. It reminds her of when they first met. "You weren't given literature on it?"

"No."

"You should've been informed of our marital traditions. I apologize." Ruger keeps his eyes on their destination as the walls of the castle come into view. Slowly, he descends and parks on a cobblestone parking lot within the walls.

"So, is it like a mandatory honeymoon?" Kira asks with a grin.

Turning the engine off, Ruger rests an arm on Kira's seat. "Coalescing is so much more than that, it's a special time every Zyandite looks forward to. It's designed not just for the physical pleasure, but the emotional connection between husband and wife. God must be first in all things, but marriage is the second most sacred bond on earth. You and I must share our deepest secrets, our favorite memories, our worst fears, and our most elaborate fantasies. Anything that could be used against us, we must bear to each other. There has to be complete vulnerability before there can be a complete seal. Things everyone keeps to themselves, both good and bad, must be out in the open before we can have any physical contact." He then lets out a deep breath. It's as though telling her this tradition relieves his soul. "It's not a time for shyness of the heart. I understand that Auctairean honeymoons were about exotic vacations, with sex as the main focus, whereas a Zyandite Coalescing is about using sex to bring our hearts and souls together as one, in order to create an unbreakable bond."

"That's beautiful," Kira whispers. "And… Foreign," she adds, making him laugh.

"You aren't afraid?"

Uncertain for how to assure Ruger she's not scared, Kira decides to kiss him.

Ruger slowly pulls his lips away before pressing his forehead against hers. "I love you."

"I love you," Kira returns, hardly able to breathe as her heart still races from their kiss.

Ruger grins before pulling an envelope from his pocket. "You're officially a Zyandite citizen, now." Stepping out, he opens her door. "Welcome home."

Kira's heart skips a beat before standing on the soil she wasn't allowed to step on, just the night before. Surrounded by high walls constructed out of cream colored stone, she admires this enclosure that's considered sacred among Zyandites. There are willow and oak trees, a few benches, and water fountains sporadically placed about. The castle itself isn't as glamorous as Kira expected. It's only three stories tall, covered with the same stone as the walls. The only resemblance of other castles Kira has seen is the tower. Other than the red tile roof, the top of this tower is constructed entirely out of glass.

"The restriction on who can enter the castle is a leftover from the Lineage. I'm taking full authority as King, and changing that law, today. Whomever I invite is now officially permitted on castle grounds. Did you know we've never allowed dignitaries in?" Ruger asks.

"No."

"It's made negotiations quite the debacle. I always have to travel, in order to get anything done. Now, people can come to me." He looks at her with the same admiration that captured her heart in Auctairea. "Our ancestors didn't believe in face value," Ruger says. "But wait until you see the inside…"

"I think it's beautiful. The stonework is bright and inviting. It looks new."

"It's six hundred and twenty-five years old."

"Two years younger than Zyandite."

"Good job."

She takes his arm and walks across the courtyard. There are several people hanging Christmas lights on trees. A few swans fly by, and several peacocks flutter their colorful wings, while some deer rest under the shade of the oak and willow trees. Ruger leads the way to cascading stone stairs, up to double wooden doors that automatically open for them.

Taking a deep breath, Kira steps inside to find the signature style of Zyandite. There are vibrant colors, everywhere. An enormous chandelier overhead sparkles with crystals and blown glass that are crafted in every color of the rainbow. The walls reflect the sunlight with golden specs. An intense, white crown molding begins at the middle of every wall, and goes down to the floor. There are red vases sporadically placed on various sized, well-lit nooks. The tile floor is blue, with bright red and orange blotches of sparkly colors swirled about.

Kira's eyes glisten as she takes it all in. "Oh, my goodness. I love it."

Ruger smiles before leading her up the spiral stairs. The railing is constructed with swirls of wrought iron, but the bars along the banister are spun with crystal strings that match the chandelier. Upstairs, the carpet is a deep red with teal specs. He stops at the middle of the top step and flips a switch. Only the chandelier remains lit, before all of the hanging blown glass lights up in rainbow colors that sporadically fade in and out. Kira gasps at the beauty of it.

"I didn't adequately propose to you." Ruger pulls something small out of his pocket before taking her left hand. "This morning, I searched every jewelry shop in Brustonite, for a ring that resembles how you make me feel." He slides it on her finger, but Kira can't pull her eyes off of his. "Will you be my lover..." He gently lifts her hand to his lips. "My best friend..." He kisses her hand before retuning his gaze to her eyes. "And my queen?"

She can barely breathe. "Yes," Kira says before kissing him.

Smiling Ruger pulls away. "Let's tell the world."

Kira kisses him again before she finally looks at the ring. A large asscher diamond is showcased by a yellow gold bezel setting, with a pattern of alternating baguette cut emeralds and rubies channel set throughout the entire band. "It's beautiful."

"You deserve it." His fingers entwine with her hair, before Ruger kisses her again.

Kira breathes him in deep. "Any woman offered your heart would be a complete fool not to take it, and never let go."

Ruger squeezes her hand before leading her down the hall, past the kitchen, and into a large ballroom. A dozen chandlers hang from the ceiling, one bearing different colors in every shade of the rainbow.

"Is this where the ceremony was held last night?" Kira asks.

"Yes." Ruger's always hated the ballroom, until today. "I was crowned in this room." He looks around and allows himself the time to cleanse the memory of his coronation, and replaces it with this moment. "The generals have tried to choose a woman for me here, many times." He blushes. "I must admit, it's satisfying to announce the lover God chose for me, from this very room."

"I feel underdressed," Kira jokes with a sheepish smile.

Ruger laughs and shakes his head. "You're gorgeous." He then leads her to a doorway, where two men stand before the balcony, talking.

Wearing civilian clothes, Major Cantor and Captain Hiledal salute their King.

Ruger lets go of Kira's hand to return it. "Are you ready?"

"Yes, my King." Major Cantor pulls out his tablet. "I'll film from the balcony. Captain Hiledal will film from the ground."

"Very good." Ruger looks at Kira with his lips curved to the side. "I want you to remember this moment for the rest of your life." He caresses her cheek, but only for a moment. "Major Cantor will give you the signal for when to come out." With a wink, Ruger steps through the doors.

Outside, Kira hears the crowd cheer. She leans against the doorframe to listen.

Major Cantor watches her with eyes that aren't suspicious, but rather, surprised. "You're nervous?"

Kira nods.

He smiles. "You don't need to worry. They aren't like the Lineage. We don't fake approval. They're cheering because you not only saved our King, but gave the intel needed for a swift victory in Auctairea. We're indebted to you."

"I don't want that." Kira looks at the floor. "I don't like owing anyone, or being owed." She gives a nervous smile. "It's too political for my taste."

Major Cantor's chin tilts to the side, and an approving smile crosses his face. He's about to say something, but Ruger's voice draws their attention. The young soldier steps outside and starts filming.

In the crowd below, one man starts chanting "Thank God for Ruger, our King for life, and for Kira, our future Queen!"

Kira's knees shake. She has to take Ruger's hand just to keep herself straight. Scanning the crowd, her eyes lock with Farrah's.

Wearing a cream sweater dress, Farrah does a happy dance from where she stands next to Brian. Everyone around them joins in Farrah's joy with laughter. As the crowd repeats the chant, Kira sees how genuine they are. She looks at Ruger and has to catch her breath. This moment is like a dream.

On the same balcony where his generals tried to arrange a marriage with a bride of their choosing, Ruger smiles and silently praises the great I Am, for God is in control. Now, not only will his line continue, but it will be intermixed with Auctairean blood. Overwhelmed by how God laughs at the bias of man, he can't contain his joy. Ruger smiles and gently holds up Kira's left hand, showing off her engagement ring. "Thank you for your support. We'll be married on the 14th of December."

The crowd cheers.

Kira looks away from Ruger to stare at the growing crowd. Their faces are so happy, so trusting.

In a breath, she no longer finds herself in Zyandite, but Auctairea. The cheering from one of Stephen Joplin's rallies fills Kira's ears as though she were there now. It was a sight to see, tens of thousands of Christians who thought they were taking their liberties back. Little did they know, they were giving their freedoms away...

Standing on stage in an elaborate golden gown that shimmered under the fluorescent lights, Kira's baby bump was just starting to reveal itself, which made the crowd adore her all the more.

With a smile painted over with her signature burgundy, Kira's dark hair was done up in flawless curls as she introduced Stephen Joplin to the podium.

Joplin began speaking, but the people couldn't care less about him.

All eyes were on her.

As Kira stepped off the platform, one woman, twice her age, took her hand and kissed it. "Thank you for being our voice!" She shouted over Joplin's well-rehearsed speech.

A man beside her nodded vigorously. "That's right. We ain't here for him, but for you."

"Yep." The elderly woman gave an approving smile.

Joplin's shouting caught everyone's attention. "Vote for me this summer, and Auctairea's inclusivity will once again, include Christianity!"

The crowd cheered, including Kira, until a voice gained her attention.

"Kira!" A woman yelled.

She turned to the voice, but now, Kira's no longer in a festive gown in an elaborate theatre. She's in her nightgown, on the floor of her old closet, grasping baby Nadia to her chest. Tears rolling down her face as her neighbor outside screams, "Kira, run!" Right before Maggie's voice was silenced, forever.

Kira watches the people of Zyandite accept her now, even entrusting her with the sacred responsibility to lead them. She doesn't deserve this. 'God, don't let me fail them. Don't let me fail *him*,' she silently prays. Outside, Kira may be cheerful, but the pain of her past continues to gnaw on her heart.

Ruger's smile rests upon the side of Kira's face, but she can't look at him, or she'll break. The shadows from her past have a hold over her. Needing God's strength to intervene where hers lacks, Kira's heart cries out in silence, 'Help me.'

The verses Farrah read from Psalm 45:11-12 snaps Kira out of Auctairea.

Forget your people and your family far away. For your royal husband delights in your beauty; honor him, for he is your lord.

If He wants to redeem Kira, who is she to argue with God?

Ruger leans his lips against her ear. "The earth is the LORD's, and everyone in it. The world and all its people belong to him." He recites Psalm 24:1. "That includes you, Kira."

Kira finally looks at him and cries. These aren't tears of sorrow or regret, but of joy.

As they kiss, the Zyandites below cheer louder. Once Kira is crowned, the idolatry in their land will finally come to an end.

***

EPILOGUE
THE MAN ACROSS THE SEA

Safely hidden behind the walls of a well-guarded mansion, an old man sits on a distressed leather chair.

His eyes were once hazel, but are now gray from cataracts. His pointed chin and sunken cheekbones would scare any child. Shoulders hunched, he glowers over a table with a wooden map of the world before him. There are tiny pieces of gold-plated steel, molded into the shapes of soldiers that occupy most of the territories.

Only Zyandite, Tunaunda, the Vulton Isles, Dulboruu, and what was once Kaddain, and Auctairea, remain free.

The rest of the world is occupied.

Both Kaddain and Auctairea are Zyandite, now. This landmass has morphed into a worthy opponent.

The backfire of his plans isn't lost on Charles.

"I will have that weapon," Charles proclaims to himself. Determined to find a way around his failures, Charles eyes ignite with the fire of resiliency. Even though his hair has aged to a stark white, there's a youthful desire for complete power that makes his frail body seem intimidating. Of course, extreme wealth, the kind that's handed down and not earned, only adds to his entitled nature.

THE LINEAGE

Nothing can escape this man's greed.

He's the living example of Proverbs 27:20, because no matter how much his aged eyes have seen, they're always starved for more. Power alone is not enough. He must own the world...

The double mahogany doors swing open. A thin woman walks in wearing a bright pink mini skirt and silver tube top, showcasing her colorful tattoos. Her clear stilettos obnoxiously tap on the hardwood floor. Her head is shaved, but like her legs, it too is covered with dozens of tattoos. The shapes of her tattoos are hard to decipher; there's so many, they almost make her face piercings invisible. There's even a chain that connects from one of her nose rings, all the way to her right ear, but even that is hard to make out with all the ink on her face.

Her blue eyes are cold, almost dead, as she stops before the old man and places her hands on her hips. "Thorton Lazeed wishes to report an update on Wilma Marshal." Her voice is far too sweet to match her eyes. It's as though she was once innocent, with only her voice left uncorrupted.

The elderly man sits back into the brown leather of his seat and chuckles. "Oh, Silver Flower, why should I care about that starlet?"

Silver Flower straightens her posture. "Because Mr. Miser, Thornton Lazeed lost influence over Zyandite command."

"I'm not surprised," Charles says with a mildly amused frown.

Her shoulders drop out of relief at his reaction. "We've also just received an influx of Auctairean refugees."

Charles hands begin to shake. "More children to feed. They're worthless." His eyes are so enraged they become bloodshot.

His colorful assistant becomes fearful of the transformation of his face. Silver Flower recoils a few steps back. "That's not all..." She glances at the floor. "The Christian King is to be married."

"To whom?" Charles asks through his teeth.

"Kira Westin."

"Kira Valeda Westin?" Charles growls lowly, as though trying to contain his anger.

Silver Flower's almost too frightened to say, and barely whispers, "Yes."

Charles immediately stands. "I want her head, NOW!"

"Should I offer another reward for her capture?" Silver Flower's voice shakes.

"No. Zyandite will protect her. You tell Thornton Lazeed that we need every man and boy from Dulboruu, to fight against these zealots."

Silver Flower nods.

"Go away now, slave!" Charles shouts, pointing at the door.

With a fearful gasp, Silver Flower runs out of the room.

Charles stares at the golden figures on the map. He grabs a handful and slams the figurines on Tunaunda. The force of his tantrum was so hard, his hand bleeds. Charles examines the abrasions on his skin and smiles. "Soon, Kira, it'll be *your* blood on the ground." He laughs.

In all his long and miserable life, there's only one thing Charles Miser loves more than power, and that's the satisfaction of revenge.

To be continued...

ABOUT THE AUTHOR

My name is Kimberly Humphreys, I am a Christian, tribal member of the Cherokee Nation, military spouse and I homeschool my three amazing kids. Writing is my passion, and while I enjoy writing fiction, it's amazing how God speaks through my blogs. You can follow me on Parler @KimberlyHumphreys. In my lifetime, I have learned that God can restore anything and anyone. I love my country and am thankful for my freedoms. In no time or place should words ever be silenced. I believe that socialism is evil, political correctness makes us weak, and dogs are awesome.

Made in the USA
Coppell, TX
28 October 2021

64824246R00154